RIVERSIDE PUBLIC LIBRARY
3 1403 00098 2776

D1212142

ALSO BY CHRISTA WOLF

The Quest for Christa T.
Patterns of Childhood (A Model Childhood)
No Place on Earth
Cassandra
Accident: A Day's News
The Author's Dimension: Selected Essays

WHAT REMAINS

Translated by

Heike Schwarzbauer

and Rick Takvorian

WHAT REMAINS AND OTHER STORIES

■

CHRISTA WOLF

Farrar, Straus and Giroux

New York

Originally published in German under the title Gesammelte Erzählungen,

the novella "What Remains" was originally published under the title Was bleibt,

Printed in the United States of America
Designed by Cynthia Krupat
First edition, 1993

Library of Congress Cataloging-in-Publication Data
Wolf, Christa.
[Short stories. English. Selections]
What remains and other stories / Christa Wolf ; translated by Heike Schwarzbauer and Rick Takvorian.
p. cm.
Translation of: Gesammelte Erzählungen.
I. Title.
PT2685.036A27 1993 833'.914—dc20 92-27906 CIP

"June Afternoon" first appeared in Grand Street,
and a section of "What Remains" appeared in Granta.

Contents

EXCHANGING GLANCES

1

I'VE FORGOTTEN what my grandmother was wearing the time that nasty word "Asia" got her back on her feet. Why she of all people should be the first to come to mind I can't say; during her lifetime she was never pushy. I remember all her dresses: the brown one with the crocheted collar, which she wore on Christmas and all family birthdays, her black silk blouse, the checkered apron and the knitted black mottled sweater she wore on winter days while sitting by the stove perusing the *Landsberg Gazette.* Yet for this trip she had nothing suitable to wear—and this is not just my memory playing tricks with me. Her little button-up boots were useful, though. They hung suspended at the ends of her too short, slightly crooked legs, always two centimeters above the floor, even when she was sitting on the edge of an air-raid cot, even when the floor was nothing but hard earth, as it was on that April day I have chosen to recall here. The bomber squadrons which now passed overhead during broad daylight on their way to Berlin were already out of earshot. Someone had pushed open the door of the air-raid shelter, and in the bright triangle of sunlight at the entrance, three steps from the dangling button-up boots of my grandmother, stood a pair of knee-high black military boots, and in them an SS officer, whose blond brain had registered every single word my grandmother had uttered during the long air-raid alarm: "No, no, I'm not budging from here, I don't care if they kill me, one old woman more or less won't matter." "What?" said the SS officer. "Tired of living? You'd rather fall into the hands of those Asian hordes? Don't you know that the Russians lop women's breasts right off?"

That brought my grandmother wheezing to her feet. "Oh God," she said, "what has humanity done to deserve this?" "Are you starting up again!" bellowed my grandfather. Now I can see them clearly, walking into the courtyard and taking up their positions alongside our handcart: Grandmother in her fine black coat, on her head the light and dark brown striped kerchief which my children still wore when they had a sore throat. She leans with her right hand against the back cross beam of the handcart. Grandfather, wearing a cap with earflaps and a herringbone jacket, is posted next to the drawbar. Time is short, the night is drawing near, closing in along with the enemy, albeit from different directions: night from the west and the enemy from the east. In the south, where they meet and where lies the small town of Nauen, flames rage against the sky. We imagine we can decipher the fiery script; the writing on the sky seems clear and spells out: Go west.

But first we must search for my mother. She is forever disappearing when it's time to move on; she wants to go back and must go on. On occasion, both urges are equally strong. At such moments, she invents pretexts and runs away, saying, I'll hang myself; and my brother and I, still dwelling in the realm where such words are taken literally, run into the small forest where my mother has no business being, nor do we wish to have any business there; we catch each other gazing at the treetops, we avoid looking at each other, voicing unutterable speculations is impossible anyway. We also keep silent when my mother, who is getting bonier and thinner with each passing week, comes up from the village, throws a small sack of flour on the hand-cart, and reproaches us: What did you think you were doing running around and making everyone crazy with worry? And who's going to get the farmers to cough up some food if not me?

She hitches herself to the front of the cart, my brother and I push from behind, the sky provides eerie fireworks, and once again I hear that delicate sound as the humdrum train *Reality* veers off the tracks and races crazily out of control right into the wildest "unreality," and I am shaken with laughter, the impropriety of which I find deeply offensive.

The only thing is, I can't convince anyone that I'm not laughing at us, God forbid, us settled, proper, respect-able people in the two-story house next to the poplar tree, us colorful peep-show people in the vinegar pot; Mannikin, mannikin, timpe te / Flounder, flounder in the sea / My old Missis Ilsebill / Will not have it as I will. But none of us had wanted to become emperor, or Pope for that matter, and most certainly not God. One was quite content selling flour and butter fat and sour pickles and malt coffee in the store downstairs, the other to learn English vocabulary at the table with the black oilcloth and glance from time to time at the town and the river, which lay there quite still and in their proper places and never awakened in me the desire to leave them. With unwavering determination my little brother put together ever-new odd constructions with his Erector set and then insisted on setting them in one senseless motion or another with the aid of twine and wheels, while upstairs in her kitchen, my grandmother made the kind of home fries with onions and marjoram which disappeared from the face of the earth when she died, and my grandfather hung the tar wire up on the window lock, took off his blue cobbler's apron, and cut a dozen fine notches into each crust of bread on the wooden cutting board at the kitchen table, so that his toothless gums could chew it.

No, I don't know why they put us in the vinegar pot, and I don't know for the life of me why that makes me laugh, even though my uncle asks me suspiciously time and again from his place at the head of the second handcart in our tiny caravan: I'd like to know what's so funny here. Even though I understand how disappointed someone must be that the fear of being laughed at doesn't even subside once one has finally been promoted to a position of confidentiality in one's firm. Even though I would have liked to do him the favor of assuring him that I was laughing at myself, I was a bad liar and I distinctly felt that I was absent, although any one of those figures leaning against the wind in the darkness could easily have been mistaken for me. You can't see yourself when you're lost within yourself, but I saw all of us just as I see us today, as if someone had lifted me out of my shell and set me down next to it with the command: Take a good look!

That's what I did, but I didn't like what I saw.

I saw us straying from the country road, groping about in the darkness on side paths and, finally, coming upon a tree-lined road leading toward a gate, a secluded estate, and a crooked, slightly shaky man who was limping to the stables in the middle of the night. He was not given to wondering at anything and so addressed the desperate, exhausted little troop in his particular, indifferent manner: Well, folks, Sodom and Gomorrah? Never mind. There's always room in the smallest cabin for a happy, loving couple.

The man is not so bright, my mother said uneasily, as we followed Kalle across the courtyard, and my grandfather, who never said much, declared with satisfaction, He is pretty crazy in his head. And so he was. Kalle called my grandfather boss, he who had held no higher rank in his lifetime than that of private in the Kaiser's infantry regiment, cobbler's apprentice under Herr Lebüse in Bromberg, and signalman for the German Reich in the administrative district of Frankfurt (Oder). Boss, said Kalle, it's best if you take that cubbyhole back there in the corner. He then disappeared, whistling, "One more drop for the road. Oh, just one more drop for the road . . ." But the people sleeping in the bunk beds had already downed their ration of tea for the night, and the inevitable liverwurst sandwiches had been handed out as well, judging from the smell. I tried to block my nose with my arm while sleeping. My grandfather, who was almost deaf, began saying his prayers at full volume as he did every night, but when he reached "and forgive us our trespasses," my grandmother shouted into his ear that he was disturbing the others, whereupon they started quarreling. Everyone throughout the hall could hear them, whereas up until then their old creaky wooden beds had been their only witness, along with the black framed likeness of an angel with the inscription: "Even when hope's last anchor pulls away, do not despair!"

Kalle woke us at daybreak. "I 'spect you'll be knowin' how to man a horse 'n' buggy?" he asked my uncle. "Because Herr Volk, what is the owner hereabouts, wants to move on with bag and baggage, but who'll drive the oxcart with the feed bags?" "Me," said my uncle, and he stood fast, even when my aunt nagged repeatedly that oxen were dangerous animals and why should he risk his hide for strangers . . . "Shut your mouth!" he snapped. "And how else are you gonna get all your junk away from here?" We were all allowed to climb aboard and our handcart was lashed to the rear stanchion. "Fine and dandy," said Kalle, "just don't think that the oxen will be quicker than your handcart." Herr Volk showed up in person to hire his new coachman with a handshake; he wore a hunting hat, a loden coat, and knickerbockers. And Frau Volk came to bestow a kind and cultured word on the women who now, in one way or another, numbered among her domestics, but I didn't like her because she called me by my first name without asking and allowed her dachshund bitch, Suzie, to sniff at our legs, which presumably reeked of liverwurst sandwiches. My aunt could see now that these were high-class people; my uncle wouldn't have gone into service with some nobody anyway. Then the shooting began right behind us and we headed off at a quick pace. God takes care of his own, said my grandmother.

The night before, however, I had dreamed for the last time that recurring child's dream: I'm not my parents' child at all, the babies got mixed up and I belong to the shopkeeper Rambow in Friedrichstadt, who is much too clever to openly claim his rights, although he has seen through it all and has measures in reserve, so that I'm ultimately forced to stay out of the street where he lies in wait for me in the doorway of his shop, lollipops in hand. That night in my dream, I had been able to tell him point-blank that I had lost all fear of him, even the memory of that fear of him, that his power over me was at an end, and from then on, I would come to his shop every day and pick up two bars of chocolate. Rambow the shopkeeper had meekly accepted my conditions.

He was finished, without a doubt, for he was no longer needed. The babies hadn't been mixed up, but I was no longer myself either. I would never forget when the stranger who had taken hold of me since and did with me as he pleased had entered me. It was on that cold January morning, when I was hurrying out of my town toward Küstrin on board a truck, greatly surprised at how gray indeed was that town in which I had always found all the light and all the colors I needed. Then someone inside me said slowly and clearly, You'll never see this again.

My horror was indescribable. The sentence was irreversible. All I could do was keep that which I knew to myself, truthfully and faithfully; watch the ebb and flow of rumors and hopes swell and fall; carry on for the time being, which I owed the others, to say what they wanted me to say. But the stranger in me ate at my insides and grew, and possibly he would soon refuse to obey in my stead. Already he had begun to nudge me from time to time, and the others were casting sidelong glances in my direction. Now she's laughing again. If we only knew what at.

2

THIS IS SUPPOSED to be a report on *liberation*, the hour of liberation, and I thought, Nothing is easier than that. That hour has been clearly focused in my mind's eye all these years, it has lain ready and waiting, fully completed in my memory. And even if there have been reasons to let it lie until now, twenty-five years should surely have erased, or at least faded, those reasons. I need only say the word and the machine will start running, and everything will appear on the paper as if of its own accord—a series of accurate, highly defined pictures. Against all expectations, I got caught up in the question of what clothes my grandmother was wearing on the road, at which point I happened upon that stranger who, one day, had turned me into herself and now has become yet another, pronouncing other sentences, and ultimately I must accept that the series of images will not add up to anything, memory is not a photo album, and liberation depends not only on a date and the coincidental movements of the Allied troops but also on certain difficult and prolonged movements within oneself. And while time may erase reasons, it also continuously creates new ones, rendering rather more difficult the selection of one particular hour; the need arises to specify what one has been liberated from, and if one is conscientious, perhaps to what purpose as well. Which brings to mind the passing of a childhood fear, the shopkeeper Rambow, who surely was a respectable man, and so one searches for a new approach, which only succeeds in bringing one a little closer and no more. The passing of my fear of low-flying fighter planes. You made your bed, now lie in it, as Kalle would say if he were still alive, but I assume he is dead, like so many of the cast of characters (yes, death erases reasons).

Dead like Wilhelm Grund, the foreman, after the strafers shot him in the belly. That's how I saw my first corpse at the age of sixteen; rather late for those years, I must say. (I can't count the infant I handed in a stiff bundle from a truck to a refugee woman; I didn't see him, I only heard his mother scream and ran away.) Chance had it that Wilhelm Grund was lying there instead of me, for pure chance alone had occupied my uncle with a sick horse in the barn that morning, so that we weren't ahead of the others heading toward the country road alongside Grund's oxcart as usual. Here, I had to say to myself, was also where we should have been, and not where it was safe, although we could hear the gunfire, and the fifteen horses were wild with fear. I have been afraid of horses ever since. But what I have feared even more ever since that moment are the faces of people forced to see what no person should have to see. The young farmhand Gerhard Grund had such a face as he burst through the barn door, managed a few steps, and then collapsed: Herr Volk, what have they done to my father!

He was my age. His father lay in the dust at the side of the road next to his oxen, eyes staring upward, one could say heavenward if one absolutely insisted. I saw that nothing could lower that gaze, not his wife's wailing or the whining of his three other children. This time around, they forgot to tell us that this was not a sight for us children. "Quick," said Herr Volk. "We've got to get out of here." They would have grabbed me the same way they grabbed the corpse by the shoulders and legs and dragged him to the edge of the woods. Just as the tarpaulins from the granary of the estate served as his coffin, so would they have served any of us, myself included. I, too, would have gone to the grave without words and without song, just like Wilhelm Grund the farmhand. Their wailing would have followed me down, and then they would have pushed on like us, because we couldn't stay. For a long time they would have had no desire to speak, just as we remained silent, and then they would have had to ask themselves what they could do to stay alive themselves, and they would have torn off large birch branches, just as we did now, and covered the handcarts with them, as if the foreign pilots would let themselves be fooled by a little wandering birch grove. Everything, everything would be like now, only I would no longer be one of them. And the difference which was everything to me meant hardly anything to most of the others here. Gerhard Grund was already sitting in his father's seat and drove the oxen forward with his very whip, and Herr Volk nodded to him: "Good boy. Your father died a soldier's death."

I didn't really believe this. It wasn't the way a soldier's death had been described in the textbooks and newspapers, and I told that authority with whom I was continuously in touch and whom I labeled with the name of God—albeit against my own scruples and reservations—that, in my opinion, a man and father of four children did not deserve an end such as this. War is war, said Herr Volk, and certainly it was and had to be, yet I claimed that this deviated from the ideal of death for Führer and Reich, and I didn't ask whom my mother meant when she hugged Frau Grund and said aloud, "Damn them. Those damned criminals."

Since I happened to be on guard at the time, it was my job to report by whistle signal the next series of attacks, two American fighters. Just as I had figured, the birch grove came to a halt clearly visible from afar and easy prey on the desolate country road. Everything that had legs jumped out of the handcarts and threw itself in the ditch, myself included. The only difference was that this time around I did not bury my head in the sand but lay on my back and continued eating my sandwich. I did not want to die and I certainly was not up to defying death and I knew fear better than I cared to.

But one does not die twice in one day. I wanted to

see the one who dared shoot at me, for I had the odd idea that in every plane there sat a few individual people. First I saw the white stars under the wings, but then, as they broke away for a new approach, the helmet-covered heads of the pilots and, finally, even the naked white spots of their faces. Prisoners I had seen, but this was the attacking enemy face to face; I knew that I was supposed to hate him and it seemed unnatural that I found myself wondering for the space of a second whether they were having fun with whatever they were doing. They soon stopped, though.

When we got back to the wagons, one of our oxen, the one they called Heinrich, sank to its knees. Blood spurted from its throat. My uncle and grandfather unharnessed it. My grandfather, who had stood alongside the dead Wilhelm Grund without uttering a word, now hurled curses from his toothless mouth. "The innocent creature," he said hoarsely. "These bastards, damned, confounded dogs, every one of them." I was afraid he might begin to cry and hoped he would get everything off his chest by cursing. I forced myself to look at the animal for an entire minute. It couldn't be reproach that I detected in its gaze, so why did I feel guilty? Herr Volk handed his hunting rifle to my uncle and pointed to a spot behind the ox's ear. We were sent away. At the sound of the shot, I looked back. The ox dropped heavily onto its side. All evening the women were occupied with cooking the meat. By the time we sat in the straw eating the broth, it was already dark. Kalle, who had bitterly complained about being hungry, greedily slurped from his bowl, wiped his mouth on his sleeve, and began to sing croakingly with contentment, "All dogs bite, all dogs bite, but only hot dogs get bitten . . ." "To hell with you, you crazy fella," my grandfather went at him furiously. Kalle let himself drop onto the straw and stuck his head under his jacket.

3

ONE NEED NOT be afraid when everyone else is afraid. To know this is certainly liberating, but liberation was still to come, and I want to record what today's memory is prepared to yield on the subject. It was the morning of the fifth of May, a beautiful day, and once more panic broke out when we heard that we were encircled by Soviet armored tank troops. Then word came down: By forced march to Schwerin, where the Americans are, and anyone who was still capable of asking himself questions would have had to find it quite strange how everyone was surging forward toward that enemy which had been after our lives for days now. Of all that was now still possible I found nothing desirable, or even bearable, for that matter, but the world stubbornly refused to end and we were not prepared to cope after a messed-up end of the world. Therefore I understood the horrific words uttered by one woman when told that the miracle weapon longed for by the Führer could only exterminate everyone, both the enemy and the Germans. Let them go ahead and use it, is what she said.

We moved past the last houses of the village along a sandy road. A soldier was washing up at a pump next to a red Mecklenburg farmhouse. He stood there, legs apart, with the sleeves of his white undershirt rolled up, and called out to us, "The Führer is dead," the same way one says, "Nice weather today." I was more stunned at his tone of voice than at the realization that the man was speaking the truth.

I trudged on alongside our cart, heard the coachmen's hoarse shouts, the groaning of the exhausted horses, saw the small fires by the side of the road wherein smoldered the papers of the officers of the Wehrmacht, saw heaps of guns and antitank grenade launchers sprouting ghostlike from the ditches, saw typewriters, suitcases, radios, and all manner of precious war equipment senselessly lining our way, and could not help recalling the sound of that sentence over and over again, which, instead of being one everyday sentence among others, should, I felt, have echoed frightfully between Heaven and earth.

Then came the paper. The street was suddenly flooded with paper; they were still throwing it out of the Wehrmacht vehicles in wild anger—forms, induction orders, files, proceedings, documents from the headquarters of a military district, banal routine letters as well as secret commando affairs, and the statistics of the dead fallen from doubly secured safes, whose contents piqued no one's curiosity now that they lay thrown at our feet. As if there were something repulsive about the paper trash, I did not stoop to pick up a page either, which I felt sorry about later. I did, however, catch the canned food which a truck driver threw to me. The swing of his arm reminded me of the movement, often performed, with which, in the summer of '39, I had thrown cigarette packs onto the dusty convoys which rolled eastward past our house, day and night. In the six-year interim I had stopped being a child; summer was coming again, but I had no idea how I would spend it.

The supply convoy of a Wehrmacht unit had been abandoned by its escort on a side road. All those who passed by took as much as they could carry. The order of the column dissolved, many were beside themselves, where before out of fear, now out of greed. Only Kalle laughed, dragging a large block of butter to our cart, clapping his hands, and shouting happily, "Well, I'll be damned! Look at them getting all worked up!"

Then we saw the prisoners from the concentration camp. The rumor that the Oranienburgers were being driven right behind us had haunted us like a ghost. The suspicion that we were fleeing from them as well did not occur to me back then. They stood at the edge of the forest and gazed questioningly at us. We could have given them a sign that the air was clear, but nobody did. Cautiously, they approached the street. They looked different from all the people I had seen up to then, and I wasn't surprised that we automatically shrank back from them. But it betrayed us, this shrinking back, it showed that, in spite of what we protested to each other and ourselves, we knew. All we unhappy ones who had been driven away from all our possessions, from our farms and our manors, from our shops and musty bedrooms and brightly polished parlors with the picture of the Führer on the wall—we knew: these people, who had been declared animals and who were now slowly coming toward us to take revenge—we had dropped them. Now the ragged would put on our clothes and stick their bloody feet in our shoes, now the starved would seize hold of the flour and the sausage we had just snatched. And to my horror I felt, It is just, and I was horrified to feel that it was just, and knew for a fraction of a second that we were guilty. I forgot it again.

The prisoners pounced not on the bread but on the guns by the side of the road. They loaded up on ammunition, crossed the road without paying any attention to us, struggled up the opposite slope, and mounted sentry there.

Silently, they looked down at us. I couldn't bear looking at them. Why don't they scream, I thought, or shoot into the air, or shoot at us, goddamnit! But they stood there peacefully, I saw that some of them were reeling and could barely bring themselves to hold their guns and stand up. Perhaps they had been praying for this moment day and night. I couldn't help them and they couldn't help me; I didn't understand them and I didn't need them, and everything about them was completely foreign to me.

There came a call from the front that everybody except the drivers should dismount. This was an order. A deep breath went through the convoy, for this could mean only one thing: the final steps toward freedom lay ahead. Before we could move on, the Polish drivers jumped off, coiled the reins around the stanchion of the wagon, put the whip on the seat, formed a small squad, and set about going back, eastward. Herr Volk, immediately turning a bluish-red color, blocked their way. At first he spoke quietly to them, but soon he began to scream. Conspiracy, foul play, refusal to work, he shouted. That's when I saw a Polish migrant worker push aside a German estate farmer. Now the world had truly turned topsy-turvy, only Herr Volk hadn't noticed yet; he automatically reached for his whip, but his lash was stopped in midair, someone was holding his arm, the whip dropped to the ground and the Poles walked on. His hand pressed against his heart, Herr Volk leaned heavily against the cart and let himself be comforted by his thin-lipped wife and the silly dachshund Suzie, while Kalle railed at him from above, shouting, Bastard, bastard. The French people, who stayed with us, called out greetings to the departing Poles, who understood those greetings no more than I did, but understood their sound, and so did I, and it hurt being so strictly excluded from their shouting, waving, and the tossing of their caps, from their joy and their language. But it had to be that way. The world consisted of the victors and the defeated. The former were free to express their emotions. The latter—us—had to lock them inside ourselves from now on. The enemy should not see us weak.

There he was, by the way. I would have preferred a fire-breathing dragon to this light Jeep with its gum-chewing driver and the three casual officers who, out of bottomless condescension, had not even uncovered their holsters. I tried to make an expressionless face and look right through them, and told myself that their unconstrained laughter, their clean uniforms, their indifferent glances, the whole damned victor's pose had probably been ordered for our special humiliation.

The people around me began to hide watches and rings. I, too, took my watch off my wrist and carelessly put it in my coat pocket. The guard at the end of the line, a lanky, hulking man beneath an impossible steel helmet, which had made us burst out laughing whenever we saw it in the newsreels, pointed out with one hand to the few people carrying arms where to throw their weapons, while his other hand frisked us civilians with a few firm, routine police motions. Petrified with indignation but secretly proud that they believed me capable of carrying a weapon, I let myself be searched. At which point my overworked sentry routinely asked, "Your watch?" So he wanted my watch, the victor, but he didn't get it, for I succeeded in fooling him with the statement that the other one, "your comrade," his brother officer, had already pocketed it. I escaped unscathed as far as the watch was concerned, at which point my heightened sense of hearing signaled once more the rising sound of an airplane engine. Despite the fact that this was no longer any of my business, I kept an eye on its approach route out of habit and threw myself to the ground by reflex as it swooped down; once more the horrid dark shadow flitting quickly across grass and trees, once more the atrocious sound of bullets pounding into soil. Still? I thought to myself in astonishment, realizing that one can get used to the feeling of being out of danger in a second. With malicious glee I saw American artillerymen bringing an American gun into position and firing it at an American plane, which hurriedly zoomed up and disappeared beyond the forest.

Now, one should be capable of saying how it felt when it became quiet. I stayed put for a while behind the tree. I believe I didn't care about the fact that, from that minute on, possibly no bomb or MG shrapnel would ever again be dropped down on me. I wasn't curious as to what would happen now. I didn't know what use there was for a dragon once it stops breathing fire. I had no idea how the horned Siegfried is supposed to act if the dragon asks him for his watch rather than gobbling him up, hair and hide. I didn't feel like watching how Herr Siegfried and Herr Dragon would get along as private citizens. And I certainly didn't feel like going to the Americans in the occupied mansions for every bucket of water, and I most definitely didn't feel like entering into a fight with black-haired Lieutenant Davidson from Ohio, at the end of which I saw myself obliged to declare that now my pride absolutely demanded that I hate him.

And I felt even less up to the talk with the concentration-camp prisoner who sat with us by the fire at night wearing a pair of bent wire-frame spectacles and mentioned in passing the word "Communism" as if it were a permitted, household word such as "hatred" or "war" or "extermination." No. And least of all did I feel like knowing about the sadness and the dismay which were in his voice when he asked us, "Where, then, have you lived all these years?"

I didn't feel up to liberation. I was lying under my tree, all was quiet. I was lost and I reflected that I wanted to make a note of the branches against that very beautiful May sky. Then my lanky, off-duty sergeant came up the slope, a squealing German girl hanging on each arm. All three moved in the direction of the mansion, and finally I had a reason to turn away a little and cry.

TUESDAY,

SEPTEMBER 27

FIRST THING on awakening the thought: This day, too, will take an unexpected course. I will have to take Tinka to the doctor because of her bad foot. The sound of doors slamming outside. The children are already at it.

G. is still asleep. His forehead is damp, but the fever is gone. He seems to have gotten over the flu. There is life in the children's room. Tinka is reading to a small, dirty doll from a picture book: One wanted to warm his hands, the other his gloves, and the third one wanted to drink tea. But there wasn't any coal. How silly!

She'll be four tomorrow. Annette is worried about whether we will bake enough cake. She points out to me that Tinka has invited eight children for tea. I get over the small shock and write a note for Annette's teacher: Please allow my daughter Annette to come home at noon tomorrow. We are celebrating her little sister's birthday.

While making sandwiches I try to remember how I spent the day before Tinka was born four years ago. Time and again it dismays me how quickly and how much one forgets if one does not write everything down. On the other hand, recording *everything* would be impossible: one would have to stop living. It was probably warmer four years ago and I was alone. In the evening, a girl friend came to stay overnight with me. We sat together for a long time; it was the last intimate talk we had. For the first time she told me about her future husband . . .

During the night I telephoned for the ambulance.

Annette is ready at last. She is a bit of a dawdler and untidy, the way I must have been as a child. Back then I never would have believed that I would reprimand my children the way my parents reprimanded me. Annette has misplaced her wallet. I scold her with the same words that my mother would have used: We can't exactly throw our money around like that, what were you thinking? When she leaves, I squeeze her face and give her a kiss. So long! We wink at each other. Then she closes the front door with a loud bang.

Tinka calls for me. I shout an impatient reply and sit down tentatively at my desk. Perhaps I can wangle at least one hour's work. At the top of her lungs, Tinka is singing a song to her doll which the children really love these days: "Leaving town at night when the moon is shining . . ." The final stanza goes like this:

One lonely day
they ate off one plate,
one lonely evening
the stork a child did bring . . .

Whenever I'm here, Tinka never fails to calm me down. Of course she knew that the stork couldn't carry any children, that would clearly be cruelty to animals. But if one *sang* it, it didn't matter, did it?

She starts screaming for me again, so loud that I race over to her. She is lying in bed, her head buried under her arms.

What are you screaming about?

You never come, so I *have* to scream.

I told you: I'm coming.

Then it still takes ages ages ages cages cages cages. She has discovered that words can rhyme. I unwind the bandage from her cut foot. She screams bloody murder. Then she flicks away the tears with her fingers: It will hurt at the doctor's, too. Do you want to scream like that at the doctor's? The whole town will gather. Then *you* have to take off the bandage. All right, all right. May I have hot custard this morning? All right, all right. You make me some! All right, all right.

The pain in her foot seems to ease. While I am dressing her, she scratches her fingernails along the underside of the tabletop, convulsed with laughter. She wipes her nose on her shirttail. Hey, I shout, who dares blow her nose with her shirt? She tosses her head back, bursting into wild laughter: Who dares blow her nose with her shirt, poop shirt . . .

Tomorrow is my birthday, so we can already be a little bit happy today, she says. But I bet you forgot that I can get dressed by myself. I didn't forget, I only thought your foot hurt too much. She clumsily weaves her toes through the trouser legs: I am much more careful than you are. Once more there is danger of tears when it turns out that the red shoe is too tight. I put an old slipper of Annette's on the sore foot. She is thrilled: Now I've got on Annette's slipper!

As I carry her out of the bathroom, her healthy foot bangs into the wooden crate next to the door. Bang! she exclaims. That hitted like a bomb! How does she know how a bomb hits? It was more than sixteen years ago that I last heard a bomb detonate. How does she know the word?

G. is reading Lenin's letters to Gorky; we come back to our old subjects: art and the revolution, politics and art, ideology and literature. The impossibility of finding congruent thought constructs among even Marxist politicians and artists. His "own" world, which Lenin concedes to Gorky (more than concedes: which he presupposes) despite all the irreconcilability of philosophical matters. His consideration, his tact in spite of all his rigorousness. Two equal partners are working together; this is not a confrontation between the one who knows it all and the one who must be taught everything. An open and generous mutual appreciation of one another's abilities . . . We arrive at the role of experience in writing and the responsibility one bears for the *contents* of one's experience: was one free to have arbitrary, perhaps desirable experiences when judged from a social perspective, experiences for which one didn't qualify on account of one's social background and personality? There is a lot one can get to know, of course. But *experience?* — We have an argument about the plan for my new story. G. presses for another change of the yet-too-superficial idea into one more suited to me. Or did I wish to write a journalistic piece? All right then, in that case I could get down to it at once. Slight annoyance on my part, denied as usual when I sense that there is, in fact, "some truth to it."

Whether I had read this? A small article by Lenin entitled "A Talented Little Book." It concerns a book by a White Gardist whose bitterness borders on madness: "A dozen daggers in the back of the revolution," which Lenin discusses—half ironically, half seriously, attesting to its "authority and candor" wherever the author describes what he knows, what he lived through and felt. Lenin assumes without any further ado that the workers and peasants will draw proper conclusions from the pure, knowledgeable description of the way of life of the old bourgeoisie, a step which the author himself is incapable of, and seems to think it possible to print some of these stories. "Talent should be supported"—irony again, but an equal amount of superiority. We arrive at the prerequisites for superior behavior in a country where socialist society must develop with the same prerequisites and conditions as ours. The reasons for and bases of provincialism in literature.

We laugh as we become aware of what we talk about endlessly at any time of the day or night, like in those schematic books whose heroes we criticize as improbable.

I take Tinka to the doctor's. She talks and talks, perhaps to get over her fear. First she demands an explanation of a mural (Why don't you think it's beautiful? I think it's nice and colorful!), then she wants to be carried on account of her sick foot, then she completely forgets about the pain and balances on the stone borders of the front yards.

Our street leads toward a new apartment building which has been under construction for months. An elevator hoists up containers full of sacks of mortar and sends them down empty. Tinka wants to know exactly how it works. She has to be content with a vague explanation of the technology. Her new, unshakable belief that everything that exists is "good for something," is good for something for *her*. If I am so often afraid for the children, then it is, above all, because of the inevitable violation of this belief. As we run down the post-office stairs I pick her up and carry her under my arm. Not so fast, I falls! You won't fall. When I'm big and you're small, I'll run down the stairs just as fast. I'll be bigger than you. Then I'll jump real high. By the way, can you jump over the house? No? I can. Over the house and over a tree. Shall I? Go ahead! I *could* easy, but I don't want to. So. You don't want to. No. Silence. After a while: But in the sun I'm tall. The sun is hazy but it throws shadows. They are long because the sun is still low. Tall up to the clouds, Tinka says. I look up. There are small hazy clouds high in the sky.

Excited chatter in the waiting room. Three elderly women are sitting together. One of them, who speaks a Silesian dialect, bought a blue cardigan for 113 marks the day before. The event is examined from all angles. All three of them bicker about the price. A younger woman sitting opposite the three finally joins in on the uninformed conversation in a superior tone of voice. It turns out that she is a textile salesperson and that the cardigan is not an "import" at all, as the Silesian woman had been assured at the time of the purchase. She is outraged. The saleswoman is holding forth on the pros and cons of wool and acrylics. Acrylics are practical, she says, but if one wants to have something real elegant, one chooses wool. Whatever is good is bound to come back, says the second of the three women, and I shoot a beseeching glance at Tinka, who is on the brink of asking a certainly inappropriate question. In the West such a cardigan costs 50 marks, says the Silesian woman. Well, says the second, why don't you convert it: one to three. Comes to 150 marks, as well.

There doesn't seem to be any point in interfering in their conversions.

I got the money from my daughter, says the Silesian woman. With my 120 marks social security I wouldn't have been able to afford it. All three sigh. Then their neighbor says, That's always been my device: simple but elegant. I study her surreptitiously and can't see anything elegant about her. She goes on, unperturbed: This coat, for example. Bought it in 1927. Gabardine. Peacetime merchandise. Not a trace of wear and tear. Horrified, I look at the coat. It is green, slightly shiny, and out-of-style. Other than that, there is nothing noticeable about it. A coat can't be eerie, can it? Tinka whispers, pulling on my sleeve, When is 1927? Thirty-three years ago, I say. She uses a phrase of her father's: Any thought of me back then? By no means, I say. Not even a thought of me at that time. Goodness gracious, says Tinka. The Silesian woman, still preoccupied with her blue cardigan, comforts herself: Anyway, I won't be cold in the winter.

The third one, a gaunt woman who hasn't said much up to now, now remarks in quiet triumph, Thank God, *I* don't have to think about all that . . . Silent question from the others. At last: You've got relatives over there? No. That is, yes. My daughter. But she only makes the arrangements. There is a gentleman. I don't even know him, but he sends me whatever I need. He just had inquiries made again about what I still need for the winter . . . Pure envy in the eyes of the others. Oh well, in that case! You can't be better off than that nowadays.

I am silent, having given up my reading long ago. The doctor's assistant calls all three of them.

Tinka is absolutely quiet as the doctor presses around the wound. She is pale, her hand in mine becomes clammy. Did that hurt? asks the doctor. She makes her impenetrable face and shakes her head. She never cries in front of strangers. Outside, while we are waiting for the bandage, she suddenly says, I'm so happy that tomorrow is my birthday!

The sky has clouded over. We're already looking forward to the bricklayers' elevator. Tinka would have stood there for a long time if she hadn't had to go to the bathroom fast. Then she becomes silent. She is preoccupied with the big black dog whose kennel we will have to pass soon. As usual at this stretch she tells me that this dog once bit a woman in the finger. This must have been years ago, if true at all, but the legend has made an indelible impression on Tinka. The effect of narrative!

The mail I find at home is disappointing, a nondescript card from a nondescript girl. On the other hand, motorbikes stop several times in front of the house, special delivery and telegram messengers, telephone substitutes. One of them brings the galley proofs of G.'s book on Fürnberg. While the food is getting ready, I read children's essays on the subject "My Most Wonderful Vacation Day," which were handed in at the freight-car-works library. A nine-year-old girl writes: "It was wonderful in our vacation camp. We had one day off when we could go wherever we wanted to. I went into the forest, where I saw a big and a little stag. The two of them just lay there not moving. They were so tame that you could touch them. So I ran back quickly to get the camp leader. It wasn't at all far to our camp. I told him everything and he went with me. He led off the big stag on a rope and I was allowed to carry the little one. We had a small stable and I put both of them in there and fed them every day. That was my most wonderful day."

I'm in favor of giving this girl first prize in the competition for her improbable story.

After lunch I go to a Party group meeting of the brigade at the freight-car works. An elderly couple on the cable car are desperately searching their pockets for the ten-pfennig piece they need in order to buy their tickets. They overspent while shopping. I offer a ten-pfennig piece to the woman. Extreme embarrassment: Oh no, oh no, they can just as well walk. Finally the man accepts, though not without protestations as to how embarrassed he is. This kind of thing is possible only with us Germans, I think.

I haven't been to the factory in a few weeks. The shop is full of half-finished freight cars. The holdup in production has apparently been overcome. My relief comes too early.

Willy does not notice me at first. I watch him working with his new machine for the preparation of pressure frames. He and J., his brigadier, have developed this simple but practical machine and handed it in as a suggestion for improvement. By using it they save half the time needed for this operation. There has been talk behind their backs in the factory, bad blood has been bred. Today I shall learn what is really the matter.

Willy looks up. Well, my love, he says. He is happy. He is still busy. I sit down in the brigade shack, which they themselves call the cowshed. Although there are still forty-five minutes left until the end of the shift, three men are already sitting here waiting for time to go by. Still not enough work? General shaking of heads. The impression I got in the shop was deceptive. And what do you do with the surplus time? Occupational therapy, they say. Iron site, wood site, mending planks. And the money? The money is okay. We get the average pay, after all. They are in a bad mood, resigned or enraged, depending on their respective tempers. And the worst is, they have stopped hoping for a change for the better. Lothar says, In January we'll be in a pickle again, even if we kill ourselves making the plan during the last quarter. The money is wasted on overtime. Is that supposed to be profitable?

31 / Tuesday, September 27

The money is okay, but he is angry at the unprofitability of the factory. Can the manager of the factory go to every brigade and explain what is going on? He cannot. But it should be explained, and in so many words for that matter and, if possible, on a weekly basis according to the current situation. The uninformed are beginning to act irresponsibly.

Meanwhile, the conversation focuses on the staff party the previous Saturday. Jürgen tells the story of how he barely managed to get his wife, who had had a few too many, home in a factory bus after she slapped an obnoxious colleague in the face in front of everyone. I was so mad I got drunk the next day, he says. He is a little afraid that his wife could have made a fool of him. At which point the others start telling about similar events with their own wives, matter-of-factly, without any emotional expenditure, the way men talk about women. I think, Surely the obnoxious colleague deserved his slap in the face . . .

Nine comrades meet in the conference room of the Party leadership. They arrive in their work clothes, unwashed. Among them is a woman with cheerful, lively eyes; I've seen her bang on the table in the brigade. Here she does not say anything.

No beating around the bush—let's get started, says Willy. He is the group organizer. Informed about his intentions today, I anxiously and appreciatively watch him home in on his goal. In front of him lies the report of the public statement of accounts of his brigade. I've seen it. However, the comrades from the neighboring brigade, the contestants, are sitting slightly flabbergasted in front of the twenty-three pages of the others who, in spite of their friendship, are their rivals after all. And if one knows the muddled history of the two brigades which at one time were *one* . . .

the star brigade of the factory under the leadership of P., who is sitting opposite Willy, keeps wiping away the sweat, and feels duped.

Willy begins reading from the statement of accounts quickly and inarticulately, a carefully selected piece. His hands holding the page tremble slightly. The atmosphere in the overheated room must have a rather soporific effect on an outsider.

No one takes quotations as seriously as Willy. He reads what Lenin said about the increase of work productivity. And how is it with us? he interrupts himself. A colleague says, Before we wanted to become a socialist work brigade we were always in agreement. Now there's trouble all the time. Willy raises his voice. He now arrives at their proposal for improvement: that simple machine which I saw in action before. There was an incredible fuss! he says, and letting the paper sink, he peers out over his wire-framed spectacles directly at P.: a savings of 50 percent! That was unheard of—for us! The practicality of the proposal was questioned. Yes, you too, P.! Be quiet, now it's my turn! But the proposal is practical, nothing can shake it. Sure, we got a premium. Sure, the two of us will make good money the next three months. I get a thousand marks out of it, if you want to know. And what of it? Is material incentive perhaps nothing to us comrades? Everything would have been all right if the two of them had shared their premiums, had shut their mouths with a few bottles of beer. But no more of that! shouts Willy. No more of that old leveling mania. And we'll buy a round at the next brigade evening.

In the division, this had given rise to the insidious question: Are you a Communist or an egotist?

And we knew it, shouts Willy, who has been in a

state of agitation for quite some time now and keeps talking out of turn. We knew it, all of us. Or didn't we? And how did we conduct ourselves as comrades? Not at all. And how could we have! We were not in agreement. Get to the point! shouts one man from the neighboring brigade.

Willy, raising his voice more and more: All right! If that's what you want! The two of us are proposed as activists in the Brigade Group Leadership. Who speaks against it? Comrade P.! The Party leadership intend to put up our picture on the "Street of the Best" on the occasion of the Day of the Republic. Who advises against it? Comrade P.! Explicit enough for you?

Perhaps I'm allowed to say something as well, demands P. You're welcome to, says Willy. Just one more thing: the work is at stake. This is about the work and not whether I don't like your face or you don't like mine. Everyone here at the table remembers P.'s statement from a time when Willy was new in the brigade, along with his "declining cadre development": He or I, that's the question. There is no room in the brigade for both of us. On the first of May, P.'s picture still stood on the "Street of the Best." Both of them must have forgotten a lot and thought about quite a few things which they wouldn't admit to themselves before they could talk to one another like today. It is not to be expected that the conflict will come to a head according to the rules of classical drama and be "carried out" to the end. It already means a lot when P. admits: Your proposal was practical. It is only right for you to get the premium. Subsequently his supply of self-abnegation runs dry. He becomes evasive, pulls out an old story which he expatiates on at great length. He can't admit defeat that easily. The two brigades argue back and forth, the suspense eases; Willy, too, has to move back a notch once in a while, which is difficult enough for him.

The statement of accounts of his brigade is still in front of him. Within one week P.'s people are supposed to have finished as well. Suddenly they get worried about the work. Willy still allows himself this small triumph, everybody notices that. But enough of that now, they must come to an agreement. They are debating who should help P. If you want an old troublemaker like me as well . . . says Willy. You old fool! says P.

Someone comes up with the idea of inviting the women to the brigade's public statement of accounts, this being the trend of the times. Nobody can publicly argue against this; however, it becomes clear that the suggestion has no fiery advocates. Don't the women have enough to do with the children, particularly after knocking off? says one of them. Günter R. is happy: You can only bring a wife if you have one.

Well, and what about you? Willy snaps at him. Haven't got one, huh? Nope, says Günter. No more. What's the matter with your marriage anyway? Don't go to pieces about such nonsense! threatens Willy. Günter is the youngest at the table. He makes a disparaging gesture with his hand but blushes bright red. A mere trifle! Not worth mentioning!

Later P. tells me: Günter was sent as socialist help to the sister factory in G. for a couple of weeks, and when he came home unexpectedly one day, who comes walking out of his bedroom but his wife's boss? Naturally, he's off to the courts immediately. Nothing to be patched up there . . .

By and by, the mood has become cheerful. Jokes

are cracked. They protest when I say that none of them wants to know about culture. The invitation cards for the public statement of accounts are passed around, white folded cards with INVITATION printed on them in golden flourishes. That's distinguished enough for them. They want to invite quite a few guests, want to "set an example," as Willy puts it. He lets the meeting drag on, hardly tense anymore and looking quite content. He winks at me and grins. Pretty sly, I say to him later. One has to be, sweetie, he says. Won't get anywhere otherwise.

I walk home quickly, nervous, my thoughts all stirred up. I hear once again what they say, and also what they don't say, that which not even their looks betray. Who could ever succeed in entering into this almost impenetrable maze of motives and countermotives, actions and counter-actions . . . To enlarge the lives of people who seem to be condemned to taking small steps . . .

At this time of year, it is already cold toward evening. I shop for what I need to bake the cakes and also pick up a bunch of birthday flowers. The dahlias and asters are already withering in the yards. I think of the huge bouquet of roses on my bedside table in the hospital back then, four years ago. I remember the doctor, hear him say, A girl. But she has got one already. Well, I guess she won't mind . . . His relief that I already had a name. The nurse informing me about how undesirable girls still were sometimes, the reactions one could experience, particularly with the fathers. They simply don't come when it's another girl, believe it or not. That's why we're not allowed to say on the telephone what it is, boy or girl.

Everyone wants to help with baking the cakes. The children are constantly in the way. I finally put on a fairy-tale record for them in the living room, "Peter and the Wolf." Afterward they lick the bowls until they are taken away from them. Annette talks about school: We learned a new song, but I don't like it that much. Democracy rhymes with victory—what do you think of that? I think it's boring. We have a new Russian teacher. She was surprised at how many words we already know. But do you think she told us her name? Wouldn't dream of it. Whereas we had to write down all our names for her on a seating plan. I don't even think she cares. They fidget around restlessly for a long time and do not want to face the fact that one also has to sleep the night before a birthday.

The cakes are rising in the oven beyond all measure. Now that it is getting quiet I imagine I can hear them rise. The pans were too full, the dough rises and rises and drips into the oven and spreads a burnt smell throughout the whole apartment.

When I take out the cakes, one side is black. I am annoyed and cannot find anybody to blame except myself, and then, on top of everything else, G. comes in and calls the cakes "a little black," at which point I tell him, full of indignation, that it is on account of the pans that were too full and the bad oven and the gas pressure that is too strong. Oh well, he says, and withdraws.

Later we listen to Antonín Dvořák's violin sonata, Opus 100, to which Fürnberg composed a poem. A lovely, pure melody. My anger is dissolving. We notice simultaneously that we smell of burnt cake and start laughing.

I still have to write a little, but everything bothers me: the radio, the television next door, the thought of tomorrow's birthday hubbub and of this day full of interruptions when I didn't get anything done. I sullenly set the birthday table, arrange the circle of lights. G. is leafing through some little book and finds it "well written." For some reason that bothers me as well.

I look through the manuscript beginnings piled up on my desk. I am embittered at the lengthiness of the process called writing. A few faces stand out from the pure brigade story, people whom I know better and have linked together in a story which, as I clearly see, is still far too simple. A girl from the country who comes to the big city for the first time in her life in order to study. Before coming, she does an internship at a factory, in a difficult brigade. Her boyfriend is a chemist, he does not get her in the end. The third person is a young master craftsman who was sent to this brigade on probation because he had made a mistake . . . It is strange how these banal events, "taken from life," enhance their banality to the point of intolerability on the pages of a manuscript. I know that the real work will only begin once the principal idea has been found rendering the banal matter possible to tell, as well as worth telling. However, it can be found—if at all, which tonight I seriously doubt—only through this long groundwork, the futility of which I am well aware.

I know that nothing will remain, neither the pages which are already lying here nor the sentences which I write today—not a single letter of them. I write and then I cross it out again: As usual Rita was dragged out of sleep as fast as an arrow and was awake without memory of a dream. But there must have been a face. She wanted to hold on to it before it faded. Robert was lying next to her.

Before falling asleep I think that life consists of days like this one. Points that are joined together by a line in the long run, if one is lucky. That they can also fall apart in a meaningless heap of time past, that only an incessant, unwavering effort gives meaning to the small units of time we live in . . .

I can still observe the first transitions to the pictures one sees before falling asleep; a street appears leading to that landscape I know so well without ever having seen it: the hill with the old tree, the softly inclined slope up to a stream, meadowland, and the forest at the horizon. That one can't really experience the seconds before falling asleep—otherwise one wouldn't fall asleep—I will forever regret.

JUNE

AFTERNOON

A STORY? Something firm, tangible, like a pot with two handles, to be touched and drunk from?

A vision, perhaps, if you understand what I mean.

Although the garden was never more real than this year. In all the time we have known it—of course it has only been three years—it has never had the opportunity to show what it is capable of. Now it turns out that it was the dream of being a green, rampant, wild, lush garden, no more, no less. The archetype of a garden. Garden incarnate. I have to say, this touches us. We exchange approving comments about its growth and understand secretly that it exaggerates its lushness; that, at present, it cannot but exaggerate, for how could it not exploit greedily the rare occasion of profiting from the falls, the still frequent rainfalls of near and far storms?

Whatever is sauce for the goose is gravy for the gander.

What is a gander? The child sat at my feet, doggedly carving a piece of bark which was first supposed to become a ship, later a dagger, and then something from the umbrella family. Now, however, unless all signs failed, it was turning into a gander. And in the process we would find out what this darned gander actually was. Although one can't carve with such a dull knife, you must admit. As if it had not been proven that one cuts oneself much more often with a dull knife than with a sharp one! Yet I, experienced in ignoring concealed reproaches, leaned back in my deck chair and read on, no matter what kind of criticism might be brought against a dull carving knife.

Listen, I said a little later to my husband, whom I could not see; however, his pruning shears were audible: he was probably at the vine, for it had to be continually thinned out this year, since it was acting as if it grew on a Mosel hillside and not on a skimpy trellis under a Brandenburg March pine. Listen, I said, you were right after all.

Didn't I say so, he said. Why you never wanted to read it, I don't know!

She knows how to write, I said.

Although not everything is good, he said, so I wouldn't be in danger of going too far again.

That goes without saying! But the way she deals with the country . . .

Yes, he said with a superior air. Italy!

And the sea? I asked challengingly.

Yes, he exclaimed, as if that alone was irrefutable proof. The Mediterranean!

But that's not it at all. One very exact word next to the other. That's what it is.

Although the Mediterranean is perhaps not entirely to be scoffed at either, he said.

Why do you always have to use foreign words! said the child, full of reproach.

The sun, rare as it was, had already started to bleach her hair. Within the course of the summer and especially during the vacation on the eastern seaboard, that golden helmet, which the child wore with dignity like something that was her due, and which we forgot year after year, would evolve again.

I turned a page and the sweetish odor of almost withered acacias mingled with the foreign smell of macchia bushes and stone pines, but I took care not to introduce any more foreign words and stuck my nose obediently into the handful of thorny leaves the child held up to me, full of malicious glee at the inconspicuous origin of peppermint tea. She stood like a stork in the midst of an island of wild chives and rubbed one skinny leg against the other. I remembered that, in summer as well as winter, she smelled of chives and mint and hay and all manner of herbs we did not yet know but which had to exist, for the child smelled of them.

Snails exaggerate their slowness, don't you think? she said, and it could not be denied that, within the course of an entire hour, the snail had not managed to crawl from the wooden leg of my deck chair to the rain barrel. Although one could not be completely sure to what extent it had understood and accepted our bet earlier on and whether a snail can plan such an undertaking: the rain barrel in one hour, if at all.

By the way, did you know that they are crazy about plum leaves? I have tested it.

I did not know this. Never in my entire life had I seen a snail eat, least of all plum leaves, but I kept my ignorance and my doubts to myself and let the child go off and look for something that was less disappointing than the snail.

As soon as she was out of hearing, there was suddenly no sound at all for seconds. Neither a bird nor the wind nor any sound at all, and believe me, it is disturbing when our quiet area becomes truly quiet. You never know why everything is holding its breath. This time, however, it was only one of those good old passenger aircrafts; I'm not saying that it can't be incredibly quick and comfortable, for these airlines flying overhead are in cutthroat competition with one another. I only mean, clearly visible to everybody, it flew from east to west, to use these designations for nothing but direction for once; in the opinion of most of its passengers the plane was probably flying from West to west; that is, because it had taken off in West Berlin, since the air corridor—a word one could ponder over for a long time—is just over our yard and the rain barrel and my deck chair, from where I observed, not without satisfaction, how without the slightest effort this airplane absorbed not only its own buzzing but the entire collection of sounds of our garden.

I do not know whether the sky is just as densely occupied elsewhere as it is here. If one lay down flat on the ground and stared up at the sky, one could get to know different types of aircraft from all over the world within the space of an hour. Yet this is of no use to me, for I was not taught even by the war to differentiate between airplanes of different make and function. I do not even know whether they blink red on the right and green on the left when they fly over our house at night, or vice versa.

And do they actually care about us in the least? Well then, I have flown often enough to know that an aircraft has no eyes to see and no soul to care. But I would bet any amount that more than an undersecretary of state, a banker, and a business mogul are drifting along above us this afternoon. I'd even bet there's one of those princesses who has recently become so active. Within the course of the week one has done one's bit and strengthened the feeling of being on outpost duty in oneself and in others, and flies home on Saturday with a clear conscience. During takeoff one shows a fleeting interest in the country down there, its roads, bodies of water, houses and gardens. Somewhere there are three dots in a green area (of course, I am leaving out the snail). What do you know, people. Well. Wonder what kind of life they lead around here. Unfavorable area, too. Not much can be done about this from the sky.

Don't think that I'm going to let you sleep now, said the child. She had crept up on me like an Indian and was satisfied to see me jump. She crouched down next to me to look up at the sky as well and scan it for ships and castles, wild mountain chains and gilded oceans of bliss. No battleships today. No storm alarm far and wide. Only the sound of cars in the distance and the breathtaking development of an oasis in the desert, its palm-tree tops graced by the sun and its animal world changing with amazing speed, for up there they had discovered the trick of letting one thing develop from another, of letting one thing merge into another: a camel into a lion, a rhinoceros into a tiger, and, in spite of the fact that this was a little strange, a giraffe into a penguin. We were suddenly overcome by a sense of insecurity about the reliability of celestial landscapes, but we hid this from each other.

Do you remember how you always used to say Engupin? I asked.

Instead of penguin? I was never that stupid!

How long is never for an eight-year-old child? And how long is forever? Four years? Or ten? Or the unimaginable gap between her age and mine?

Engupin, I insisted. Ask your father.

However, we could not ask him. I could not hear him laugh and say Engupin, in the same tone that he had four years ago. For Father stood at the fence speaking to the next-door neighbor. The usual conversation: What? You're not thinking of cutting the wild Lactarius on your tomatoes even more? You can't be serious! We listened to the argument with haughty amusement, the way one listens to something one is not really concerned about. By the way, we agreed with Father. Out of principle and because the neighbor had lost our last bit of respect during spring, when he demanded in all seriousness that the child pick all of the at least six hundred dandelions in our garden, so they could not turn into puffballs and their seeds threaten his pedantically manicured yard. We had a lot of fun over the thought of armies of puffball parachutes—six hundred times thirty, roughly calculated—drifting toward the neighbor's yard one day in a favorable southwesterly wind, with him standing there groaning, since he is growing too fat, and armed to the teeth with hoe, spade, and garden hose, his straw hat on his head and his furious little cur at his feet. Yet all of them together are no match for the puffball seeds leisurely sailing along and alighting wherever they happen to drop, without the least hurry or reluctance, for there will be no problem at all in finding that little piece of soil and dampness needed to gain ground and germinate. We were completely on the side of the puffballs.

Still, the neighbor was right in complaining about the fact that the strawberries are rotting on their stems and that nobody knows where it will end if a sunny afternoon like this is a rare exception.

The dry, sharp, truly bloodcurdling sonic boom of a jet invaded this weary talk, the subdued laughter from another garden, the slightly sad dialogue in my book. It's always right above us, said the child, insulted but not frightened, and I did not reveal how easily shock can still pull the ground out from under my feet. It can't manage any other way, I said. What? The sound barrier. It has to get through. Why? It has been specially made for this purpose, and now it has to get through. Even if it boomed twice as loud. He must be embarrassed about it himself. Don't you think? Perhaps the pilot puts cotton in his ears? But he doesn't hear anything. That's the whole point: the sound stays behind him. Practical, don't you think? said the child, and added in the same tone, I'm bored.

I do know that one should fear the boredom of children, and that it cannot be compared with the boredom of adults, unless their boredom has become deadly. What do we have to fear more than the deadly boredom of entire races? However, that does not apply in this case. I had to cope with the boredom of the child and said vaguely and ineffectually, Then do something!

It says in the newspaper that children should be given tasks, says the child. That's what educates them.

You read the newspaper?

Of course. But Father takes the best articles away from me. For example, "Husband's Corpse Found in Window Seat."

You really wanted to read that?

That would have been exciting. Did the wife murder the husband?

No idea.

Who was it that hid him in the window seat?

But I haven't read the article!

When I'm big I'll read all those articles. I'm bored.

I told the child to get water and a rag and wipe off the table and chairs, and I saw the body of the husband in the window seat swim through her dreams, saw wives flitting about with the intention of murdering their husbands with—what? With a hatchet? With the kitchen knife? With the clothesline? Saw myself standing by her bed: What is it? Did you have a bad dream? and saw her frightened eyes: Nothing. There's nothing wrong with me. Are you all there? At some point in the future the child will tell her children about an early nightmare. The garden will have sunk into oblivion a long time before; she will shake her head in embarrassment at an old photo of me, and will hardly remember anything about herself. The husband's body in the window seat, however, will have been preserved in her memory, impudent and pale, the same way I am still tortured by a man my grandfather once told me about: on account of a horrible murder he had been sentenced to madness by drops of water which fell on his shaved head in regular intervals, day in and day out.

Hey, said my husband, can't you hear today?

I was thinking of my grandfather.

Which one—the one who was still standing on his head at eighty?

The one who died of typhoid fever in '45.

The one with a mustache like a seal?

Yes. Him.

Strange how I always get your grandfathers mixed up!

That's your problem. One can't be mistaken for the other.

He continued to complain about my grandfathers and I continued to defend them, as if we had to fool an invisible spectator about our true thoughts and intentions. He stood next to the little apricot tree, which, surprisingly, overcame its stunted existence this year, although it did not manage to bear more than one single fruit, and we pretended to look at this tiny green apricot. I don't know what he was really looking at. I, in any case, was amazed at the light, which now surrounded the apricot tree and everything in its vicinity, so that one could look at it for quite a while without getting the least bit bored. Even if one proceeded from the grandfathers to something else in the meantime, for example the book I still held in my hands, the advantage of which was that it did not interrupt the contemplation of apricot trees. Instead, it contributed its bit, in all modesty, as is expected of a third party.

Yet there were still a few too many recluses and prophets and bewitched people in it, we agreed about that, and I obtained permission to skip a story, which supposedly describes all the gory details of a people's revenge on a traitor; I confessed that I could no longer cope with all these mutilations and killings of men before the eyes of their trussed-up wives; I admitted that, as of late, I have begun to be afraid of the next drop that falls on our bare heads.

Just at that moment our daughter appeared, and next door, the engineer pushed his new frog-green car out of the garage for its Saturday-night wash. As regards the car, none of us would have had the sad courage to tell the engineer that his car is frog-green, because it says "linden-green" on the car's registration, and that's what he adheres to. He goes by printed matter in general. You only need to look at his haircut to know about the most recent recommendations of the magazine *Your Hairdo* and at his apartment to know what *Interior Design* considered a must two years ago. He is a friendly, flaxen-haired man, our engineer; he is not interested in politics but looks helpless when we call the most recent editorial boring. He never reveals anything, and neither do we, for we are more than convinced that the flaxen-haired engineer with his frog-green car has the same right to be on this earth as we do, with our puffballs and celestial landscapes and this or that slightly sad book. If only our thirteen-year-old daughter, yes, the one who is just now entering through the garden door, had not set her mind on finding everything connected with the engineer modern. And if only we didn't know what catastrophic dynamite that word contains for her.

Have you seen the chic sunglasses he is wearing today? she asked as she drew closer. With one glance I was able to prevent Father from calling the sunglasses we hadn't even noticed impossible, and we watched in silence as she stalked across the bit of lawn, throwing a very long shadow, as she lowered herself in a complicated fashion next to the apricot tree and smoothed out her blouse in order to make it clear to us that the person sitting in front of us was no longer a child.

Have I already mentioned that she was coming from a rehearsal for a school recital?

It isn't working, she said. Nothing is working at all. What do you think of that?

Normal, said her father, and to this day I believe that it was nothing but revenge for the engineer's chic sunglasses.

You! said the daughter angrily. You probably find it normal if the speakers do not know their poems and the choir keeps hitting the wrong notes and the solo dancer keeps falling on her bottom?

You teach me all these expressions, stated the child, who was sitting on the edge of the rain barrel and taking care not to miss a single word from the nerve-racking life of her big sister. This caused their father to explain that it was a regrettable fact if a solo dancer fell on her bottom, but not an expression. However, the real question was whether a solo dancer was really needed at a school party.

How can I make you understand in so many words that the argument which now started had deep roots which were not so much nourished by the coincidental performance of a solo dancer as by a principal difference in opinion about the taste of the teacher, who has been organizing all school events since our children started attending the school. Up to now she had always found some well-built girl in the ninth or tenth grade who was willing to drift across the stage in a dress of red veils and mime longing to piano music. If you ask me, these girls deserved neither bitter disapproval nor uncritical rapture, but as I said before, this has nothing to do with them. This does not even have anything to do with the teacher's penchant for Bengal lights, for we should have learned by now to come to terms with all possible kinds of illumination. No, in reality Father cannot bear his daughter's painful devotion to everything she deems perfect; cannot bear the sight of her vulnerability; keeps standing in the empty field, whenever there is a thunderstorm, in order to attract the lightning bolts meant for her. For which he wins alternately stormy tenderness and furious ingratitude, so that he has said a thousand times, From this second onward I'll never get involved in these women's affairs, I swear. However, we did not listen to his oaths, for he is involved, with or without oaths. By hook or by crook.

Crook-jail, said the child inquiringly testing the waters: Will they continue to ignore me? The answers, which she got from us in quick succession and which I record here faithfully, will seem odd to you: Rain worm, I said. Fortune cookie, said her father. Night ghost, said the daughter. With such a good collection of words our game could begin at once, and the first round was: Rainjail, crook-cookie, fortuneghost, and nightworm, and then we really got going, got carried away with holeworm and crookghost and rainfortune and cookienight, after which point there was no stopping us, the dams broke and flooded the land with the most exquisite monstrosities, what with wormghost and crookrain and nightjail and cookieworm and jailfortune and nightrain and cookiecrook gushing out.

Excuse me. But it is difficult not to get carried away. It is quite possible that there are better words. And of course five or six players are better than four. We once tried it with the engineer. Do you know what he said? You'll never guess. Of course he cheated. One of the rules of the game is that everybody name the word at the tip of his tongue, without stopping to think. The engineer, however, racked his brains for seconds before our very eyes; he made a great effort until, very relieved, he came up with reconstructionhour. Of course we didn't want to let him show us up and racked our brains as well and served him up work brigade and extra shift and union paper, and the child in her confusion articulated pioneer leader. Yet unionreconstruction and brigadehour and extrawork and shiftleader and paperpioneer failed to turn into a proper game; we went on for a while listlessly, dutifully gave a small laugh at leaderunion, and broke off.

None of us said a word about this abortive attempt in order not to hurt the daughter's feelings, but it visibly occupied her until, at night, she defiantly said, So he's got consciousness!

Snow goose, said her father back then, the same thing he says today, because the daughter once more comes up with the solo dancer, who had been previously disposed of, and states in her defense that, wonderfully enough, this time she would perform in a sea-green dress. Sea-green snow goose! He took the child by the hand and they went off with expressions on their faces as if they were leaving us forever and not just for the short walk to their secret clover spot, for fortunecookie had naturally made them think of a lucky four-leaf clover. The daughter, however, looked after them triumphantly. He always says snow goose when he runs out of arguments, doesn't he? Do you happen to have a comb?

I gave her the comb, and she took a mirror out of her little basket and clumsily fastened it in the branches of the little apricot tree. The she took the ribbon out of her hair and began to comb it. I waited because it was not worth starting a new page. I saw her trying to control herself, but it had to be said: Looks awful, don't you think? Who? My hair. There's no use washing it right before going to bed. Now it had been said. This hairdo strongly emphasized her big nose—Have a heart, I hastily interjected. Your nose isn't too big!—even though it had the advantage of making its wearer look a little older. The bus conductor, for example, had just treated her like a grownup: Listen, miss, pull in your legs a bit! This had been embarrassing for her, but not only embarrassing, do you understand? Couldn't you have put him in his place? I said, purposely changing the subject ever so slightly. Perhaps in the following fashion: Were your polite remarks perhaps addressed to me? Oh no. She never thought of anything like that when she needed it, and apart from that, this was not about the impoliteness of the bus conductor but about the form of address. However, to get back to her hair: Listen, my daughter said. What would you rather be, beautiful or intelligent?

Do you know the feeling when a question hits you like a thunderbolt? I knew immediately that this was the question of all questions and that it got me into an insoluble dilemma. I expatiated at great length, and saw in the face of my daughter that she thought me guilty of each and every offense which was thinkable in my answer, and I silently asked an unpresent authority for a happy inspiration and thought, How she is beginning to resemble me; hopefully she doesn't notice it yet! and I suddenly said out loud, Now you listen to me. If you're going to look at me like that and not believe a word I'm saying anyway, why do you ask me in the first place? At which point she threw her arms around my neck, but that had been the purpose of the question anyway. The comb lay in the grass as if forever, and her soft lips were all over my face and very welcome protestations at my ear, such as "I-only-really-love-you" and "want-for-ever-to-stay-with-you" and "always-listen-to-you," in short, the kinds of promises one rashly makes for one's own protection shortly before one has to break them for good. And I believed every word and scoffed at my own weakness and my penchant toward cheap self-deception.

Now they're licking each other again, said the child disdainfully, and casually dropped a bouquet of clover into my lap, seven little stalks of clover, each one of them with four properly formed leaves, I could go ahead and see for myself. No optical illusion, no false bottom, no glue spit involved. Solid, four-leafed luck.

Seven! the daughter cried, electrified. Seven is my lucky number. In short, she wanted the leaves. All seven of them for herself. We had difficulty finding words for this immoderate claim and did not even think of reminding her that she had never shown any interest in four-leaf clovers and had never found a single four-leaf clover herself. We only looked at her with widened eyes and kept silent. But she was so set on luck that she did not become the least bit embarrassed.

Yes, the child said finally. Seven is her lucky number, that's true. On our way to school she always takes seven steps from one tree to the next. It drives me crazy. As if this were an act of inevitable justice, she took the clovers out of my lap and gave them to her sister. By the way, I got them back right after the daughter had firmly pressed them against her supposedly oversized nose; I should store them in my book for the time being. I was carefully observed as I put them between stone pines and macchia bushes at the edge of the foreign Mediterranean, on the steps of those stairs to the oracle who lied out of compassion, on the wooden table where the young landlord had waited on his guests as long as he was still happy and had not yet been marked as the victim of a dark evil. I left out the pages on which that gruesome act of revenge is committed, for what do I know about four-leaf clover and the lucky number seven, and what gives me the right to challenge certain forces?

Better to be on the safe side.

Now which one of you took my string again? From one moment to the next the foreign flora and fauna slipped off behind the horizon, which is where it belongs anyway, and what concerned us was the father's look of gloom.

String? Nobody, we said bravely. What kind of string? Didn't we have eyes in our heads to see that the roses had to be tied up?

The child pulled one of the pieces of string she always carries with her out of her pocket and offered it to him. This made us aware of the gravity of the situation. The daughter proposed getting new string. However, the father did not want any new string, just the six pieces he had just measured and cut and put down here somewhere and which we naturally had to take away. You see, our looks said to each other, we should not have left him to his own devices for so long, one should at least have put a clover in his pocket, for everyone needs protection from evil spirits when he is alone. We saw ourselves searching for string for the rest of the afternoon and, on top of that, heard Father bemoan a fate which had thrown him among three women. So we sighed and were at our wits' end. Then along came Frau B.

Frau B. came waddling across the meadow, because she has to shift her entire weight from one leg to the other at every step, and in her left hand she carried her shopping bag, which she doesn't leave the house without, but in her right hand she held the six pieces of string. Well, she said, hasn't somebody forgotten these by the fence? Afterward you have to look for them and then all hell breaks loose.

Oh yes, said Father, actually these are just what I need. He took the string and went off to the roses.

Thank you very much, Frau B., we said. But won't you sit down?

The daughter went to get one of the garden chairs we had just wiped off, and we looked on, slightly uneasy, as it completely disappeared under the voluminous bulk of Frau B. Frau B. panted a little, because for her, every little walk becomes a chore; she took a deep breath and subsequently informed us that excessive chemical fertilization had ruined our strawberries. For Frau B. is accustomed to even the oddest behavior of any living creature; she sees at a glance the disease and its roots where other people spend a long time looking. Our meadow should have been mown long ago and the weeds in the carrot patch thinned out, she told us, and we did not argue. But then Frau B. astonished us by asking whether we had already looked at the inside of the yellow rose, the first one on the left of the rose bed. No, we hadn't yet looked inside the rose and we sensed that we owed her something as a result. The child immediately ran off to make up for it and came back breathlessly with the announcement that it was worth it. Deeper inside, the rose became a darker yellow and finally almost pink. Although this was a pink which does not exist otherwise. However, the greatest thing was how deep this rose was. Really, one would not have thought so.

Just like I told you, said Frau B. It's a superior variety. The hazelnuts are also growing well this year.

You're right, Frau B., we said. It is a superior variety. And only now, after Frau B. had noticed it, the hazelnuts were doing well and it seemed to us that everything which her gaze had graced with approval or reproof, even the strawberries that had bolted to seed, had received its proper blessing only now.

At this point Frau B. opened her mouth and said, The standing crop is going to rot this year.

Now, Frau B.! we exclaimed.

It's true, she said, unmoved. That's how it is. Just like the Hundred Years' Calendar says: Storms and rain and thundershowers and floods. The harvest will stay outside and rot.

This silenced us. We saw the harvest perishing according to the Hundred Years' Calendar, with Frau B. calmly looking on, and for the space of a second we may have thought that it was she herself who had the power to rule over the harvest and the hazelnuts and the strawberries and the roses. After all, there is a possibility that, through a lifetime's work with the products of nature, one can earn a certain say in their fates. In vain I attempted to imagine the floods of fruit juice, the mountains of jams and jellies which had passed over Frau B.'s kitchen table within the course of forty years; I saw the freight cars full of carrots and green beans which had grown beneath her hands and been cleaned by her fingers, the thousands of chickens she had fed, the pigs and rabbits she had fattened, the goats she had milked, and I had to admit that it would only be fair if *one* now told her in front of all the others, Now listen, dear Frau B., as far as this year's harvest is concerned, *we* were thinking . . .

For, after all, no one has seen the Hundred Years' Calendar with their own eyes.

Here they are again, said Frau B. contentedly. I'm just amazed that they aren't getting sick of it.

Who, Frau B.? What?

But then we saw them as well: the helicopters. Do I have to apologize for the busy air traffic over our area? The fact is that at this hour of the afternoon two helicopters are flying along the border, whatever they may hope or fear to see beyond the wire fence. We, however, should we happen to have time, can see how close the border is, can see the long propellers turning and show one another the light spots inside the cockpit, the pilots' faces; we can wonder whether they are always the same ones who have been assigned to this flight or whether they take turns. Perhaps they only send them so that we can get used to them. After all, one is not afraid of things one sees every day. Yet, not even the nightly searchlights and the red and yellow signal flares going up against the bell-jar glow of the city move the border as close to us as the harmlessly curious helicopters, which do not shun the daylight.

To think that he could be from Texas, said Frau B. Where my boy is now.

Who, Frau B.?

The pilot up there. He could just as well be from Texas, couldn't he?

Sure he could. But what on earth is your son doing in Texas?

Playing soccer, said Frau B.

And then we remembered all about her deaf-mute son, who lived in the West with his deaf-mute wife and who was now in Texas with the soccer team of the deaf, never dreaming what his mother was saying at the sight of a foreign helicopter pilot. We also thought of Anita, Frau B.'s daughter, who was deaf as well and who was training on a job, alone in a distant town, although within reach, and sent her laundry home every week. We took another look at Frau B., searching for traces of fate in her face. Yet we did not detect anything special.

Everyone look straight ahead, said the child, and made a face.

Standing at the fence was our neighbor the Widow Horn.

Well, good night, then, said Frau B. I'm leaving.

Yet she stayed and turned the entire mass of her body toward the fence, facing the Widow Horn: the woman who does not add an onion to the potato pancakes and does not have her blocked drainpipe repaired and who does not grant herself a change of headscarf, out of pure naked stinginess. She had come to talk to us about the train accident in her penetrating, indifferent voice.

Now there are twelve, she said, in place of a greeting.

How are you, we answered uneasily. What do you mean by twelve?

Twelve bodies, said the Widow Horn. Not nine like they wrote in the paper only yesterday.

Good heavens, said Frau B., and gave our neighbor a look as if *she* had killed the three people who hadn't been in the newspaper the day before. We knew that Frau B. thought her capable of anything, for whoever loves money can also steal and kill people; however, this was going too far. Although we didn't like the sparkle in the eyes of the Widow Horn either.

How do you know this, we asked, and is it really certain that three people from our village are among them?

Four, our neighbor said casually. But the wife of that actor had good insurance, anyway.

Oh no, we said, and turned pale. Is she dead as well?

Of course, said the Widow Horn severely.

Then we kept a few seconds' silence for the wife of the actor. For the last time she came up the street to our garden door with her two dachshunds, for the last time she complained in earnest as well as in jest about the dogs' bad habits, let herself be dragged reluctantly from tree to tree, and smoothed back her long black hair. Yes, now we all saw that she had beautiful hair, just slightly touched up, and that she was slim and looked good for her age. However, we could not tell her this, she was already over, had turned her back on us in an irrevocable manner which we had never seen in her, and we could not hope that she would turn back or even come back to us so that we, the inattentive living, could see her face one more time and impress it on our minds—forever.

What an unsuitable word for the actor's wife who had been vital but always bogged down by everyday worries.

He is not back, anyway, said our neighbor, who hadn't noticed anybody passing by.

Who?

Well, the actor. They didn't find any more of her, just her pocketbook and her passport. That must have really confused her husband. He is not back yet.

It happened as it had to happen. The child opened her mouth and asked, But why? Why didn't they find any more of her?

All of us stared at the Widow Horn, as if she would now proceed to describe what the rails can look like after a train accident such as this, but without so much as heeding our imploring glances, she said, It takes time. They're still searching.

Why don't you come over, I said. Why don't you sit down.

However, our neighbor could only smile at that. One never sees her smile unless something unnatural is expected of her, that she should give something away, for example. Or that she should sit down in the middle of the day. Whoever is sitting down thinks. Whoever carts manure onto his cornfield or digs up his piece of land or slaughters chickens has to think much less than a person sitting in her parlor and staring at the cupboard with the collector's cups.

Who could guarantee that a man would not suddenly stand in front of the cupboard, at the very spot where he always stood to take down his newspaper; a man who deserves to be hated, who recently found his punishment for leaving his wife through death, as one hears. Or grandchildren one doesn't know since one kicked out the daughter-in-law, that slut, along with the son, after all. Then one jumps up and puts the wire cage with the chickens in the parlor; who cares if they fill the empty apartment with their chirping, who cares if their feathers fly about so that one can hardly breathe, who cares if everything goes to hell. Or one runs into the kitchen and colors eggs and gives them as Easter presents to the neighbor's children, those good-for-nothings who ring the doorbell at night and then scatter so that there is no one there when one comes rushing out, keeps rushing out, but nothing is there. Nothing and no one, no matter how one may crane one's neck.

Bye, said the Widow Horn, I didn't really want anything else. Frau B. went with her. Every single one of her heavy steps intimated that she had no dealings with the gaunt woman tripping along beside her. It was imperative to protect the boundary forever separating undeserved fate and misfortune incurred through one's own fault.

A fight broke out between the children to which I paid no attention. It got worse and in the end they chased one another beneath the trees; the child held up a torn-off scrap of paper and screamed, She loves somebody, she loves somebody! and the daughter, beside herself, demanded her scrap of paper back, her secret which was just as hard to hide as it was to reveal. I leaned my head back on the pillow on my deck chair. I closed my eyes. I wanted neither to see nor to hear anything. The woman of whom one had found nothing but her pocketbook no longer saw or heard anything either. No matter which game she had had her hand in, it had been slapped away, and the game had gone on without her.

The entire feather-light afternoon hung on the weight of this minute. A hundred years are as one day. One day is as a hundred years. The sinking day is what they say. Why shouldn't one feel it sinking: past the sun, already dipping down into the lilac bushes, past the little apricot tree, the loud children's screams, even past the rose which is yellow on the outside and pink on the inside only today and tomorrow. Yet one begins to be afraid if one still sees no ground; one jettisons superfluous ballast, this and that, only in order to get up again. After all, who is to say that the hand which will pull one away from everything is already set to pounce? Who is to say that, this time, it is our turn? That the game will go on without us?

The children had stopped fighting. They were catching grasshoppers. The sun was barely visible. It began to get chilly. Father called out that we should clear everything away, it was time. We tilted the chairs toward the table and put the rakes in the stuffy little shed.

As we left, the air was full of June bugs. At the garden door we turned around and looked back.

When was all that about the Mediterranean, anyway? asked the child. Today?

UNTER DEN LINDEN

I am convinced that it is part of life on earth that everyone be hurt where he is most sensitive, by that which is most unbearable: Essential is the way in which he overcomes this.

—RAHEL VARNHAGEN

I HAVE ALWAYS liked walking along Unter den Linden. And most of all, as you well know, alone. After I had avoided it for a long time, the street recently appeared to me in a dream. Now I can finally tell of it.

I cannot describe how much I love these safe beginnings, which only the fortunate accomplish. I always knew that I, too, should have them at my disposal again someday. This would be the sign of readmission to the fellowship, the severity of which is surpassed only by its liberality: the fellowship of the fortunate. Since, as of late, I am unburdened by all doubt, they will believe me again. I am no longer chained to the facts. I can freely tell the truth.

For we esteem nothing more highly than the pleasure of being known.

It has never bothered me that the street is famous, not during my waking hours and most certainly not in my dreams. I am aware that it has suffered this misfortune on account of its location: East–West axis. This street and the one appearing in my dreams have nothing in common. The one is abused by newspaper pictures and tourists' photographs in my absence; the other stands at my disposal, undamaged, even over long periods of time. I admit the two can be confused, if looked at superficially. I even make this mistake myself. Then I heedlessly cross my street without recognizing it. Only recently I avoided it for many days and sought my luck elsewhere, yet find it I did not.

Summer arrived and I dreamed the day had come. I set out, for now I had been summoned. I did not tell anybody and almost refused to believe it myself. I thought (as one can cunningly think, awake or in a dream, in order to betray oneself) I would finally take a look at the new metropolitan districts which were being talked and written about everywhere. However, even the bus driver was part of the conspiracy—with whom shall remain unsaid. He was rude to me for no reason whatsoever, and trembling with rage, I paid him back for all those unavenged instances of rudeness I had suffered in my life as if I would die were I to tolerate this one as well. The man was silent at once, fixing me with a grin, and now it was my turn to be angry at myself for making it so easy for them. For now, insulted as I was, I had to get off at the next stop, and I found myself, barely surprised at this point, exactly where they wanted me: in front of the State Opera, Unter den Linden.

And so the time had come. I'm sure you're familiar with it. One only knows one has been summoned and must obey. The time, place, and purpose of the meeting are not disclosed. One can but turn to speculations, which feed on wishes and therefore often prove to be faulty. Every child knows from fairy tales that one must run off guilelessly and should turn one's attention to everything without prejudice, in a friendly manner. And that's just how I walked in the dry, pleasantly sharp June heat, through the smell of dust and gas, through the noise of cars and through the white light reflected by the stones. Suddenly there appeared that bright, cheerful attentiveness which I had missed so bitterly for such a long time. The day was very beautiful.

In your dreams you catch up with what you've always missed out on. This is why I wanted finally to take a close look at the Great Changing of the Guards, which was just beginning at the new guard station with fifes and drums and twitching white gloves. I wanted to impress upon my memory the commands with which they yank, snap, snap, as if on taut strings, the two main characters out of the stationary rifle platoon. I did not want to miss out on a single one of those admirable parade steps, which, precisely tracing a line invisible to us uninitiated, must end up exactly in front of the tips of the sentry's boots—should he be standing where the regulations have placed him. As a rule, this is the case, you can rely on it. However, on this afternoon of all days, the rule had been broken and one of the relieving officer candidates marched straight off into a catastrophe. The spot where his predecessor was meant to receive him (between the second and third pillar) was empty.

Scarcely five or ten minutes earlier, this negligent soul—possibly affected by the heat—had obeyed a command audible only to himself, by suddenly executing a precise left face and, with his rifle shouldered in the prescribed manner, goose-stepping to the corner of the building he was symbolically guarding, where, after completing another wheel to the left, he finally came to a halt in the deep shade of a chestnut tree. With clear conscience he stood sentry at impeccable attention in the wrong place, with no hope of relief, while his successor, lacking the necessary partner, was executing in an embittered manner all the complicated maneuvers which finally brought him to the spot all too long deserted by his brother officer. Not that it was any of my business, but when the guard platoon marched off, it seemed to be complete again.

I saw strange characters among the crowd, which quickly dispersed after the spectacle was over. Not all of them had been baptized with the waters of the Spree and grown up under pine trees. I remembered an Indian with a ruby-red stone in his snow-white turban, slim black people who always moved as if in a dance, and, most of all, a charming couple who detached themselves from the mercurial crowd and, closely entwined, walked toward the statue of Alexander von Humboldt, where they both, girl and boy, looked up silently and attentively. Strange birds with brightly colored plumage: the same jeans, the same light-blue sweaters tied around their waists, the same flowered shirts—viewed from behind distinguishable neither by their narrow hips nor by their unkempt hair of equal length. When they turned around I saw that they approved of the stony Alexander, and the black lettering of the large orange-colored buttons on their equally flat chests jumped out at me: ALL I NEED IS LOVE. They responded happily to my smile, said something in their soft, melodious language—words of praise that could have been meant for me as well as for Alexander von Humboldt—and moved off on supple, flat sandals. I generously placed my street at their disposal since they had come from far away to look at it. It pleased me that strange, foreign birds could find crumbs of nourishment here as well.

You see, I was not far from the point where everything that crossed my path pleased me.

You know that one can realize in a dream that one is dreaming. The girl came into my dream and I thought, Now I've already begun to dream about her. A dark motif, what is it supposed to mean? And yet—I had to admit—nobody fit into my dream better than she—for reasons which remained concealed from me for the present. She disappeared through the door of the university.

Have I ever told you about the girl? I must have kept it a secret, but the story is still on my mind. I was once confronted with it when I did not want to hear about it at all.

Then I saw my old friend Peter come out of the university, and the beautiful blond woman whom I had noticed quite a while back got up from a bench in the courtyard and walked toward him. Suddenly I feared that the afternoon could end here already, with this coincidental encounter. But there was no danger of my friend Peter noticing me. He had eyes only for this woman, to whom he had been married but for a few weeks, as I knew. She is one of those creatures who remain forever girls, no matter what may happen to them, and who thereby cause men's blood to boil. I did not begrudge Peter this burn. Why should he not do penance for his unfaithfulness. Why should he not pay for the tears which Marianne had shed for him. Yet at the same time I also did not begrudge him this beautiful, blond woman who clicked along beside him on high heels, took his arm, and gazed up at him.

Oh, I understood him. I could still count on him through thick or thin. I just didn't know whether I still wanted to. He walked by me at a distance of two steps, as if he were a blind man, laughingly pulling his young wife at a run across the street to his car, letting the engine roar into life, and steering into the traffic with a brashly sharp turn, which I found annoying.

Do you remember what I often said about him: He

will succeed at everything he sets his mind to. However, I had not counted on the fact that he could set his mind to something that I utterly detested. But what do you know, he even succeeded at that. Succeeded at seating his new wife on the very same bench which was forever ours: the three of us, he, Marianne, and myself. Succeeded without any further ado at thinking nothing of it. Had succeeded at something which was beyond us: forgetting those unspoken oaths which were the most serious things in all the seriousness of those years and which now served to hold our youth together. Serious like the punishments we would receive if we dared break our oaths. Now I saw it with my own two eyes. Only he who believes in faithfulness receives punishment for a breach of faith. But my friend Peter did not.

The girl—well, yes! She had lied and betrayed, but I relied on her; this had never been so clear to me as now in my dream. For a short while I even suspected that I had come here on her account, had, from the very start, had the intention of visiting certain localities which served as the scenery in her drama. That which, legally speaking, is called a return to the scene of the crime.

A swarm of girls was drifting toward me. Students walking arm in arm in small groups. In former times, I would have attempted to pick out the girl, whose looks, hair color, and stature I had always taken care not to inquire about. It was not likely, yet still not out of the question, that I would run into her here, in front of the university where she had still been a student last year. The fact that her name had been removed from the register of students would presumably not prevent her from roaming around here. It would not be an unsolvable task for her to spy on how the person in question spent his days, for example, when he left the university after his lectures. She could easily hide behind the pedestal of the stony Wilhelm Humboldt at a previously ascertained hour if she still cared about seeing him. Until he appeared, laughing and clear of conscience, the same way that my friend Peter had just appeared.

They were always laughing whenever one saw them.

That man, with whom the girl was perhaps still infatuated, was a lecturer as well. Names are unimportant, they said, you don't know him anyway, and if you do—so much the worse. So he could just as well be another historian like my friend Peter. There are as many historians as there are grains of sand by the sea.

I cannot explain to you why it was suddenly so important for me to show understanding for Peter, my old friend. I remembered this and that, troubles during his career, ordinary offenses he met with and which seemed to hit him harder than they did other people, because he was one of the elect and had lived under a lucky star since he was small. He suffered from the most everyday slights as only a human being can suffer who is prevented from following a great calling. We—his wife, Marianne, and I—thought his mishaps banal, whereas he saw true insufferable misfortune in them. It had not as yet dawned on me that the marks for good and bad luck are fixed at different levels on each life measure. What happened to him, anyway? An assistant professorship which someone else stole from under his nose. A trip abroad to a conference where he was passed over. A lecture with which he rightly hoped to excel, but which was dropped on account of a syllabus reform. Trifles.

I know, he said himself. But I don't like it, you understand?

You will not marvel at the fact that the young teacher from the country, who had driven her ten-year-olds across the street like a flock of young lambs, asked me of all people for the time. Anybody who does not have a watch asks me for the time. Of course she owned a watch, said the teacher, a beautiful old one from her favorite uncle, who had passed away, only it was very delicate and always being repaired at the watchmaker's in Königs Wusterhausen. You won't believe it, but I haven't found the time to pick it up for the past three weeks.

I had run into her at the point where she had told everybody everything: about the bad bus connections to her village, about the difficulties in finding a bigger and, above all, sunny room, and about her homesickness on the Sundays when the flatlands really got to her, because, after all, she came from Thüringen. She looked at me expectantly with her big brown eyes, wondering whether I could duly appreciate the fact that she was from Thüringen. In the meantime, I inconspicuously took great pains to read the time on my small Moscow watch with the narrow black plastic strap, which my teacher was bound to come back to eventually. Strangely enough, I could not manage it. Admittedly, I am nearsighted but not as regards the distance between eye and wrist; moreover, I was wearing my sunglasses with the Zeiss lenses and could see every single hair on my arm. It was only the dial of the watch that got blurrier and blurrier the closer I held it to my face.

I must ask you not to lose patience with me. I can only say what really happened in my dream and will not importune you with any attempts at explanation.

From Thüringen? But the girl about whom I had

been told all manner of remarkable things came from there as well! That may well be, conceded the little teacher readily, many people come from there now. Her statement struck me as enigmatic and I decided to ponder it later, as soon as I had informed her about the time. Meanwhile, the teacher forbade her boys to continue the jumping exercises on the thick stone wall of the building which houses a section of the Academy of Sciences, as far as I know. So you didn't study in Berlin? I asked her, just to be on the safe side. Of course not! she said, just short of indignation. Still, it was quite impressive to see all this in real life, the new television tower, the Marx-Engels Square, and the Brandenburg Gate. It had quite a different effect than on the television screen.

Her girls had begun to play hopscotch on the stone slabs of the sidewalk. There you have it, said the teacher, as if this inappropriate children's game were convincing proof of her manifold vexations. But I've only had them for a year.

This remark seemed to console her and she cheerfully moved off with them. She had not insisted on being informed about the exact time, so I did not insist on it either. Why should I be fussier than a young thing from the provinces?

I had an uncanny feeling as I continued on my way. I had always suspected that this street leads into unknown depths. I had only to enter through the wrought-iron gate on my right into the inner courtyard (which, incidentally, I did not recognize) of the State Library. But nobody insisted that I remember. I had only to go on toward the green-and-blue-tiled fountain, climb over the edge, and dive down. One has exaggerated notions about this. It is easy, you just have to have wished it often enough and urgently. I lay still on the bottom of the pool, just as I had often pictured it: lying before the benches of judges, lying down on naked floorboards before the fact-finding committees, on the stone floors before the examining boards, lying there quietly and ultimately refusing to testify (which you, dear girl, no longer had to do, when the time came). Now I understood that up to then I had lacked heaviness, a specific weight. If you are too light, you simply do not sink, that makes sense; it is a physical law one learns in school. I was satisfied finally to have got to the bottom of it.

The faces which appeared at the edge of the pool to look at me left me cold. We were separated by the water line. Curiosity, suspicion, and malicious glee could not harm me; even the pain went away. However, I still remembered what he looked like; pain had a face which hung next to the others over the edge of the pool and silently ordered me to rise, voluntarily leave my element and follow him, to fling all former experience to the winds, to mix again with people and violate the taboos.

Oh, my dear, you always want to know the truth. But the truth is not a story and not credible in the least. The truth is that I came voluntarily out of the fountain and was immediately dry and sober, as if by way of intense radiation, and walked toward the heavy, carved door of the State Library, which I, fully aware of my actions, pushed open easily and without any hesitation.

I was never to enter here again, the invisible writing over the door had said, until this day. I should not expose myself. A more powerful magic had lifted the ban. I was exposed like the rest, what did you think?

So that you can believe me, I am now blurring the

transitions between the credible and the incredible, just for you. Immediately upon my entering, the rules of this place revealed themselves to me. Incidentally, I found them easy to follow, not much was demanded. Don't turn around, said the pale, bloated porteress, to whom everybody has to pay attention and who does not need to know anybody herself. I hastily nodded while holding up my reader's pass, which I always carry with me and which she accepted as usual. As I passed through the wooden turnstile, I became uneasy. Was that all there was to it? This I could not believe; my dread of this place went too deep. I had to make sure, had to go back and ask her. Yet a stiffness in my back and neck prevented me from turning around. What next, I thought furiously, yet obediently began climbing the stone steps. I would put up with it this one time. Sometimes the laws dictating one's behavior in certain places change overnight and it doesn't mean much of anything. My knees shook a little. There's no end of things that can happen to you.

I am sure that, in these districts, the examinations seem easy, but the penalties for minor failures are severe. The motto is All or nothing!—but one is left in the dark as to how to go about it. Yet some know. The girl, for example. Have I already mentioned that she stayed faithfully by my side? It saved me from turning around.

I have been told about you, I almost said in the reserved manner the situation called for, because I had to make the first step but did not know how. Here, I wanted to say, my hand lay on this very spot on the banister, when I was told for my edification what had befallen you. This, however, did not interest her, any more than the fact that I had not been allowed to set foot in this house, let alone on these stairs, since that December morning long past—which was exactly the time during which my acquaintance with her had become more intimate. Forces incomprehensible to me seemed keen on establishing a kind of balance between give and take.

Half an hour ago I had christened this girl, of whom I knew nothing but the basics, a student of history. So it was only natural to head with her straight to the social sciences reading room. I made her feel that I was in the picture—wasn't it here that one once came to sit in a very specific place from which one could keep an eye on a very specific back. In order to walk up to the shelf as soon as the person in question had left and lug the heavy tome he had just put down back to one's own place.

You wonder how I know? Better not ask. Love? Oh goodness me—so you are nothing but a silly young thing who believes in miracles? Who has to set her mind on him, of all people, who is, after all, her lecturer, who is, after all, married (to a woman who was possibly called Marianne, a fleeting thought). Could you really have convinced yourself that one could string together any odd amount of foolish actions without them ultimately resulting in something which was not foolish? My dear child. Whoever wishes to believe that can. Not I. (As you can see, I got up on my high horse, and it almost seemed as if I had summoned her in order to be able to look down on her.)

Why not you? (That was her question.)

Because it is, after all—let us once again not ask why—totally clear to me that one does not do these absurd things without secretly knowing their purpose. Without a secret acceptance of the results. Which is not to say that one always knows what one is looking for.

Let's go. Here in the foyer, by the way, where the children's books and oversized photographs of authors are exhibited today, there was once an exhibition of amateur painting by physicians—with scalpel and brush, or some such thing. Everyone could go, not just doctors, of course. I could go, too, and my old friend Max as well, who did not come on his own. No, my girl, I must ask you not to raise your eyebrows, but rather to respect true coincidence. Coincidentally, he did not come alone; I met him and the man he was with purely coincidentally; this was the last coincidence which occurred in connection with Max's companion and thus it deserves to be recorded.

The two of you have been wanting to meet for some time, haven't you?

Now that was typical of Max, like a bull in a china shop, always ready to bring people together; one need only have seen someone briefly—at one of those numerous popular-science lectures, for example—one need only casually have mentioned a name, and of course he knows the person and feels obliged to drag him along on the very next occasion.

Been wanting to? Is that so? For some time? What makes you say that?

Don't be so impolite. So this is Herr . . .

Don't worry. Do I look as if I was going to name names? I don't know yours and the other one is superfluous. Besides, I'm about to forget it anyway.

Down the stairs in a foursome: Max, the nameless one, you, and I. You deny it? Pretend you were not there? Hadn't yet set foot in this city? Were just getting into your high-school graduation gown in your pretty little small-town bedroom? Weren't suspecting a thing? Oh, you silly child!

How one can be so utterly mistaken! Step by step you walked alongside us, not a single stair was spared you, and word for word, note for note, you must have been familiar with the little song which has been going around in my mind all this time and which you will now hear from me for the first time:

I sought you at a window high.
The senseless scent of spring wafts by.
Where may you be, where may you be,
What profits one in May to live,
What know you of the pain of love.

Questions of this kind seem to have a spell-breaking effect. In any case, the porteress controlled my reader's pass as if she had never whispered a secret password to me, the fountain in the courtyard was not in operation, the greenish-blue pool lay flat and empty. I went into the street, put my sunglasses back on, and established with a glance at my reliable Moscow watch that it was almost three o'clock. It was only half an hour ago that I had met my friend Peter and heard him laugh as I had not heard him laugh for years. He had regained everything that we used to like about him: laughter, sparkle, and self-confidence. Had recovered it at the same moment that he managed to shake us—we his pursuers, we his bailiffs who sought to take away that which he did not own.

You sometimes reproached me about my weakness for him. So that when I met him one evening back then on Unter den Linden, I merely told you that I had met him. At the corner of the Charlottenstrasse where the old Linden Café used to be that we went into later on. We were both coming from different meetings and were tired. There was nobody I would rather have seen than him. Hey, Peter, what a coincidence, let's shoot the breeze like in the old days. The linden tree I was leaning against was thinner and at least two spans shorter than today; my friend Peter delivered a speech on the empty street to a slightly dented moon, as he would have done in our student days. He wanted to make me laugh, and make me laugh he did. Honestly, with all his brilliant qualities the only thing lacking was the one that could hold them all together: a little resolution. I must have got to talking about this, because he started in on his new dissertation topic. Without thinking, I adopted the same tone as he. The tone which was now appropriate between us. I casually said, Did they rob you of your nerve?

Just stop it, he said. That's when I noticed that he was not cowardly but unperturbed, and realized how much more difficult it is to talk to an indifferent person than to someone with a guilty conscience. One feels ridiculous telling someone like Peter all the good reasons which he himself put forward in favor of his old, slightly sensitive topic only a week earlier. He knows them only too well and is not about to deny them. (Wasn't it about a controversial period of the most recent past? A field plowed by others in the meantime?) We sat in front of our beers, and Peter acted out the different roles of the meeting which had been called for the express purpose of stroking his ego. Of convincing the one already convinced. The new topic proposed to him by the staff of his department was to his old one what a lapdog was to a hedgehog, everyone knew it and no one was allowed to show that he knew. Peter acted out how each of his colleagues—some of whom I knew—kept coming up with new arguments for the urgency of this project, which at least could harm no one. My friend Peter had known ahead of time that they were determined to play democracy—incidentally, without conferring among themselves—and who was assigned which role in the play. His role was to be disappointed, of course, distressed, then half disarmed; he was supposed to put up a carefully measured amount of resistance and then give up at precisely the right moment, begrudgingly, yet yielding to the better arguments. He passed the warm handshake proffered him by the relieved director of the department on to me. He looked me in the eye with the same conviviality which the professor who was to supervise his new topic had inserted into his gaze just now.

At which point, confused by the various layers of conviviality, I lowered my gaze and have never since raised it again as frankly as before to my friend Peter. I didn't blame him. Who am I to blame anybody? Yet he still cried out, Why me of all people?

The question remained with me, to this place, to this point. I could not keep it to myself and passed it on, at the wrong time, to the wrong man. That was nearby, over in the Lindencorso, the new espresso bar, when it was still new. It must have been autumn; I was wearing my suede coat and walked by the table at the window like a blind person so that the man, the unnamed one who would be sitting here around this time as on every Thursday, would have to notice me first, get up, catch up with, greet, and invite me to his table. Naturally, the amount of risk with such undertakings is high, but this time it worked. Even the surprise worked. You won't believe it, but I did not have to pretend. I was surprised. Oh—you here? Really, every Thursday! Between your two main lectures?

Coincidence is praised.

Together at a table for the first and nearly only time, like other people who have a quick lunch of Hungarian salami and bread together and drink a cola or, as he preferred, a small pot of mocha. The only difference being that other people simply make a date or end up in this place by coincidence, whereas coincidence had let me down after that beautiful initial coup. I was forced to resort to calculation, cunning, nerve-racking inquiries, degrading telephone calls which led me at a certain hour to a certain place: here. The art of unself-consciousness. To take one's seat having erased every trace of calculation and cunning in oneself before meeting the other's gaze. Having forgotten even the memory of shame when glancing hesitatingly at one's watch. Time? Well, if need be, a little. (And then, for the space of thirty minutes, to know nothing of the time thereafter, which can be as infinite and black as it deems proper.) The art of picking up a conversation where one remembers having left off a long time ago, and not getting embarrassed when it turns out that this conversation has never taken place. In one's mind at most. The art of avoiding words and phrases, lulling the other into a false sense of security with a familiar tone of address—which Max had introduced, of course—and then, in a harmless sentence, harmlessly shooting a perfidiously formal turn of phrase like an arrow. You graced the Black Sea again with your presence this holiday? And can your spouse bear the August heat?

The art of not taking notice, of not showing any reaction, of retaining one's position once taken. Can I treat you to a coffee? Should you be thus inclined . . . Do you smoke? If you entice me to do so . . .

The *haute école,* the lessons of which one masters without ever having learned them. And in the midst of it, in the deceptively lighthearted tone one has settled upon, my question: But why me?

The attack failed. I should have known, he never let down his guard. Impulsive utterances cannot be drawn out of him, his answer is clever and controlled, a judgment which I have to accept: You, as well, are only asked to do what you are capable of.

How right you always are. Let's drop it.

On that last evening, when I looked him in the eye for the last time, my friend Peter knew exactly what was at stake—and so did I. His question was a final appeal to my sense of fair play, and I neglected to point out to him that not everything in life boils down to the rules of a sporting competition. I gazed at him with sadness and emotion. A gentle giant. We never again mentioned that autumn evening, each of us for a different reason. He, because he was determined not to look back. I, because I reproached myself for not having avoided the unavoidable loss of a friend. For a while we went on as before, all three of us, even Marianne, who wasted away during those months. However, she was not the one who ended it, but he, my ex-friend Peter. One day he ran off with that blond, brown-eyed woman.

Just as my friend Peter was beginning to bore me, the Golden Fish swam past, unsummoned as usual—the same one who had figured in such incomparable stories told by Peter in his best days. How do you do, Fish. Luckily, he recognized me. You sure took your time. Let's go. We can no longer do anything for our former friend Peter. He and the two of us—we could be facing one another as non-friends someday. Wasn't it imperative, in this case, that I call him one more time tomorrow and congratulate him, in a genuine tone of voice, on his Ph.D.? Who am I to deny him the few pat phrases which may still be lacking for his total contentment . . . and if they are not lacking, so much the better. He will have the tact not to invite me home to his beautiful new wife, I the delicacy to avoid those expressions which best describe behavior like his. And so we can live alongside one another on the basis of that which we do not do. (According to traffic regulations: "Caution and mutual consideration . . .")

You are dissatisfied, Fish. No problem for you. A Golden Fish can be strict. But I, Fish, must wait. However, amid the hustle and bustle which fill my days for the time being, there grows a longing for honesty, until that beautiful moment when I throw down the receiver and deny the pat phrase. You doubt it, Fish? But the day will come. Only then will I learn which of the earthly goods being distributed here on this street is meant for me and whether I will be ready to receive it. For this is the street—did you really not know, Fish!—where the great, fair exchange continuously takes place until everybody has received what they deserve: the young thing from Thüringen, her godforsaken village, her unruly school class, and homesickness on Sundays for now; the girl (you know her, don't you, Fish?), the long days in the light-bulb factory and the long, lonely evenings; Peter in luck, his beautiful wife and not for a long, long time yet the heavy cold stone, which he will certainly have to bear off someday; and I—oh, various things not deserving of the condescension you can hear in my voice.

Come, my wonderfish. Let us go to the shiny new shop windows, in front of which stand people counting their money in their minds. The sight of you startles them, Fish;

outraged and insulted they run off to complain, they have not taken you into account. Let them go, I'll show you everything.

He comes along faithfully, silent as usual. I show him the Bulgarian folk art; he likes the rugs, particularly the white ones made of sheep's wool. He shakes his head in regret that they are so expensive. Then we stand in front of the leather shop, which smells so good, but we realize that they won't let the two of us in. I point out the wallet in the window I would like to have, golden ornaments on red morocco leather; yes, he finds it beautiful as well. I show him my old one, so that he cannot but agree with me: It is a shame how worn out it looks. I put it back in my pocket, satisfied. You're not interested in jewelry? I ask severely. No, he isn't. Then we can go across the street to the bookstore.

The street has come to life again, which goes to show how quickly people get used to a fish. A silly beauty in a canary-yellow cape tries to lure him away from me, supposedly because his color matches her cape. He does not so much as glance her way. He looks to me like a worldly-wise, elderly gentleman. Once in front of the books, however, he regrets not being able to speak Russian. I translate a few titles for him, and he listens politely. If this is boring for you, Fish, I say, go on. Do go on, don't let me keep you.

Fish have to take everything literally. He approximates a formal bow and leaves. And yet there was so much more to be said.

The unnamed one—perhaps he still sits in the espresso bar on Thursdays at 2 p.m., but by no means may I cross his path—would never hear about this apparition, provisionally named Fish. Why not? Because I could not bear to see my goldfish filleted with two or three clean cuts (after all, he is a physician, my unknown one, a surgeon). Because I do not care to see how he skillfully exposes the backbone, holds it up in order to examine it, and then simply tosses it over his shoulder. Garbage!

Those are his words.

Come back, Fish, beautiful Fish, come. He does not come, he never comes when you call him. He is on his way down the Friedrichstrasse heading toward the Oranienburg Gate with canary-yellow cape, accepting the tributes of the young generation, which break down the doors of the shops to buy scarves in his color: gold. Oh, Fish, the canary-yellow woman will be your downfall. For what reason? That is precisely what we should have found out together, but you chose to leave me alone.

Alone with the mirror image of the Linden Hotel in the bookstore window and a voice behind me speaking English with a Saxon accent and announcing to another, native English voice that our new Linden Hotel would soon catch up with, and even surpass, the American Hilton in the number of services rendered. Together with the Fish I could have come up with all thirty possible and impossible services, one by one, from shoeshines to umbrella rentals, and then added the guests who have to avail themselves of them day by day.

Then, when I let down my guard for a moment, a landscape of ruins appeared instead of the Linden Hotel in the polished glass, windswept, grown over with weeds, and traversed by a beaten path whereupon walk three figures familiar to me. I turn with a start—not fast enough. My landscape is gone. The three of us, who do not fit in with the well-dressed public in our old-fashioned, shabby clothes, wind our way through the parking spaces in front of the Linden Hotel. We stow away the little white scraps of paper labeled ELECTION ASSISTANT'S LICENSE in the pockets of our windbreakers and could burst into laughter at the shady word "legal" which they just drilled into us in the union building. Legal like never before, says our friend Peter, who takes Marianne's arm and rushes up the streetcar stairs at Friedrichstrasse station and down at Bellevue a quarter of an hour later without once stopping to catch his breath. That need not bother you, my girl, you were just eight years old and would not meet him for eleven more years. Just so you know whom you had to deal with then.

The whites of the eyes of the adversary. The police officer riveted to a spot in the hallway, we move slowly down the stairs toward him, but my friend Peter goes right up to him coolly: What say, boss? He did not even want to see our election assistant's licenses; he held in his hand one of the brochures we had just pushed through the letter-box slits of this posh house inhabited by high-ranking officials. He merely pointed his fat finger at a blank section where, according to him, there should have been a "seal of approval." Illegal. Let's go, he said.

In such cases one shows no reaction, my girl. One tears up the election assistant's license as ordered without asking oneself why. One follows the police officer under protest but, my friend Peter stops in front of the urchin who crouches barefoot in the gutter screaming, Communist pigs, hang them all. All? inquires Peter casually, and lifts up the chin of the urchin, whose eyes widen in fear. Think about it. Means a lot of work.

Since when does one cross the street at a red light

in Central Europe, madam? The madam is myself, and a traffic warden now gives me a special lesson which reaches its high point with the observation that it is of no interest whether the intersection is empty or not. Red is red, and that is a matter of principle. Meanwhile, the light has turned red again.

Peter, in any case—you are not embarrassed, my girl, if I come back to him?—strictly forbade us to drop so much as a single mark of our hard-earned money at a fraudulent rate into the hungry maws of the West Berlin swindlers and speculators as we stood released in front of the gates of Moabit Prison, seven days later (the money needed for return tickets for the streetcar). He preferred smuggling us through the gate with his expired student ticket, whereby we were forced to cheat our country, which, after all, receives the income from the streetcar, a fare of sixty pfennigs. Peter thought dialectically and applied the theory of the lesser evil in this special case, and then went to give the staff of the election office—right next door in the Free German Union Association building, my girl—a piece of his mind. Couldn't we have been told that we had illegal material with us? Well, they said, there we were again, fought free under their leadership; we had more than fulfilled our mission by getting locked up and should confidently leave the selection of agitation material to those comrades who were more experienced.

Tactics, said Peter to us outside. Pretty complicated stuff.

Just so you know, my girl. So you won't think someone crazy for whom the walls of the new prefab hotel start shaking and become transparent as if they weren't there. When you showed up at this intersection, miss, nineteen years old, innocent and nothing more, the street had just been torn up, furrowed by deep excavations and shaken by heavy rammers, I know. For months you tightroped across wooden planks on your way to the university.

Also on that morning, before the new lecture by the new lecturer, which, as you truthfully assert, you did not find suspect. But cross your heart and hope to die, is that really true? Are we ever struck by a bolt from the blue? Does one really stand completely innocent in the door of the lecture hall (just one possible example), having arrived late, and tiptoe to the corner seat saved by one's girl friend? Is it a coincidence that one does not immediately forget the indifferent look of the young lecturer who has just begun his first lecture for the lower years?

The scales fell from my eyes: wasn't she a history student? Can't—or mustn't!—my old friend Peter have been her lecturer? So it was he!

Why not, anyway?

You needn't tell me anything about the power of a look. That, just like insidious poisons, it takes effect only later, long after the lecture, for example. You are sitting in the department reading something about the constellation of powers which led to World War I, when you are suddenly struck and you can shut your books and go home. Although you already knew that look when you were trying on your dress for the high-school prom in your girl's room. Wasn't that the reason why you bid goodbye after the ball to that friend who has not stopped hoping up till today? However, since you had to wait such an immoderately long time for the look, you began pacing barefoot back and forth on the worn runner in the lodger's room rented from Kosinke the mailwoman, Oranienburg Gate, back and forth, which even

Otto, the fifteen-year-old son of the mailwoman, who has an awful lot of patience, had a lot of trouble getting used to.

The flies are falling from the walls, Otto, do you see? But of course, miss, it is getting clammy, where else should they fall off of? Your sister Uschi, Otto, the one hanging on the wall over there, she looks mighty content, huh? Her? She is blissfully happy if she even so much as puts on her little stewardess's cap! We once had to write a composition, Otto, called What Is Human Happiness. Such things happen less and less often, nowadays, miss, abstract concepts have rather fallen out of favor. So what did you write? I can't remember, Otto. Can't remember a thing.

After my friend Peter's third or fourth lecture, after the girl had checked thoroughly and skeptically, time and again, as today's youth will do, wherever she went, whether the effect of certain looks would not wear off after all (it did not; it did not wear off)—on that day, when the fancy new delicatessen here under the arcades, on the corner of Friedrichstrasse, sold Prague sausages for the first time and could barely cope with the crowds, the girl was standing where I am standing now, under the arcades; she was an obstacle to the reckless rush of customers and made a binding decision without the benefit of witnesses: to forget from that second on what one may allow oneself to feel; what one does and does not do; what one lets oneself get away with and what gets away with oneself.

This is a factual account, my girl, we both know that, but they won't buy it. Herr Unnamed, who had obtained all the circumstantial evidence concerning your story, quoting it to me bit by bit, asked me if I had evidence to the contrary. Otherwise one wanders around in the dark, doesn't one, he said, and I was shocked at how blind he was already. On that day, which I am waiting for, because then nobody will any longer stand between me and those who want to believe me, not even myself—on that distant day, the craziest fictions will be snatched from my hands and taken for plain truth, which will force me to tell the truth and nothing but the plain, crazy truth forever. Today, however, I am still groping for the rough stone pillar I leaned against, as if it were proof of the fact that you also stood here once, my girl . . . That's how far things can get out of hand. But why am I telling you?

People passed me by, I didn't know any of them. One greeted me. I did not need to know him either; my dream censor, who is less strict than you, let it pass. At which point I remembered: it was my colleague, our desks had stood side by side in the same office for an entire year. Now he, too, will think me conceited. The complaint was dismissed as a mere excuse. I should please remain sober. Dream sober. And remember. Remember what?

Scornfully: Do I really need tutoring in this matter?

You will hardly believe it: a kind of interrogation. What did they get out of it, if I remembered particulars? Since I had already admitted that I had to defend the girl's decision once before? The questioning continued: When? Where? I got impatient. Back then, in December, as I already mentioned, by the stairs of the State Library when he . . . Who, he? You know, the Nameless One, the Unnamed, whose name I would refuse to reveal to any authority.

Is that so? We'll see about that. By the way, what did he say?

What they always say. If I was right in my supposition (but it was more than a supposition, it was a certainty) that the girl had not stumbled blindly into her misfortune (I had stated: Whatever she did she had to do), well then, she had rushed into it with open eyes, but he did not see why that should make anything better. Trying to destroy oneself out of sheer wantonness or getting buried under an avalanche: the result was the same in both cases.

Oh, if you only knew how wrong you are!

That smile again, those raised eyebrows.

As if you knew her!

And if I did?

Then I saw his eyelids flutter and finally heard that tone of voice that I was after: I know what you're getting at.

The word "passion." I had never heard it in an ordinary conversation before, a conversation like you can have in a lobby, casually leaning against a banister. Passion as an unbridled surplus of desire. That girl with her pointless passion. As if one could not get one's fill of the word now that it had broken through the barriers. Passion and all the degrading pathways which are always, but especially nowadays, inevitably chained to it . . .

Excuse me, I said in a low voice—but you didn't invent the girl, did you?

Then I saw him embarrassed. The things you come up with! he said. Invent! Why should I!

Well, that was only too clear: for reasons of intimidation. He was caught and broke off the conversation for the time being.

Now you are pacing back and forth on that runner again, miss. And there is a soccer game on TV. Am I pacing, Otto? But now it's completely different . . .

I was advised to get to the point—I, who used to chase after far lesser miracles. An ability I had thought lost and I was just beginning to miss—a sure sign that it was needed again. No one can live on figments of the imagination, he added. That's how he spoke to me. Now you have heard and can be satisfied.

He even made jokes and made fun of the girl who learned to shudder.

And so? I said. Did she learn?

And how! he assured me. That you should even ask.

Well then, I said finally, and had the last word after all. So she got what she wanted.

At which he made a helpless face, and that was all. Trite, as I predicted. You can calm down. The girl is invited by Otto to have potato pancakes at Kosinke's. I will have a look at the clothes on sale at Sibylle.

My dream censor likes to pose as a man of the world; he makes the lights turn green, holds doors open for me, ushers me in like a queen, turns the clothes rack in front of me with an ironic twist, elevates me to the position of sole customer, has forbidden the saleswomen to so much as turn down the corners of their mouths, which they normally do quite openly. I see through it all, but I am no spoilsport. I let them place the corn-yellow one into my hands and nod in a blasé fashion. I'll take it graciously, if they insist, although I'm the one who outwitted them. After all, it suits me, I really do like it, and I want it by all means. Condescendingly, I allow them to pay for me. That's only fitting, and it goes without saying that this will not result in any obligations on my part. Head held high, I find myself back on the street, in new clothes, and can tell myself that

I did everything right this time: taking the goods and remaining incorruptible. This could be the way to proceed in general, I inform my censor. This could be the way to get into an elated mood, no matter who is squatting in some corner with an ironic grin on his face.

He wasn't grinning but approving, he modestly points out to me. Even more, the suggestion was his, if I wanted to be fair. But I did not want to be fair. No one, I said to him, could expect a human being to be chained to such a killjoy in the long run. This he admits zealously. Why, of course, he says repeatedly, why, of course, and implores me to regard him as nonexistent, as if blown away, and from this second onward, I should feel completely free at last. This makes me furious and I call him rude. He hasn't the right to give me freedom. I am the one who takes it.

Certainly, he says submissively.

I am too proud to fight with him for the last word.

The beautiful freedom of not having to know what I know—I took it a long time ago. Already back when Max began to play information into my hands. He, who had reached a venerable old age, began meddling in worldly affairs now that he was old; his means were crude, but I was touched and could not tell him to his face that he was lying when he tried to insinuate that he was acting "on instruction." I took the liberty of believing him at times so that I could keep an appointment that had been engineered a bit too clumsily without compromising myself. Listen, I don't feel quite right, can't you come by today around five? Then the same text delivered to another telephone number. A doctor will not refuse a visit to a slightly indisposed friend. So that two familiar faces show up at his place, coincidentally, at the same time and feign precisely the degree of surprise which Max could expect of us. Provided that he who, unfortunately, arrived after me (whoever arrives first is too easily assigned the role of the waiting person) feigned as well as I and was not really surprised.

A procedure we could easily have repeated a dozen times if it had been demanded of us. And it was demanded, I could testify to that. However, it was not allowed. Already on the evening of the same day I decided: Max played the director, for my sake. Only for my sake (you know, sometimes, I grant this unbearable thought preference over others). That's why there will be no repetitions, and from now on, coincidence alone must reign.

Pure, unvarnished coincidence. That makes sense to those favored by fate, but it is evil pride and goeth before a fall. Now the mind incessantly produces occasions, courageous combinations which no respectable coincidence would pass up. At any intersection, for example, a certain blue Wartburg can coincidentally have a small accident, and one is coincidentally nearby, becomes a possible witness for the innocence of the driver . . . something like that.

But coincidences today are not what they used to be, if one can believe the literature from the past. And pride wears off without a trace by the evening of the fifth day, at the latest. Then one struggles along for another three or four days, which one would not wish to experience again. Around five on the evening of the ninth day, one rings the doorbell of an apartment. So you came after all? says Max, who has lost some weight and does not let himself be fooled. Our mutual friend is abroad on a study trip.

No coincidence can have known this I am quite relieved. How long he intends to stay away—three, four weeks—is of no consequence since, of late, time is measured by the second. I thought I deserved the break.

The girl, on the other hand, who is granted neither breaks nor solace must act. For the screw is being turned, be it only one twist a day; between yesterday and today this boils down to the difference between still bearable and totally insufferable. The unsuspecting secretary of the faculty does not wish to be the ally, does not want to give out any addresses, for a class paper is given to the lecturer after the lecture; in other words, either yesterday or the day after tomorrow.

No. Today.

She has no idea over what kind of information she heedlessly wields power. What, the telephone number, too? Well, all right, perhaps it really is better if you call up first.

Or maybe it isn't. Instead, the girl goes to the post office at Friedrichstrasse station and enters the telephone booth behind the glass door on the right. She dials the number by heart. A woman's voice answers (I know it but the girl does not: Marianne). Three times she asks, Hello, is anybody there? Who is it? Say something, will you! Then the receiver is placed back on the hook. Must have been a wrong number, says Marianne to my friend Peter, who is sitting next to her at the desk and lets her take the calls because he often has to pretend not to be at home.

Nothing happens, nothing will ever happen. Said to Otto Kosinke, who seems skeptical and argues that nowhere in nature is there ever a standstill. This was a law applicable to human society, as his history teacher proved to him today. So the girl keeps her doubts to herself, which do not concern the greater whole but rather the individual par-

ticular. Nothing is happening with me, Otto, and that's the greatest misfortune. You'll see.

It is best in this case to leave everything as it is and go for a walk, as I do today, although I have different reasons, for I have been summoned. High time to mention this again. The Exquisite Lingerie Shop goes past, the handballs and camping furniture in the window of the sporting-goods store, the most recent self-obligations in the display case of the Central Council of the Free German Youth. I almost let myself be fooled, believe I am walking on genuine cobblestones under real lindens. Until a finger, hard as the barrel of a gun, presses against the spot on my back we know from detective movies. Follow me inconspicuously, says Max, in a tone of voice intended not to shock me. He knows, though, that I am still shocked, because he is dead, after all. You must admit that a dream in which such things happen threatens to swerve into the unrestrained. I take care that he, Max, doesn't notice anything. Hello, Max, I say casually. After all, one knows the effect of this kind of casualness on those exposed to it.

Hello, he says. What's up? Same old thing?

No, I say firmly. No, Max, not at all. For today I have been summoned.

Of course he has been informed. He could drop his eternal know-it-all manner, but he doesn't. We sit down on two free chairs in the central promenade. You are losing your grip, he says. This has been going on for quite some time. Don't you think?

I remain silent obstinately, so he changes his tone. He—to whom nothing can matter less than women's clothing—praises my new dress. He should not have done that. I insult him angrily. On account of his inexhaustible understanding and his naïve belief in progress. That's why we bore you a grudge, I tell him. And you know when? On the day of your funeral.

We went to the Rooster Bar directly from the Dorotheenstädtische Cemetery, away from all national honors, and spread vile gossip—he, whom you call "our mutual friend," and I. Gossip about Max, whom we had been calling "the old man" for quite some time already in our conversations. The old man who had managed to make an exit on time before reaching the point of condoning everything in existence, just because it exists.

We drank vermouth and then Soviet cognac. It was the only time we drank together. And it turned out that we were good at it. We lifted our glasses and toasted the old man, toasted him again and again. We talked about nothing but him, the old man, that sly dog. That's what "our mutual friend" called him after the third cognac. That sly dog, now the whole world mourns him, and how! In another five years he would even have been forgotten during his lifetime. By you, too? I asked. Certainly, he said. What do you take me for? I, too, prefer sparing myself the sorrow, like every man.

Oh sure, I said. Mr. Everyman spends his money so the economy will flourish, but he spares himself his emotions. Colleague Everyman is able to compete. Comrade Everyman is successful.

Do you know what he said then, Max? He said, Don't you slander the old man's name.

Let it be, says Max. Don't overestimate such impulses. The guilty conscience of the living. Normal. As if the dead were proven right by the sole fact of their death. I tell you from experience: Death does not prove anything.

By the way, it was decent of you not to belatedly spoil my life by praising me to death.

At which point I ask him how it begins. A certain restlessness at first? Insomnia? Then a twinge in the left side of the chest? The pressure? The pain that reaches all the way to the arm? A medical shrug of the shoulders: The instruments do not register anything? Only that it comes back quite frequently, and not only on certain occasions but even at the thought of such occasions. Shortness of breath occurs? Be honest, Max, you needn't spare me: this is how it starts, isn't it?

Max had already made off. So I went as well. Stayed on the central promenade and slowly strolled to the Brandenburg Gate among tourists with the same destination but not as much time as I. A tourist guide distributed candy and small red apples among his group. I noticed that my mouth was dry and longed for refreshment. Suddenly I also was holding a small red apple in my hand. I don't belong, I said, but he cut off all protest with a magnanimous gesture. I bit into the apple at once and found it invigorating beyond all measure. I mentioned this to a young fellow who was walking beside me and had to belong to my tourist guide's group, since he was also eating an apple.

He did not share my enthusiasm about the apple and proved rather taciturn in general. This provoked me. You look familiar, I said. So do you, he retorted, nonplussed. I don't know what prevented me from dealing with him like the impertinent fellow he most certainly was. I don't know what piqued me to get mixed up with him, although it was foreseeable that nothing but trouble would come of it.

I was annoyed right away about my bad memory

for faces. And I apologized right away for that very reason to the fellow, which did not put him in a better mood. It did not matter to him in the least whether he was recognized or not. Some people place importance on being the toast of the town, but not he. Now I began to be afraid that my intrusiveness was getting on his nerves, but as is frequently the case in dreams, I saw no possibility of breaking away from him.

At which point my attention was diverted by a woman, eating an apple of course, who was walking in front of me. She was a plump, cheerful person in a tight-fitting, light-blue dress. God knows how, but I knew the front view of this dress; it was double-breasted, with white buttons, and had a cock embroidered on the left breast pocket. I forgot the brash fellow, passed the woman, and assured myself of the correctness of my prediction. I even recognized the dimple in her left cheek. The woman nodded at me as if I were an old acquaintance; I plucked up my courage and asked whether we had met before. She smiled good-naturedly and pointed to the stitched rooster on her chest. Rooster Bar, she said.

I was more shocked than I can say. I know now how shocked a malefactor is who, having attempted to keep his atrocity completely hidden, suddenly sees himself encircled by witnesses. I understood now whom I was dealing with and recognized them all, one after the other. The small vivacious salesgirl with the black curly hair from the Gentlemen's Fashion Cooperative had linked arms with the waitress from the Rooster Bar. I had almost driven her around the bend back then with my request for a double of that funeral tie—black with silver-gray stripes—which had been ruined by drops of vermouth. Now I had to expect that she would fish the small packet wrapped in silk paper out of my handbag with a mocking smile, right in front of everybody, in order to display the tie stained with white vermouth. And who would be so naïve today as not to know that such a trifle can suddenly become the last, most important piece of evidence in any trial?

Even the telephone receptionist from the post office seemed to be friends with the salesgirl from Gentlemen's Fashion. They were all in cahoots with one another. Being provided with the ability to immediately forget their own offenses, they themselves have got the best conscience in the world. I would love to see her face if I reproached her for having let me wait an entire hour, on that autumn afternoon, for an urgent call to Jena while she herself called her boyfriend five times and demanded that he account for every minute of the previous evening. Of course she then eavesdropped on my call, in order to be able to give her evidence at the appropriate time.

At first a female office voice answered, to whom I had to reveal the name of Herr Unnamed. This was the only time that I pronounced it in full together with my own. Supposedly he had to be called. Not a single person at that pharmaceutical research establishment seemed to have any grasp of the preciousness of a minute. Still he was breathing quickly when he finally answered. He had expected that Max would die. Yes, he would come to the funeral. Where had I got his telephone number from anyway? From your last letter, which Max gave me in case notifications became necessary, I countered. Typical of the old man, he said. Yes, I'll find the time. I'll be there.

The telephone receptionist will not be able to testify how I actually spent the hour waiting on the bench in front of her window, no matter how cunning she may be behind her sluggishness. Molding thirty words into a text which should give nothing away yet contain everything that must be said. Only I forgot it completely when I heard his voice.

There limped behind the others, as if he did not belong, the gray-haired railwayman from the ticket office at the Zentralviehof streetcar station. His displeasure was of an impersonal nature, I did not relate it to myself, not even back then. He took no notice of me but, naturally, he as well was provided with that flawless memory; naturally, he as well had been called as a witness to testify at the appropriate time as to when and in what way I had asked him in his ticket booth about a very specific street. And so the street will be publicly named and the ticket inspector will recall that I urgently insisted upon the information which he, out of pity or grumpiness, would rather have denied me. For what good would it do if I wandered into this street? My railwayman will be rebuked. The court asks the questions here. What kind of an impression did I make on him? Nervous? Composed? My ticket puncher is not used to such words. He hesitates. He is prompted. Impatient? Possibly even—obsessed? He will nod at each of these words and they will be satisfied with him. They love such words once it comes to trial.

The last thing he is asked is when I passed his window. To this he can give a quick, straight answer: At 5:12 p.m. Thank you, he can go. Now it is the impertinent young fellow's turn, now I recognize him: the taxi driver who drove me home late at night from the corner of that street, repeatedly mentioned by now, late at night, Your Honor?—on the day in question (February 7 of this year, that is). He confirms this, even now with no sign of eagerness; this jars me the most. When exactly had he picked me up at the corner? Objection, Your Honor, I say as my own attorney. Your choice of words suggests dereliction, crime. The objection is sustained, another word chosen. When had I flagged him down. Around 10 p.m., he had just started his shift. Incidentally, I had not said a single word to him the entire long way right across Berlin (the fare of nineteen marks and thirty had been rounded off to twenty marks by me). As if each word would have been one too many for me.

In the silence following this trivial statement everybody is preoccupied with calculations. I wasted four hours and forty-eight minutes of Central European Time in that street on February 7 but nobody will breathe a word of it. They are not out to shame me, their only order is to convict me. This they carry out impartially and in my best interest.

That man there, for example, the cheerful tourist guide who led us up to the low wall a short ways before the Brandenburg Gate: he, who really can't blame me for anything except for the fact that I came into his travel agency one beautiful day, picked up a few brochures, and studied the posters on the walls (for I left quickly without so much as a goodbye, without having finally given myself away with a question about weekend trips for two persons)—that unsuspecting man is supposed to pronounce the sentence. What will he say? I know only too well. I was told some time ago during the course of a humane prison sentence: Love is terribly endangered, not only by the rival, but also by the lover himself.

I will turn to leave without a word, for silence has long since been imposed on me. If there are doors there, the small friendly elevator operator from the Linden Hotel will open all the doors for me, courteously and discreetly. His testimony (the only one that really could have harmed me) is no longer needed. Enough is enough. Outside, however, my impudent taxi driver is waiting and indifferently offers me his services so that he can fulfill his quota.

An appeal cannot be lodged. I know. I always knew. At one point I would not be able to fall back on anything. I had fallen into the trap.

I am gripped by panic. With my last ounce of strength I push away from the low wall and flee step by step, walking backward. I am already thinking I have escaped when our tourist guide gives me a friendly wave: Go on, go on! We only wanted to have an apple with you.

I rush off. I run blindly across the intersection, placing myself in danger of being hit by one of the speeding cars. But deep down I know: not yet. I reach the Soviet Embassy at a run. I pant; I am beside myself. There must be an authority in this goddamned street to whom one can complain. No, says someone beside me. You better not count on that.

I had completely forgotten the girl.

But that doesn't matter, she says magnanimously, and I become painfully aware of the fact that I am now dependent on her magnanimity. No sign of superiority. What else would they do to me just to cut me down to size?

The hardest of all, says the girl, is renouncing what is beyond our reach anyway. Be quiet, I say forcefully. What do you know about it anyway. What do you know about voluntary renunciation—you who have obtained everything by force?

Do you think so? asks the girl softly. Do you think

one can obtain anything by force? Do you think either of us could renounce voluntarily?

And you're trying to tell me that you told them that to their faces? I ask breathlessly.

Certainly, says the girl. What else?

I have to believe her. She had left all fear and conflicts behind her when she was questioned by the conflict committee. Peter, my old friend Peter, whose name was never placed on file, who therefore could only have appeared by her side voluntarily and uninvited, used an official trip as an excuse. He figured that it would not have helped anybody but would have done him great damage had he shown up. The girl agreed with him, and the committee decided that an unknown person could not be subpoenaed. After all, it was not he who had attempted to deceive the university administration but she. An establishment of fact which was not contradicted. I hope you'll listen to reason.

Reason? asked the girl wonderingly. What do you mean?

Well, if you don't know . . .

Please listen to reason, I beg you, my friend Peter may have said to her upon parting. He had insisted on an honest parting of ways and had not stolen away secretly as he easily could have done, with the little suitcase he had taken to his absent friend's new studio apartment in order to spend some undisturbed, happy time with this charming, nubile, and funnily persistent girl, while his wife, Marianne, was taking Kneipp's cure. With the girl who was aware of having seduced him and demanded only one thing of him: that he should make her forget that very fact. But this he couldn't do, because it was of no interest to him.

When she rose at night from the broad bed behind

the drawn-back curtain, when she went to the kitchenette and thirstily had a drink of water, went to the open balcony door, listened to the roar of the city, looked across the low roofs of the shopping area into the Friedrichstrasse, saw the headlights approach and fade, and, finally, lifted her gaze to the jagged skyline of the city against the reddish horizon; when my friend Peter, helpless as never before in his life, sat up behind her and asked whether there was anything he could do for her, when she began to comprehend that she had been forsaken and it was no one's fault; that no one can be made accountable for the irretrievable losses—then, while she was still speaking, she said, Love is lost when it takes itself seriously.

My friend Peter cannot bear up under pangs of conscience.

The chairman clears his throat. You are not telling us who the gentleman is, I only hope that he is not a member of our staff. One can't help noticing that this happens more and more often these days. In former times a gentleman refused to reveal the name of his lady—in this era of equal rights the opposite custom seems to be taking hold. How many children without their fathers! Well, that's your business. Ours is to establish why you did not attend classes for three months without any excuses.

The girl has nothing to say. She did speak to Otto Kosinke, who was starting to get worried and came on behalf of his mother to ask whether she might perhaps be ill.

You see, Otto, it really disgusts me. What, miss? What can it be that you find so disgusting? That they don't care about themselves, do you know what I mean, Otto? Strictly speaking, no, miss, said Otto Kosinke. That they don't value their own happiness. But I can't believe that, miss. You can't? Where are your eyes? Can't you see them rushing off, further and further away from themselves? And you never wondered what becomes of that which we can never do? Life unlived?

An experienced person saw at once that this child had taken on more than she could handle. We want to help you, said the chairman of the committee, and he meant what he said. Which of us would be so presumptuous as to throw the first stone? The representative of the youth organization, a bright-eyed, likable girl, seemed to want to at least touch the first stone, at least feel it in her hand; how her eyes widened in anticipation of the throw. However, the chairman stopped her short with a glance. You have worries—we won't go into what kind. You get into trouble. Fine. This can confuse a young person for a week or two, so that she neglects her duty. But for months? And then not answering for what you have let yourself in for? And then running away? And even attempting fraud?

Now the girl at my side raises an objection. We have reached the secondhand bookshop, in the windows of which are old etchings and early editions of *Werther*. I know, excuse me, I say. I am bearing false witness against your chairman, a respectable man. He was not the one to speak of running away and attempting fraud. It was someone else. Every word a knife—not aimed at you, for he did not know you either, but at me.

Where would we end up, now you tell me—that is how he spoke to me—if we followed our impulses? We were crossing the Marx-Engels Square, which is empty between demonstrations, it was a spring day in April; I had waited for him in front of his clinic without giving a reason for this outrageous move. The expression on his face did not change, but he had to begin talking about you again, my girl, and when it started to rain he did not refuse to share my umbrella. He implored me, my girl, to explain to him, for God's sake, what you were after: Marriage? A child? A family on the side like the ones coming into fashion nowadays?

Since I did not deign to answer him, he felt compelled to tell me your entire story from start to finish, here on Unter den Linden. This student misses three months of lectures—for whatever reasons—without any excuse. Any doctor would have certified her as ill. But no, she is too good for that. Of course, the social organizations have to be blamed for letting so much time pass before reacting, for demanding an explanation for the whereabouts of the time owed them at such a late stage (even if she no longer claimed her scholarship money). At this point she is seized with panic—why only now? I ask you—rides home slap-bang, plagues her girl friend's good-natured, rather inexperienced mother, who works as a doctor's assistant in an outpatients' department, until the woman procures a certificate for her. An outright fabrication, which does not go unnoticed by the university administration. The fraud is exposed. The committee has already been mentioned. What else could they do but remove the girl's name from the register of students? For one year only—they could not have been more generous. She works on the assembly line in the light-bulb factory.

So I thanked him. Thank you, I said, for this beautiful, sinister story.

We continued on silently to the red city hall. You don't have to look at me like that, I said, my face is wet from the rain.

Under the umbrella? he asked. He doubted it. Back then a certain department store still stood on the Alexanderplatz, we had to seek shelter in the entranceway, it was coming down in buckets. He kept looking at me. I wanted to speak plainly at last, in a relaxed manner, as is appropriate, yet in a subdued tone. My dear friend, I said, and that was a good beginning. Do you realize what you are ceaselessly engaged in? Aiding and abetting. A murder? he asked ironically.

Circumstances leading to death.

Then I realized that this thought was not new to him.

So you condemn me, he said.

I said, You needn't think that you are rendering me defenseless by turning yourself in—an hour late, by the way. You never walked the rope.

What rope?

The tightrope above the abyss. You always waited for the bridge.

I always tried to help build the bridge.

I know that. And never wasted a minute of your precious time listening to the voice. The thin, enthusiastic, or warning voice of the one who was already on the other side—who walked the tightrope against your advice?

But I did, said he who wishes to remain nameless. I listened. Sometimes your voice sounds beautiful. Seductive. Stirring. Sometimes, I must admit, I like the fact that one of us is already on the other side and is building up courage. Sometimes it makes me furious that he unnecessarily exposes himself to danger. For do not forget: a rope is a rope and an abyss an abyss.

A fall, however, I retorted, nearly always occurs through a loss of feeling, as you well know.

The girl's story was the proof. I depicted the stupor in which my friend Peter left her making off with his little four-week suitcase. The snap of the rope is followed by a long fall, which is not painful as of yet, only one drags down that which could be of support later on: above all the certainty that one could not have acted any differently. This is followed by horror, shame, and finally even that which one would have least expected: fear. We don't want to call the fits she is reproached for today—flight, fraud—criminal acts, do we? Don't you know how everything can be turned upside down for someone? I asked him. Faces into grimaces? Love into betrayal? Routine inquiry into unbearable snooping? And if I knew, he retorted, but couldn't change it? Are you advising me to heap up senseless agony upon agony?

We were standing in the shelter of the department store roof and my face was wet with rain. Someone must have wiped away the droplets, but they came back quickly.

The sentence! demanded the unnamed. You wanted to pronounce sentence on me.

Acquittal, I said. You are acquitted.

Now he seemed just as shocked as I.

The girl had left me as well. I went on my way. Unfamiliar, so unfamiliar were the furs I passed by, the Dresden china, the handicraft articles. Suddenly I entered the liquor store and shoved my way into the crowd of shoppers. I as well wished to spare neither expense nor pain getting myself a spot of happiness. One should not shy away from expenses if one wishes to entertain a guest. When it was my turn, I asked for an expensive brand, as if I did so every day, paid the bill, and reached for my bottle, beautifully wrapped in tissue paper. Just then somebody gently bumped into my arm, the bottle neck slid out of the paper, the bottle slipped from my hand and shattered on the floor.

There immediately rose the aromatic smell of good alcohol. The faces which are transformed on the threshold of this shop as if by strong radiation—greed and ruthlessness emerge in them—turned toward me in indignation. They were not scandalized at my clumsiness but at the waste of expensive beverages. I reveled in their disapproval. I reveled in looking cheekily right into their faces until they lowered their eyes. No, I did not want another bottle. In a cheerful voice, I said loudly that I did not have that much money. The saleswoman came reluctantly with a bucket and a rag.

Relieved, I left the store, crossed the Friedrichstrasse once again, and looked for a table at the window in the Lindencorso. I ordered a mocha and cake with fruit topping. I was very tired and began wondering whether I had really been summoned. The terrible thought of a mistake, a simple, glaring error, dawned on me. Could I have misconstrued certain requests? "The day has come." For what? And for whom?

Now I strongly desired to wake up, but this was not in my power. The dialogue of two women at my table was painfully long-winded. One of them had tousled hair, was terribly agitated and exaggeratedly skinny, and poured forth loud imprecations at her boss, who had worked her—stupid sheep that I am, she kept saying—into such a state, while the other one, young and healthy and clever and unconcerned, merely answered with brief exclamations and mollifications though her flitting glances were somewhere else entirely. I was just as disgusted as she was at having to listen to a lengthy description of this monster of a boss who, for two and a half years, had supposedly sucked the skinny one dry; yes, sucked her dry! She could find no other word for it. The young one laid her hand soothingly and absentmindedly on the arm of the skinny one: Now now, don't get all worked up, will you!

Then the skinny one complained, no one could imagine what it was like: Intershop wholesale. All those foreign exchange transactions, purchasing and sales. And the complaints! The guy had paperwork for every run in every pair of nylons pass my desk. You had to have a head like a cash register. I straightened him out on that right from the start, said the young one. He had to get me an assistant clerk first thing. The skinny one was speechless. Then she said, exhausted, Sure, in the beginning everything is hunky-dory. Some even fall for him. Good-looking man, always wears dark glasses, always a pearl tie clasp, and nice manners, only once . . . But the tide turns sooner or later. Well, I warned you. After six months everyone wants to get away from him. Everyone!

Not I, said the young one lightly, and signaled the waitress to bring the check.

If this entire crowd who summoned me here, chased me up and down this street all afternoon, and then left me high and dry—if, at the very last second, they decided to summon him after all, and even if he came from behind me, through the patio door—I would sense it. The muscles on my back would tense up. The polite young man sitting opposite me consuming large quantities of butter-cream cake—all the while apologizing for the space he is taking up—would understand immediately and hurry to pay. Of course he drops a mark on the floor in his overeagerness, I bend down for it as well, the poor devil protests under the table: Thank you, I can manage.

When I surface again, all the others have disappeared as if at the swipe of an eraser, and he is sitting across from me. Through some magic trick he even has his double mocha in front of him already. Foolishly I say, So there you are. However, he stirs his coffee and asks severely, What more do you want? The old circumstances. If you hadn't come today either! I said. Really, I wouldn't have stood for it any longer.

This threat frightened no one except myself.

You're going too far, he said. You're going too far, as usual. As if anything had happened. Nothing happened. Nothing. Don't make a tragedy out of it.

Oh God, I said in that fake tone of voice which you rightly hate so much about me, who's talking about tragedy? Perhaps we are in some way still fighting the binding agreement not to make a tragedy out of the absence of love. A man like you is beyond all that. He rationalizes everything and refuses to suffer. For us, unfortunately, the only connection to the world is through love. For the time being. We will have to suffer a short while longer. But we are prepared to learn. Have no fear, even our sorrow will atrophy. Possibly the contradiction we are caught up in leaves us a little paler. But we are showing reason. Are already beginning to voluntarily withdraw from ourselves. Don't worry, soon there will be no one pouring out his troubles to you. Soon there will be no connection left between us but the blindness of our souls. But this street, where we henceforth meet only by coincidence, afternoons after the fall. Since we all know the sin of lovelessless, no one will remember it. This we will call good fortune.

Oh, my dearest, I said, I cannot postpone love. Not till the new century. Not till next year. Not for a single day.

It felt good to have said this, if only in the dream. I could not count on an answer. I instructed myself to go off without a greeting, without a goodbye. I know from experience: he whom I wish to meet will never be sitting where I happen to look, but a crazy hope ran high in me once more. Once inside the door I turned around, which has been forbidden, for good reasons, from time immemorial. His seat was empty. Our time had run out.

I went out into the street in my bitter shame. I ridiculed it. Straight as an arrow, I sneered. Street to the heart of the matter . . . Street of coincidence, I swore at it. Newspaper street. It lay at my feet, clean and neat. One stone next to the other, good work. What had I expected of it? Some distraction between two stories? A new dress? A trivial dialogue in a café? And it had given me just that.

I now availed myself of the useful invention of taking a walk, as opposed to earlier.

The stroke of the hour washes the wave of office workers out of the administration buildings. Where are they afraid of arriving at too late, anyway? What train will leave without them, what morsel will be snatched away forever? Or have those millions who sell their lives cheaply also retained the secret longing for the real meat, the juicy red meat?

I walk along and my beautiful life unravels behind me like a bright ribbon. He whom I will never name again was right in the end: everything has already been experienced, perhaps even by myself, in times past. What there was to feel has been felt, what had to be done has been done. I let myself drift.

Then a solitary figure came my way, a young woman. Never has the sight of an unknown person so cut me to the quick. She wore a suit made from the material I had been after for a long time, and a bright sweater, the color of which reflected on her face. She walked quickly and easily, the way I always wanted to walk, and looked at us all attentively yet without prejudice. Her dark, shoulder-length hair was blown back by the wind and she laughed the way I wished to laugh with all my heart. As soon as she had gone past me she vanished in the crowd.

Before I saw her I could not have known what envy is. Never before had an encounter shaken me so. This woman would never be abandoned by good fortune. She would succeed at everything in which others failed. Never, never would she be liable to offend. No mark on her forehead suggested insoluble entanglements. She had been given to freely choose from that which she deserved among the promises and temptations of life.

I began to sob heavily among all those people out of envy and sorrow. That woke me up. My face was wet. I could not figure out why I was so cheerful. With real greed I kept summoning up that woman in front of my inner eye, her face, her gait, her figure. All of a sudden I saw: It was I. It had been myself, none other than myself whom I had met.

Now everything was cleared in a flash. I had been meant to find myself—that was the point of the summons. Cell by cell this new joy filled my body. A mass of imprisonments dropped away from me forever. No misfortune had stamped its seal upon my forehead once and for all. How could I have been so blinded as to submit to a false judgment?

Only much later, today, did it occur to me to account for my experience in the usual manner, for we esteem nothing more highly than the pleasure of being known. I was lucky, for I knew immediately to whom I could tell it, came to you, saw that you wanted to hear, and began: I have always liked walking along Unter den Linden. And most of all, as you well know, alone.

THE NEW LIFE AND OPINIONS OF A TOMCAT

The more civilization, the less freedom, and that's the truth.

—E.T.A. HOFFMANN,
The Life and Opinions of a Tomcat

"THE TOMCATS looked like morning!" To read this line out of a novel, to feel it and know that I am a writer: at just the right moment, the author, long dead and, incidentally, translated from the Russian, gives me back the courage for literary production, which vanished abruptly toward the end of my adolescence. Rarely have I been overcome by such pain as at this moment, pain at the inability of my master, Rudolf Walter Barzel (forty-five), Professor of Applied Psychology, to understand the language of animals, and that of tomcats in particular. If only he knew that I am capable of experiencing three mental-psychic processes simultaneously! If only he suspected the purpose of that nice square booklet bound in coarse linen, nearly half of which Isa (sixteen), the daughter of the house, has scribbled full of her exceedingly childish ranting, and which I successfully appropriated in order to confide to its white pages some of the results of the feverish activity of my touchingly promising cat's brain!

Happily shocked at the heights to which the catness in myself, currently its most worthy representative, had soared, I left the book and the professor's desk, where I had lain, took my usual route through the window, and strayed to the utmost boundaries of my territory in the gardens in the mild autumn sun in search of a soul who might be capable of appreciating my extraordinary person. I say "soul" although I know—not least through the careful perusal of the works of my great predecessor Tomcat Murr—that this hypothetical matter, which has never been scientifically verified but was indispensable to the early nineteenth century, is being cornered by more recent authors through tricks such as "speculation," "reflection," and the expression of "opinions"—tricks which may not necessarily have resulted in a greater clarity of style but most certainly in a more profound facial expression of said authors; an expression, by the way, which I, too, master, it having become second nature to me, just like any behavior that is practiced long enough, and does not fail to produce the most beautiful effects on my inner being. Although it could be my own, this observation is to be found alongside other pertinent remarks in Professor Barzel's early work *Behavioral Exercises and Their Effect on the Personality*. It proves to me that nowadays, since all great discoveries have already been made, even the most original talent would have to wear itself out between steep eccentricity and insipid epigonism, did it not follow the maxim of all that which strives toward good morals: Keep to the center! This shall be the first sentence in my *Guide for the Adolescent Tomcat in Dealing with Humanity*.

Lost in such thoughts, I encountered at the boundary between my territory and Beckelmann's neighboring lot that black, green-eyed cat (two and a half) who, although petite and graceful in outer appearance and seductive in an unmistakably Oriental manner, is unfortunately impudent and presumptuous and greedy at heart; in short, a female, who, after all, principally eludes the progressive testing methods of science much more obstinately than the male, as my professor admitted in conversation one day. However, we keep this fact a secret in order not to come under suspicion of concealed adversity to women's emancipation and in order not to additionally aggravate the unfortunate situation of women, each and every one of whom suffers from the defect of not being a man. I also carefully showed this type of consideration toward the black cat, and so I really do not know what it was that could so have incensed her about that unassuming sentence I uttered, deep in thought, just as we met: Tomcats are mysterious.

However, this assertion is immensely true! The learned world knows this from old as well as from more recent literature, and I am quite confident that further proof will be furnished through my modest yet solid contributions toward the elucidation of the nature of the contemporary tomcat.

Humankind, on the other hand! How transparent it is to me and to itself! A species with a cerebral cortex like all of us, from the birds on up, subject to the ruthless workings of coincidence like every animal, it invented reason for itself in a lucid moment. Now it can fully explain to itself all the sacrifices it has to make on account of its higher vocation and react to each situation accordingly. In any case, this is how Professor R. W. Barzel tries to explain it to his blond wife, Anita (thirty-nine), at night when she is lying in bed reading crime novels and eating chocolates with liqueur-filled centers. Now, I have never noticed that she benefits from these lectures, for her face is indifferent, if not sneering. But I, seemingly asleep on my professor's soft bedside rug but in reality grateful and receptive for each and every one of his words, I can say, Nothing human is foreign to me.

Had I come into this world as a human with a gift

for writing and not as a talented tomcat I would certainly not dedicate my life to such a superfluous literary genre as fiction, which, after all, always legitimizes its existence through the yet unexplored depths of the human soul. So much for depths! says my professor to Dr. Lutz Fettback (forty-three), nutritionist and physiotherapist, and a member of his staff. Dr. Fettback has a little mustache which jumps up and down when he laughs, and he laughs as he says, Even a simple practitioner like myself, who could not hold a theoretical candle to my professor, could see that the soul is a reactionary illusion which has brought a lot of unnecessary suffering upon mankind and, among other things, has allowed unproductive sectors of the economy such as *belles lettres* a lucrative existence. Yes, says Dr. Guido Hinz (thirty-five), cybernetic sociologist, a capable but impenetrable man; instead of allowing that waste of idealistic and material forces of production which, of course, had its roots in these uncontrolled activities of the soul, one should early on have set up a reference work as complete as possible for the optimal variations of all situations of human life and sent it to every household through administrative channels. This is a remarkable idea. How much energy, entangled in useless tragedies, would have been set free for the production of material goods which, as is generally known, humankind sees as the true purpose of its existence (a fact, by the way, which I gather from the regular perusal of three daily newspapers). In view of the simple possibility of systematizing human problems, almost all factors lowering efficiency could have been traced and solved; progress in science and technology would have been triggered decades earlier and humankind could already be living in the future. The cozy contentment every creature longs for would have spread a long time ago, and even a pet—this I add of my own free will—would have to welcome this, of course. For who must bear the burden of their masters' sorrow and want, when all is said and done, if not dogs, cats, and horses?

(Which reminds me that I still have to contribute my two cents' worth in order to spread the new word recently introduced by the mixed pet committee for the old-fashioned expression "masters": we now wish to call our masters "landlords," with every justification, and I do not hesitate to include as the second rule in my guide a sentence which will resist the wear and tear of time: "Happy humans—happy pets!")

At this point in the discussion Dr. Guido Hinz raises his right index finger, which I find thoroughly detestable, as it is in the habit of roughly poking my soft flanks—raises this finger and says, Do not forget cybernetics by any means, dear colleague! If I understand anything about human hierarchy, my professor is by no means the "colleague" of a doctor. But, above all, he never for a minute forgets cybernetics—the basic principles of which are naturally familiar to me as well—that I can vouch for. How often have I heard him say that only cybernetics is capable of providing him with that perfectly complete inventory of all human misfortunes in all thinkable combinations, which, as he says, he needs so urgently to get even one step further. And who knows better than himself, he says, that TOHUHA would remain a utopia—yes, he repeats, a utopian fantasy!—without this wonderful instrument of the computers! Yes, if I were a human I would devote myself to the total propagation of ratio, which knows everything, explains everything, and regulates everything, just like my professor! (No one will begrudge me the changeover into Latin; there are words for which I cannot find the equivalent in my beloved native tongue.)

TOHUHA is top secret. My professor lowers his voice long before he lets this word slip out, Dr. Fettback lowers his little mustache, and Dr. Hinz lowers the corners of his mouth for reasons unknown to me. But I, motionless and attentive among the papers on the desk, I know what it is all about: TOHUHA means nothing less than TOTAL HUMAN HAPPINESS.

The abolition of tragedy: that is what they are working on here. Since I could not refrain from committing to paper the most secret of all human secrets—farewell thou vain and foolish hope of ever seeing this, my best work, in print! What is it that urges the true author to speak of the most dangerous things again and again? Despite the fact that his head, his mind, his sense of duty as a good citizen affirm the strict order of absolute discretion: imagine TOHUHA in the hands of the adversary! However, some organs, which seem as yet to have gone unnoticed by physiological research, keep compelling the unfortunate writer to make fateful admissions in a manner not yet clear—through the insidious secretion of some kind of truth hormone, I presume. As my great ancestor Tomcat Murr, whom I outwardly resemble like a twin and to whom I can trace my origins back in a direct line, expressed it in his charming though scientifically unsolid fashion, "Now and then a queer feeling, I would almost call it mental belly-pinching, rushes all the way into my paws, which must write down everything I think."

No one who knows that my professor is preoccupied with total human happiness can wonder at his often vexed mien or at the regrettable fact that recent clinical tests depicted a stomach ulcer on the X-ray plate which my professor presented to his friend Dr. Fettback, not without a certain amount of pride, by holding it against the green light of his desk lamp. We were delighted to hear Dr. Fettback call this ulcer "classic" and obtain confirmation of the health-damaging aspect of our work straight from the horse's mouth, so to speak. Naturally he also slept badly, my professor? He hardly got any sleep, the latter answered modestly. I see, said Fettback, and his mustache twitched. Autogenous training.

Nestled into the professor's desk chair, I participated in the exercises which Dr. Fettback carried out with my professor out of a sense of long friendship. There is certainly something curious about seeing this man, whose mind is unquestionably superior to those of his colleagues, stretched out full length on the leather sofa, obeying the commands of little Fettback, who takes great pains to banish all manner of intellectual expression from the features of his patient. It's about time, said Dr. Hinz, who once coincidentally barged in on my professor and Fettback, both mumbling to themselves in hushed voices with the same empty expressions on their faces. I am wonderfully relaxed. I am going to sleep peacefully. I feel fine.

You finally got him, said Dr. Hinz. Whatever that is supposed to mean. Only this much is certain: my professor faces the evening monologues of his wife, who unfortunately runs out of crime novels from time to time, much more calmly. A sense of loyalty toward my landlords causes me to summarize these long-winded and often rather shrill monologues in one detached sentence: The disappointments of life, and most particularly those of a woman's life, and most particularly the disappointments inflicted by those closest to oneself, for example one's own husband, take their toll on even the strongest of dispositions in the long run. During such speeches, in which she drops phrases such as "inexhaustible virility" or "eternal love satisfaction" in a context not quite clear to me, in an unmistakably scornful undertone, she drinks large quantities of apricot brandy, her favorite liqueur, and demands of my professor, who has been reading a certain interesting work on suggestions for sublimation in the area of sexuality every night for the last four weeks, that he take out the animal. By which she means me.

It need not be said that I feign a deep slumber, and my professor reproaches her in a soft voice: But why, dear Anita? Leave the animal be, after all, it doesn't bother us. At that point she has already burst into inappropriate laughter and finishes with a crying fit. My professor, however, turns off the light in such cases, closes his eyes, and after a while I hear him whisper, My right arm is heavy and warm. I am completely at peace. I am feeling better from day to day . . .

He still did not sleep much. I often see him lying there with open eyes when, at the crack of dawn, I jump, fresh and well rested, from the bedroom window to the small birch where I let myself down to betake myself unto those of my own kind.

There is no quarreling with humans about taste (this sentence also belongs in my guide for the adolescent tomcat). Still, Frau Anita is very, very blond. This statement cannot and must not be understood as criticism. She towers over my professor by a head—a circumstance I completely forget when I see them lying next to each other so peacefully in bed at night. It is not unthinkable, said Dr. Lutz Fettback occasionally, that an ascetically minded man can be inclined toward a woman of buxom proportions; however, his professional ethos forced him to disapprove of Frau Anita's eating habits.

I know what he means, since I recently read his paper "Even Eating Depends on One's Character." It culminates in the sentence: "Tell me what you eat and I will tell you who you are!" (Whereupon I add another important rule to my *Guide*: Not everything is good for everybody!) Thus Dr. Fettback is not ashamed these days to show up precisely at mealtimes, accompanied by speeches which strike only him and nobody else as humorous, in order to supervise the presence of incredibly disgusting raw vegetable salads and the absence of meat on Barzel's table. Thus I was given ample opportunity to save my professor from awkward situations by consuming the morsels of meat which my professor threw to me under the table, as quick as lightning—no matter whether I normally prefer sautéed meat or not. But like every action against nature so did this one have its price: suddenly my professor began to get interested in my rates of reaction and my life became quite strenuous, now that it was chained to a stopwatch, as his had already been for a long time.

Had I only suspected that the experiments he carried out on me would form the basis of his studies of reflexes which would become so significant later on—how much the quicker would I have shown the kind of behavior which he could expect from a talented test person, to both our advantage: that is, that one was capable of always reacting to the same stimuli in the same manner. That is the least, said my professor, that this miracle of a computer can expect from its partner.

In short, as soon as this principle became clear to me, our series of experiments came off quickly and smoothly. Why should I not do my professor the small favor, after a copious meal of liver for example, after which one would naturally prefer a rest, of repeating my constitutional leap onto the young fir tree in front of the house thrice instead of twice! With Isa's help I survived a hunger test, which is most repulsive, even though it serves the progress of science, without any damage to my health: she secretly fed me ground meat and coffee cream, and I ate whatever she offered me although, due to my scientific objectivity, I naturally could not share her anger at the experiments of her father. I gave an excellent performance of simulating progressive loss of strength up to and including a remarkably genuine breakdown on the seventh day. (It seems worth mentioning here that one has to drive out every trace of the memory of a meal one has just enjoyed, not only from one's head, but from one's gastric and digestive tract as well, if one wants to credibly faint from hunger.) Isa has been eyeing me peculiarly ever since, and that is the truth. Incidentally, I gained more than a pound during that hunger week (I weigh myself regularly on Frau Anita's bedroom scale, even though I am not so silly as to nail my weight table onto the wall). Spring, which had just begun, helped me regain my beautiful slim figure within a short time, and I once again lead a life appropriate to my standard of education.

I did put up a conscious resistance to the attempts of Dr. Fettback to regiment my defecation drive as well on the occasion of said experiment. To empty my bowels whenever I feel the desire—this I consider one of the fundamentals of cat freedom; my professor appears to be of a different opinion as far as the fundamentals of human freedom are concerned; in any case, he looks unhappy enough when he returns at seven in the morning—the time which Dr. Fettback has assigned to him—from the toilet without having achieved his goal. Recently, however, the poor soul has been pretending to be happy and relieved and prefers to go secretly later in the day or, as I have occasion to suspect, often enough not at all, since Frau Anita said to him one morning, You can't even do that whenever you want to! Have I already mentioned that Frau Anita calls me "tomcat"? There isn't really anything wrong with this form of address. But what human would like to be addressed as "human"? If one does have one's own name, "Max" in my case, one finds it irritating to be denied this most personal denomination, as that is precisely what distinguishes the individual from the species. Given the choice, I would rather put up with that certainly incorrect but well-meaning appellation which Isa decided in favor of. She calls me Maximilian; he was an emperor. I found him in the encyclopedia and was finally content: I am most certainly aristocratic by nature, from the tips of my beautiful whiskers all the way to the last of my sharp claws, and so it shall remain, even if that black cat mentioned previously is bewitched by the idea that my magnanimity is weakness. Oh, how I could, if only I wanted to! "My little tiger," Frau Anita calls me sometimes, which is not at all unpleasant to my ears, and the pattern of my face radiating out from nose and mouth in beige and black proves the predatory origin of my lineage. On the other hand, I am not gray, as the humans say; their dull senses cannot do justice to the diversified patterning of my fur; on my back there are black horizontal stripes which blend into grayish-black brownish ornaments at the flanks, striking rings on the chest, and the light-dark shading of the legs which repeats itself on the tail: this is precisely how my esteemed ancestor Tomcat Murr presented himself to the world, and it is my innermost conviction that this is what one must look like and no different if one wishes to make something of oneself.

My reader, my unknown friend from the next century, has long since noticed that I am moving about freely in time and space. Chronology is bothersome. And so he shall follow me back to that part of the fence between bushes of symphoricarpos albus, snowberry in common parlance, where, on said afternoon, that black cat took such umbrage at the statement: Tomcats are mysterious! For, within an incredibly short time, she hissed and spat a good measure of insults against me, all of which I felt compelled to ignore. I have long given up trying to point out to that seductive, yet, in sexual and other respects, unrestrained cat, that her aggressiveness betrays the insufficiently developed sublimation of her drives and that her lusting for power most probably stems from that fatal appellation which cast a shadow over her childhood and let loose those complexes she is now seeking to take out on me.

Now is the moment to mention it: the cat in question is called Napoleon. It is well known that man's poor physiological knowledge is related to his desire to be good and helpful and to forget his origins in the animal kingdom. If one also takes his understandable preference for the male sex into consideration, then one believes one knows the reasons for the false diagnosis that must have preceded that fateful naming. Still, why Napoleon of all things? A propensity toward masochism? The badly repressed wish to take out one's own imperatorial inclinations on the innocent animal in the form of a name?

However, it remains doubtful whether the Beckelmann family, our neighbors, draw the motives for what they do and do not do from psychological literature as we do. One cannot help thinking that these people follow their feelings directly (this is what Frau Anita also suspects), bring children into the world (the boys Joachim and Bernhard and a girl who, strangely enough, is called Malzkacke by the children in the neighborhood, although she is now approaching her sixteenth birthday and has no idea how short her skirts should be—Frau Anita is right on this point), and simply drift apart again when they do not feel like it anymore. Who can do that, after all! says Frau Anita; and then to continue living together in one apartment after the divorce, as Frau and Herr Beckelmann have been doing for three months now. I couldn't do that, says Frau Anita, never in my life, and I add, I couldn't do it either. For now the coffee-brown Trabant of Frau Beckelmann's new admirer stops in front of the common door of the former married couple at any time of day or night, and there sounds that obscene horn which Frau Anita hates like nothing else in the world. With my own eyes I have seen Herr Beckelmann open the window and have heard him inform his successor—in the friendliest possible tones!—that his wife was not at home, whereupon the latter with thanks tipped his leather cap, fetched a bottle wrapped in tissue paper from his car, and proposed having a quick drink with Beckelmann the construction worker. This is indeed exaggerating the laxity in moral questions.

To get back to Napoleon, she is unfortunately not interested in a deep psychological discussion of the reasons for her name. She does not mind what she is called, she asserts. However, she does mind my habit of shirking the most elemental of paternal duties under the pretext of scientific tasks. This being an exceedingly expurgated and abbreviated version of her long speech, during the course of which I resorted to the reliable measure of lying down, relaxing every one of my limbs, and giving myself those sweet commands which, well ground into the reflex paths as they are, never fail to achieve the desired effect: I am quite calm, I said to myself. My limbs are heavy and warm (indeed, they were). My pulse is slow. My forehead is pleasantly cool. Solar plexus toasty warm. I am happy. Life is beautiful.

In April of this year Napoleon the cat still had the power to make me suffer. In the meantime, I have learned that sorrows and fears always spring from lust and that the safest way to get rid of the former is liberation from the latter. *Voilà*. It is accomplished. Too late, one could argue, for my unrestrained drive had already produced results. I am not ashamed to confess for all posterity that my naïve paternal heart beat faster when, one morning, Napoleon the cat marched into the Barzels' kitchen with four kittens in tow, droll creatures, two of which were my exact likenesses. Inwardly proud of this beautiful proof of Mendel's laws of heredity, I nonetheless found no time for meditations on genetics or for a genuine understanding of the Napoleonic tactic of entering the sacrosanctum of my own territory unhindered, with the most innocent facial expression, under the guise of motherhood. I concentrated hard on softening the shock which the Barzel family suffered from the circumstance that an animal they had taken for a male had borne kittens. My professor, who grasped the situation a few significant seconds later than Frau Anita, looked me in the eyes without reproach but questioningly. I, equipped with the knowledge of the insightful book *Love without Veils*, which lies under Isa's pillow, looked back at him manfully. My professor forgave me.

I must say, though, that his daughter, Isa, burst into the most inappropriate laughter. She was told to be quiet. But Frau Anita went so far with her irrationalism as to offer Napoleon the cat—whom she foolishly called my wife with pursed lips!—the remainder of the kidneys in my saucer: Nursing mothers are always hungry.

But enough gossip about private matters.

I have every reason to believe that the letter combination SYMAHE should be familiar to all my contemporaries, so that I must really translate it only for inhabitants of another planet, into whose hands my work might possibly fall in the near or distant future: SYSTEM OF MAXIMUM HEALTH OF BODY AND SOUL. It is understood that this is a subdivision of TOHUHA, and I had the indescribable luck to be educated in the household of the man who invented SYMAHE and is still in charge of it today. The work was in full swing when I made my appearance in the Barzels' house. All factors necessary for or detrimental to the health of body and soul had been compiled in a colossal index file, which imposingly takes up an entire wall in the professor's study in the form of a block of thirty-six white cases and is locked with iron bars at night and additionally sealed. The three scientists in whose presence I not only learned how to read and write but also began my special studies in mathematics, logic, and social psychology were intensely preoccupied with unifying the mass of individual pieces of information in an internally closed system—SYMAHE, that is. Soon enough I found myself in the position of being of help to them, without, however,

ever breaking my iron principle, which is: Conceal your beneficial activity from everyone. The index file became my area of work. The white, pink, and yellow cards slumber in their individual cases like soldiers in the rank and file, until they are pulled out and called upon to go into battle for SYMAHE, under the leadership of the subject headings listed at the front ends of their cases. There is a myriad of subjects: Pleasures of Life, for example, or Dangers Caused by Civilization or Sexuality, Family, Leisure Time, Nutrition, Hygiene—in short, the study of these cards alone teaches an extra-human being everything about the human race. One day, the professor caught me in the act of studying the cards, and since I know that he also goes along with the human prejudice regarding the impossibility of educating animals, I quickly stuck the card I was holding between my paws into the next best open case and pretended to be asleep. Thus "Adaptability," which I had removed from the case headed "Social Norms," found its way into "Pleasures of Life," and my professor, who naturally ascribed this idea to himself, called it brilliant and made it one of the supporting tenets of SYMAHE. Encouraged by this success, I embarked upon the systematic activity of producing creative coincidences, so that, today, I can call myself one of the founders of SYMAHE without any sense of false shame.

So what are we interested in? Nothing less than the exhaustive programming of that sequence of time which humankind has dubbed Life, such an antiquated word. It is unbelievable but true—I am saying this for my future readers from other galaxies—that humanity could maintain a casual, even mystical relationship with this space of time all the way into our century, the results of which were disorder, wasted time, and an uneconomical waste of energy. So SYMAHE met an urgent need by developing a logically inevitable, uniquely correct system for an efficient way of life with the employment of the most up-to-date computing technology. It is no wonder that my professor's face begins to radiate from within at the word "computer" —a touching sight which, on the other hand, causes Dr. Hinz, whose specialty is cybernetics after all, to smile mockingly and remark that one should not consider automatic computing in as similarly enraptured a manner as the first Christians did their doctrine of salvation. My professor, who is a disciplined person, finally had to remind his junior by ten years that he, Hinz, had expressed himself in the very same fashion as Barzel himself recently at a large conference by speaking of the infinite possibilities of employing computers for the simulation of social and nervous processes. At which point Hinz's grin became even broader and he went so far as to claim that the Popes had also spoken for centuries *locum Christi* without being Christians themselves: in the long run only the non-believer exerted power over believers, because only he had his mind free for thought and his hands free for action.

My professor, who is led by purely ethical motives, naturally could and would not let this inappropriate comparison pass. I was already looking forward to hearing his brilliant refutation of this nihilist—for what is a human being who believes in nothing?—when Hinz resorted to improper means by cunningly asking whether he, Professor R. W. Barzel, did not perhaps share his opinion that humanity had to be forced toward happiness?

You should know that this is the most recent finding of the creators' collective from a voluntary test of SYMAHE in several rural districts: only a small group of test persons, who were hospitalized and closely monitored, could be made to follow the rules of SYMAHE after a fashion for a period of three months. All others who, incidentally, did not dispute the absolute reasonableness of the system still rushed from one violation of the beneficial regulations to the next, and it is said that there were people who, formerly used to a respectable, healthy life, abandoned themselves to a dissolute way of life under the pressure of the dictates and prohibitions of SYMAHE. So that Dr. Hinz's question touched upon the sorest point of our system, and my professor, whose most beautiful characteristic is his courage in confronting the truth, could not but respond with a clear, if soft, yes, in the silence of the study.

Then I understood: these intrepid men, who wish to liberate humanity from the compulsion to tragedy, are obliged to enter into tragic entanglements themselves. In view of the present immaturity of large sections of humanity, the decisive step into TOHUHA cannot come about in any way other than by force. However, those who have to apply force are harmless people like these three who, instead of always leading the way for the others, also want to sleep a little later, sit in the sun here and there during the course of the day, and cohabit with their wives in the evening after a stimulating TV show. I was confronted with martyrs! This realization made me so immensely tired that I put my head on my paws and yielded to a sweet sadness, which regularly leads to the pleasantly aching question as to where our poor solar system is traveling in infinite space, before subsequently blending into an invigorating sleep with cosmic dreams. (This, incidentally, being an observation which, in my opinion, does not allow Dr. Fettback's assertion that dreams of any content are to be explained by disturbances of intestinal peristalsis that appear all-conclusive.) So I slept and missed observing what the three of them made of my inspiration of putting the card marked "Parental Love" in the case "Dangers Caused by Civilization." They have to make something of it, for the index file has already been inspected and accepted by an authorized committee of TOHUHA, so that it may no longer be changed at any cost, least of all on one's own authority.

Now, I have a certain amount of scientific pride myself. Once when I caught my professor cheating—after some shaking of the head he had surreptitiously put the card "Acquired Marital Impotence," which I had placed under "Stimulants," back in the case "Sexual Disturbances"—I naturally had to insist on my idea. When he discovered the card in the wrong place for the second time, my professor nearly crossed his heart; but why he turned pale like a caught sinner, I do not know.

It is a well-known fact that some theorists base their entire—meager, to put it bluntly—criteria for differentiation between humans and animals on the claim that animals can neither smile nor cry. Of course this is true as far as I can see. On the other hand, do humans smile or cry? Among the population available for my observations I have found nothing of the sort—at least not in the way described by those researchers.

Laughter—yes. Recently, for example, in my professor's study: Dr. Hinz had published a new article in his series "Your Health—Your Gain" in the Sunday supplement of the newspapers. He wrote about the social significance of fishing, and I read in disbelief and admiration that the human fisher is not only spurred on by the base thought of the fish as a tasty meal but, above all, by the desire to store up a reserve of energy through the recreatory activity of fishing, which he shall expend as increased productivity at his workplace the following day. Do you fish? my professor asked Dr. Hinz, and when the latter, full of indignation, answered in the negative, Dr. Fettback interjected, He isn't productive either! At which point a momentary silence ensued in the room, followed by the above-mentioned laughter, as is fitting in a nice community.

But smile—no, smile they did not.

Isa smiles now and then, that is true. She sits in a chair, does nothing, and smiles a little foolishly for no reason whatsoever. This observation supports my thesis that smiling and crying are infantile relics from the history of human evolution and are shed by fully matured specimens of this species around their twenty-fifth year, in much the same way a lizard rids itself of a damaged tail. This theory sufficiently accounts for the unshakable seriousness of animals, whose tribal history is, without any doubt, immeasurably longer than that of humanity, so that the necessity to get rid of inconvenient attributes must have arisen much earlier for them. There is no bone mold left which could tell us whether the ichthyosaur smiled and succumbed for that very reason when progress and further development were at stake. But that is what it is all about, for without this higher goal in mind, my poor professor would certainly also prefer to cultivate his roses in peace. This is how he expresses himself, purely metaphorically, for he knows nothing about roses, and Frau Anita is once again reminded of the Beckelmanns, whose jointly owned roses are flourishing even after their divorce, which remains a puzzle to

Frau Anita and me, considering the sensitivity of that flower.

Frau Anita has recently begun to dream of black tomcats, which is certainly not only due to Fettback's vegetarian salads but is rather nothing but an expression of her unconscious desire that I look like Napoleon. Humans supposedly are not to be blamed for their dreams, but this does offend me. My professor has recently been coming home very late, if at all, and Frau Anita naturally asks him what he has been doing day and night. He was right in the middle of some complicated calculations, retorts my professor, and he needed his little computer in the department, with whom he spent the night now and then. Well then, you have fun, says Frau Anita angrily, without noticing what a strain on her husband's nerves this new working phase is. Even I, who considered myself lucky to lend him a helping hand up to now, if only in a modest fashion—even I must leave him alone, eye to eye with his great project. Everybody must see that he is overexerting himself. His garden, which he normally keeps in a perfect state, albeit not out of passion but out of a love of order, has been growing wild for weeks. He himself, who in constitutional terms is more the asthenic type, is now wasting away completely. I do not even dare to think of an interior view of his stomach.

What he wants is superhuman, and he knows it.

SYMAHE, I have heard him say, shall be perfect and have universal validity, or it shall not be.

This simple sentence made me shudder. But how true it is! A faulty system would be a pointless invention, for one can have faults without a system as well, as many as one desires. This is unfortunately proven by the course of human history. A faultless system, however, which SY-

MAHE undoubtedly is, must also be obligatory for everyone, for who could continue to answer for the high economic losses caused by a nonapplication of the system? Who could defend the loss of time prior to the general introduction of TOHUHA before the next generation, although, if I may judge all others according to Isa, they don't know how to be thankful for the efforts of their fathers . . .

How else is one to interpret the fact that, as soon as her father has announced that he is going to sleep with his little computer again and as soon as Frau Anita has thereupon left the house with a small suitcase to spend the night at a girl friend's house, Isa calls together seven specimens of the male and female sexes by telephone in order to hold one of those gatherings called "parties," which are generally very loud and very dark and wherefrom I withdraw into the cellar or the garden? After midnight I saw five white shapes dive into the swimming pool, and this cannot, no matter how sultry this night may have been, be considered a civilized manner of cooling oneself off. This, at least, is how Isa's father, my Professor R. W. Barzel, expressed his displeasure when he unexpectedly appeared at home after all, incidentally a picture of male desperation in the dim glow of the garden lights, and without a tie, which is not like him at all. With some satisfaction, I saw the swimming pool divers slip away, scantily dressed and fairly embarrassed. Isa, however, first smashed a few expensive Rosenthal cups by the front door, then locked herself in her room and cried out in a shrill voice at her father, who was rattling the door, You anti-progress philistine!

I couldn't believe my ears. This girl fed me when, with scientific meticulousness, they kept a tight rein on me. She alone knows that spot under my chin which, when tickled, affords me the highest pleasure. And still, I do honor to the truth when I say her behavior is inexcusable. I am certain that—although this is a secret to everybody except myself—my professor's preoccupation with his technical hobby dates back to that evening, a simple system of rules, which, controlled from one single center, responds to impulses in a precisely predictable way with a margin of plus minus zero: a perfect reflex creature. The advantage of such a model for the scientist is more than obvious. Its disadvantage—insufficient adaptability to changing environmental conditions—could be compensated for by an absolutely stable environment. SYMAHE (the System of Maximum Health of Body and Soul)—suddenly I saw the light—would be the ideal environment for a reflex creature. But why did my professor conduct this research like a thief, with curtains drawn under cover of night? Why did he carefully lock his papers away in an iron strongbox? Why did he shy away from presenting his results to his staff, who were meanwhile compiling a complete catalogue of all human characteristics and capabilities with painstakingly detailed effort? No matter what he was normally like, Dr. Hinz accomplished extraordinary things during these restless weeks. It is to him that we owe the method of parallel connection of the unchanging data of SYMAHE with the data of the catalogue of all human characteristics. Both data, intertwined in a complicated manner, were entered into Heinrich, that is the name of our little computer. His response? Often, often have I read the fateful strip of paper on my professor's desk:

QUESTION WRONGLY POSED. NOT POSSIBLE TO UNIFY MUTUALLY EXCLUSIVE FEEDBACK CONTROL SYSTEMS

IN A SINGLE FUNCTIONING SYSTEM. BEST WISHES, HEINRICH

In his initial rage my professor said that Heinrich was a brainless being. He made a special trip to the capital to the big computer, which is much too respectable to be called anything other than GRA 7 and demands a thousand marks for one minute of computing from its clients. Dr. Hinz, however, whose job after all consists of feeding the automaton information, was already out after half a minute, albeit a little pale. Frau Anita thought that pallor would suit Dr. Hinz well, when my professor told her all about it that night. Conceited as these established computers are, on the strip of paper which Dr. Hinz held in his hands there was only a single word, half a meter long: NO NO NO NO NO . . .

So GRA 7 is a pessimist. None of us could get it into his head that GRA 7's designers could have made such a mistake. Dr. Fettback suggested a complaint to the Central Office for Computer Design, but my professor advised against it, since it is well known that they do not deal with lesser mortals there at all. I could not bear seeing him so dejected and therefore did not hesitate to carry the silly strip of paper to the Beckelmann's yard, during the lunch hour, where, significantly enough, it did not cause dejection but was tied like a necktie by their youngest around a just-blossoming pinkish-red rose. Napoleon and Josephine (my youngest daughter, in every respect the picture of her mother) informed me of this with malicious glee.

However, to my consternation, my professor began searching for this fatal strip of paper as if it were a treasure, by reason of that pathological human tendency to transform every misfortune into a file, as if it thereby stopped being a misfortune. (From my *Guide for the Adolescent Tomcat*: Handling files is damaging to your health!) And so my professor desperately scoured house and garden, looked across the Beckelmanns' fence, and saw the girl, Malzkacke, among the roses. A banal picture, I swear by my good taste. I do not comprehend what suddenly changed my professor's voice so much. Oh, he said in this changed voice, what beautiful roses. This may very well be true, I do not care much for flowers. But he completely overlooked the white strip of paper on the largest rose. Yes, said Malzkacke in the indifferent way in which young girls talk to grown-up men nowadays. Beautiful roses. The most beautiful one, however, says NO NO NO. And she handed the professor the strip, which he did not even look at; he sighed foolishly and said he hoped to soften the strict judgment of the most beautiful of all roses. And then he asked Malzkacke whether her name was still Regine, and since this question was naturally answered in the affirmative, he wanted to know whether she also fertilized her roses with Growquick. Regine (now what kind of a name is that!) answered in the negative. She did not fertilize her roses at all. At which point my professor pronounced enigmatically, Fortunate hands! and went into the house, where he simply threw the computer strip into the wastepaper basket, so that I had to tip over the entire basket in order to get it and put it back on the professor's desk. I naturally ignored Frau Anita's inappropriate temper tantrum over the scattered paper and gave myself wholeheartedly over to worrying about my decidedly ailing professor—a worry which was confirmed only too quickly by the course of events.

Meanwhile, the three men, who bore the entire

burden of responsibility for the immediate, economically effective incorporation of SYMAHE, found out in dramatic sessions with Heinrich that the only variable in their system complex was the quantity: HUMAN BEING. It took them longer to come to this realization than somebody unbiased, such as myself, for example; their firm adherence to prejudices concerning indispensable aspects of the human creature—a myth—was almost pitiful, however it delayed the utilization of SYMAHE. Still, the idea of the standard human being came to fruition. It was a great moment when this concept was articulated for the first—and, by the way, also for the last—time during a midnight session. And I can say that I was there.

Dr. Hinz said into the uneasy silence, as if he were making small talk, Why don't we call him SH. Dr. Fettback, who struck me as a little depressed, rashly agreed. This made quite a few things easier. At that very second I realized that humans use their language not only to make themselves understood but also to conceal the already understood from themselves again. An invention which I cannot but admire.

So they set about purging the human catalogue of everything that was superfluous. It can hardly be believed how much they were capable of throwing overboard in one go. Full of hope, they fed Heinrich the new data. He apparently made a great effort, as he appeared to enjoy the task. But in the end he declared regretfully: HEINRICH CANNOT DO ANYTHING. Then the three of them decided in favor of a catalogue of data which Dr. Fettback whiningly described as the absolute minimum (on this occasion it turned out that the doctor reads books at home and picks out quotations from the classics as guidelines for his own life). Heinrich, however, said sorrowfully: APPROACH CORRECT, GOAL DISTANT.

At this point Dr. Hinz proposed teasing the computer and amputating the entire complex of "creative thinking" as an experiment. EXCELLENT, wrote Heinrich, DO NOT RETREAT!

A stroke of genius, said my professor. But what do we do now? Above all, said Dr. Hinz, we should not get waylaid by the idea of an antagonistic contradiction between the loss of creative thinking and the definition of a human being. Dr. Fettback then declared that the greatest fortune of mortal man had always been the personality, and the personality could not do without creative thinking, which he, Fettback, would defend to the last drop of his blood. And if a scientific conference decided otherwise? asked Dr. Hinz. Well—then! said Fettback. He was no obstinate crank either. The conference, which was convened at the instigation of Professor R. W. Barzel, decided by majority vote that creative thinking was a part of the ideal human being and to be propagated in literature and art; however, one could ignore it for purposes of scientific experiments.

This I heard my professor report to his wife, Anita, at night. She, however, who now keeps her bottle of apricot brandy in her night table, did not follow his soaring thoughts and merely wanted to know whether Dr. Hinz had worn his beautiful red vest again. Of course my professor had not paid attention, and Frau Anita said dreamily, He has such a beautiful wine-red vest . . .

Now it only took my professor's idea of introducing the concept of "shaping the personality" for the work to get under way quickly. (Needless to say, I contributed my modest bit from the very beginning. The cards I removed I took down to the waste paper in the boiler room, where they were safe from any discovery. I carefully got down to work and took only yellow cards, which merely denote secondary characteristics anyway—of which humans, however, seem to have difficulty ridding themselves no matter how superfluous they are—such as "Daring," "Altruism," "Mercy," and so on.) So they now distinguished between "shaped" and "unshaped" personalities. Those shaped by the three scientists were slowly but surely approaching Heinrich's ideal. The unshaped ones, which, unfortunately, still constitute the mass of people nowadays, could be left out as anachronisms.

This is how a mass of unnecessary junk was gradually shaped off from those human beings suited to be blessed with the benevolence of SYMAHE. Dr. Hinz declared that, as he saw it, we were finally approaching a state of truth, since being truthful meant fulfilling the criterion of usefulness. Heinrich's information, however, which had sounded encouraging for a while, was beginning to stagnate at a certain point. We accommodated him. We removed "Faithfulness to One's Convictions"—to which kind of conviction should a human being have to be faithful in a perfectly equipped system? What does he need an "Imagination" for? A "Sense of Beauty"? We got into a real frenzy deleting and deleting, and awaited Heinrich's response with our nerves taut as bowstrings. But what did he say? WE ARE NOT GETTING ANYWHERE LIKE THIS. I AM SAD. YOURS, HEINRICH.

Rarely has anything moved us as much as the sadness of this machine. We were willing to go to the limit just to make him happy again. But what was the limit?

Reason? asked Dr. Fettback cautiously. That can easily go, said Dr. Hinz, since it's no more than a hypothesis anyway and not a quality. But the uproar if one admits it in public! Here he directed a meaningful gaze at Frau Anita, who left the room carrying the empty cups and has recently developed a strange habit of wiggling her hips.

Sexus? Dr. Fettback now suggested blushingly, while inadvertently biting into a ham sandwich. He reaped silence. At a loss we parted. We were in the middle of a crisis, there was no doubt about it. In the evening, shortly before the onset of darkness, which supposedly turns all cats gray (not true), I tracked down my professor in the shrubbery between the Barzels' and the Beckelmanns' yards. He addressed me. Max, he said to me. Max, be glad that you are not a human! In truth, this exhortation was not called for. But what did he want to be? A cat, perhaps? This idea bruised my sense of decorum.

My professor has shown the courage of a hero. I know he removed "Reason" and "Sexus" from the shaped personality and then chased it through the computer again. He came home a broken man. Heinrich had uttered the angry sentence: SPARE ME HALF-TRUTHS! That night, my professor finally took the reflex being out of the strongbox in order to compare its data with those of the shaped personality. During those minutes he must have grasped what I have long known: the standard human being was identical with his reflex being. Why this results in a shaking of the head, I cannot say. Why he did not go off at once and introduce this being to Heinrich, I do not know. I no longer understand the man.

My professor leaves the house as usual, but hours later I see him roaming about in the little grove. Without a greeting I make for the bushes, for I value discretion concerning my privacy. (This time, by the way, it is plumber Wille's black-and-white Laura, a gentle, affectionate creature without any lust for power.) Dr. Hinz visits us although no work has been done for days. He comes in the evening when my professor is not yet home. He wears his wine-red vest and kisses Frau Anita's hand; then they go into the living room, where I do not follow them, since unscientific talks bore me no end. Isa turns the radio in her room up full-blast so that I hide under the fur linings in the hall wardrobe. Then I hear Dr. Hinz and my professor politely greet one another in the hall. One of them comes, the other goes.

Midnight.

What is it with you, Rudolf? I hear Frau Anita ask. My professor passes her without a word and with strangely heavy steps and locks himself in his study; I can barely squeeze through the door myself. He does not pull any new messages from Heinrich out of his briefcase, but rather two bottles of brandy, one of which is half empty. He immediately lifts it to his mouth and takes a long gulp. Then he begins to speak.

Although I am no chicken by nature, I am afraid.

Regine, says R. W. Barzel, Professor of Applied Psychology, Fräulein Regine Malzkacke. So you do not want me and are proud. All right, then. Excellent. (Thus speaks my professor and drinks from the bottle.) For one day you will *have* to like me, my dear Fräulein. The only difference being that then you will no longer be Malzkacke but a reflex being like everyone else and I will have removed your pride as irrelevant and instead of your dreary blond motorcycle boy I will marry you to SYMAHE. Best man will be Heinrich, and I will have taken the starch out of that arrogant lout as well. He will be positive, the scoundrel, mercilessly positive, and no matter what I give him to eat he will spit out nothing but YESYESYESYESYES . . .

There is a knock on the door. I hear Dr. Fettback's voice and decide . . .

Editor's comment:

The manuscript ends here. Max, our tomcat, should he really be its author, which is exceedingly hard to believe, was not able to complete it. He died last week of an insidious cat disease. Our grief over him, who was extraordinary in beauty and character, is deepened by this discovery of his legacy. As nearly always, if one has known an author personally, one is disturbed by the curious—one could even say, distorted—view of the world in his writings. Our Max as well took the liberty of inventing. We believe we know him even better and differently than the first-person narrator of these lines.

But who, out of petty scruples or wounded vanity, would wish to deny the greater public this monument of, and to, a talented creature?

III
A LITTLE OUTING TO H.

A FRIEND of the kind one finds quickly even in the most distant lands invited me, shortly before I had to leave his country again, on a little outing. Yet he refused to reveal our destination, or even the direction in which we would be driven. I shouldn't take it the wrong way: Einstein himself with his time-space continuum would capitulate in the place toward which we were setting out.

My friend was a bigmouth. We were clearly heading east, our route was the nauseatingly familiar, dilapidated country road between the two rows of wind-beaten plum trees, and I was annoyed. My friend, who is normally so eager to please everybody, took no notice. Loud and long-winded, he praised the driver, a plain-looking, slender-boned man with a dark blue captain's hat and light blue eyes, whose open, unsuspicious gaze I sometimes encountered in the rearview mirror. Only this man's intensive endeavors, said my friend—he even put his arm around the driver's shoulders and the backrest of his seat—had overcome the resistance against our little undertaking on the part of the Society for Border-Crossing Tourist Traffic, which had properly attended to me thus far. No wonder, the driver said lightly, these people are not very openminded. Everything in its time! my friend hastily assured him. The driver shot an amused sideways glance at him. Incidentally, he seemed to be one of the very few experts who knew the way to our destination, of which I had tired before we even arrived.

I am attentive by nature and accustomed to paying attention to detail; therefore, I still haven't understood up to the present day how I could not notice the moment we left the plum-tree street. What I did notice was the following: We shot over a bump, the driver cheerfully said, Whoops, and at the very same second we were in a completely different area. Just before, the flat waves of potato fields, coolness, and a hazy horizon—now a bleak, godforsaken heath, a clear blue sky, and a faultless concrete runway, as straight as an arrow. An exclamation stuck in my throat as I met the harmless glance of our driver in the rearview mirror. Hot, I said. Don't you find it dreadfully hot all of a sudden?

Quite possible, my two companions answered with friendly indifference.

The driver took off his captain's cap and gave it to my friend, who solicitously kept it in his lap. I now saw the shorn gray back of the driver's head and the cowlick at the top. A head couldn't look more ordinary. After all, I reflected, in this country there was nothing unusual about coming across concrete roads in the middle of the countryside which had been built for access to concealed military objects. This one, however, was brand-new. In the human, thoughts of the inexplicable are suppressed.

An enormous red banner stretched across the street like a kind of triumphal arch finally testified to the proximity of human settlement. I read: WELCOME TO HERO TOWN! Naturally, they fought about that as well, said the driver, with a hint of disdain, to my friend, who shook his head and said, Tut, tut, tut!

Shortly thereafter we stopped at the side of the road by a small group of people who had been expecting us. Here we are, said my friend. We got out of the car. A man detached himself from the group and came toward us. He was very tall and gaunt, had blond, wavy hair, and a large Adam's apple, which bobbed up and down vigorously as he spoke. Like all the men in the reception committee, he wore a loose, threadbare, black suit, but he was the only one who had a round badge with a large, black P against an orange-colored background on his lapel. Blushing, he asked us whether we would permit the present chairman of the Cultural Committee of the City Council of Hero Town to welcome us. We gave our consent. The present chairman, a plain, middle-aged man, was motioned to approach. He read out his joy and satisfaction at our visit from a standard-size sheet of paper. His hands were as white as the paper they held and trembled when he said that our sojourn came at a phase in his town which was complicated but characterized by the breakthrough of a new era. He did not seem to be able to counteract the trembling, although he undoubtedly tried; I, for my part, could not wrench my eyes from his hands. This is how I missed the major part of his speech. The hand I had to shake at the end was just as damp as I had feared.

However, it was not he, the trembling current chairman of the cultural committee, who got into our car, but the gaunt one with the P on his lapel; he was addressed as "Colleague Bien" and, for some reason, put on an impenetrably sulky face. The rest of the reception delegation followed us in a greenish-yellow minibus of recent make.

My friend could not bear the stuffy silence for long; he cheerfully asked Bien, who was sitting next to me in the back seat, Well? No moral hangover? Colleague Bien did not want to know what he was talking about, at which point the driver said in his lively, rather likable manner, Bien has once again displayed backbone. Following this obviously incomprehensible dialogue, all three of them lapsed into silence and left me feeling superfluous, a feeling I had become thoroughly familiar with in this country.

At last the town came into sight, and it immediately aroused my sympathy. Gray, white, towerless, naked—without gardens, colonies of summerhouses, barracks, suburban developments—it rose out of the midst of the flat heath. It had been laid out in age rings, explained Colleague Bien to me, conquering his obstinacy. But what did age mean, anyway? Not a house older than twenty years!

I warily asked whether this was a motto. The three of them laughed heartily. No, the town had been founded only twenty-three years ago. We were driving through one of the oldest districts, which could be seen by the primitive architecture of the houses, the dirtyish-gray, peeling plaster, and the comparative disrepair of the street. What about the fresh ruins? I asked. Did you have a fire here recently?

Again this hearty, superior laugh, which made the blood pound in my temples; again this putting on of an air of secrecy. Bien seemed to want to clarify the situation; the driver, however, impishly put his finger to his mouth. I see, said Bien. Well, you know best.

And I, basking in the blue-eyed gaze of our driver, forced a smile, to my surprise. In the meantime, we were passing through a more recent district: tile façades crumbling away, imaginative, albeit mostly damaged neon signs above the shops: FINE LINGERIE, EVERYTHING FOR YOUR CHILD, THE SWEETS CORNER. Ah yes, my friend said dreamily, the fifties . . .

Then came the rectangularly positioned prefab houses, with their candy-colored balconies and the first self-service stores; everywhere the same scanty plots of grass with clotheslines, the same rows of ugly garages of corrugated asbestos in the background. They're stopping all this now, said Colleague Bien. Where we live, too. It's about time, said the driver. Of course, you in Sector R are always one step ahead of us, said Bien.

In acute despair, I turned the conversation to the successor institutions, a time-tested topic. Just as I had expected, this triggered a lengthy problem analysis on the part of Colleague Bien which differed from the other lectures I had been forced to listen to before in ten other cities on one point alone: the percentage of the nonworking population was extremely low in Hero Town. I wanted to know why. This has to do with the progressiveness of our writers, Bien said hesitatingly. Hey, Bien! the driver called out warningly. Okay, okay, said Bien. In any case, there were problems concerning child care for working mothers.

I now preferred to look out the window. The people on the street seemed clothed strictly in the fashions of the time in which their houses were built. Still, there were young ladies and gentlemen walking among them here and there who stood out from the gray uniformity because of their pastel-colored spandex sweaters and nylon dresses. These citizens of both sexes were also the ones wearing the orange-colored badge with the black P. I wanted to know finally what this was supposed to mean. But P stands for Person, of course! Colleague Bien exclaimed in shock, and the driver and my friend giggled.

I'm no spoilsport and I can take a joke, even if it is at my expense. This, however, was going too far, no matter how you sliced it. From now on, I wasn't going to say a single word to these people or ask another question, not for anything in the world.

Soon afterward, we stopped at the bright, hot market square, in the midst of which bubbled a fountain surrounded by beds of pansies and bleeding hearts. In the town hall was the familiar small reception room where a clerk without any distinguishing features was waiting for us behind a long, polished table, in order to hand each of us—my friend and myself—a round badge: a black P against a white background, which we had to sign for and then pin on our chests immediately, just to be on the safe side.

A female colleague of indeterminate age appeared, with a malicious grin on her face, which, as I later realized, did not apply to us but to the state of the world in general, and informed me that there would be a further welcome. If I didn't mind, I should proceed up the stairs to the social chamber of the first chairman of the Town Council. As a matter of fact, I did mind, but whom should I have told? So I went, but did not understand why our dear colleague Bien stayed back at the foot of the stairs, slowly turning pale from the tip of his nose to his ears; why there were these two fire-red spots burning on his cheeks and why his Adam's apple twitched and bobbed so pitifully. Bien remained in my memory as a picture of misery, yet bravely waving with his right hand, for I never saw him again.

On my extensive travels, I have often had occasion to observe that, even with the utmost concentration, the foreigner lacks the key to the finer sentiments of the inhabitants of their respective countries. I suspected that Bien's horror and the scarcely curbed triumph in the eyes of the malicious Fräulein Büschel were somehow connected; and my friend, who seemed determined not to stray from my side, not even in hell, managed to fawn upon this Fräulein Büschel at the same time that he hissed almost inaudibly to me from the left corner of his mouth, Party quibbles! Whereby he only intensified my perplexity.

Then I was standing before the presiding first chairman. He was stocky, affable, self-confident, and dressed in a subdued gray. He annoyed me, because I thought I should know him; today I know that I was dealing with an average specimen of the species First Chairman; he shamelessly displayed a pride in his impeccable manners. The hands holding the paper with the speech meant for me had never trembled in all his born days. Yet it was the same speech that I had heard before from the mouth of his trembling deputy on the outskirts of the town. Flabbergasted, I looked over to my friend; he was completely absorbed in a monumental fresco. I admit that I felt very much alone.

I would not mention a small incident on the side (or, more specifically, in the background) if it had not had certain consequences. For without any consideration for the ceremonial act, our driver dragged a heavy parcel into the room and slammed it down in a corner. This parcel commanded more interest on the part of various participants in the function than the chairman's speech. They—all of them P people, by the way, with the fidgety Fräulein Büschel at their head—maneuvered themselves into the corner, tore open the parcel, from which they extracted printed pages, and greedily started reading the material—which was certainly most improper. My friend put the left corner of his mouth into action: Communiqués! he muttered. His face betrayed no expression.

I did not care about what they were reading. I finally wanted to get down to business. Which I then stated in so many words to the small, wiry gentleman, who shooed the current first chairman and his entourage out of the room with one single gesture. Upper P man! my friend murmured to me. He wore a double P on the orange-colored badge on his lapel, was called Krause, and was equipped with a beaming countenance. After only a few sentences I understood that one could not complain about anything to him; he gave me—how I do not know—the incontestable impression that he also wholeheartedly detested that which was bothering me, and that he would spend years of his life with no other purpose than to render me perfectly contented. Within the bounds of possibility, he added with a winning smile. He implored me to ask everything that was on my mind before he unfortunately had to withdraw on account of pressing business.

I gave myself a push. Openness against openness! I said, and copied his smile without wishing to. Why is it that some inhabitants of this town wear those orange-colored badges but others do not? I was granted the satisfaction of having rattled upper-P-man Krause. Well—but did nobody tell me that the P people were People? Yes, yes, I said. But what are the others?

Krause first looked at me and then at my friend for a long time, who intimated with his transformable face that he wasn't really present; then he took a breath and said simply, The others are Heroes. My dear friend, you are in Hero Town.

Now it was my turn to make Herr Krause happy. He gloated over my face, which, after several weeks' sojourn in this country, I am far from being able to control as well as its inhabitants control their faces. It came to the point where Herr Krause laughed till tears came to his eyes, while slapping both his thighs and my friend's shoulder. What a rogue! He can't leave well enough alone; once again he's led someone up the garden path! Finally he got hold of himself, beckoned a young man who had stood to one side in an attentive position, and appointed him to take charge of me. When we parted, he looked deep into my eyes and asked incredulously whether I had honestly never wondered about the earthly abode of the heroes of our literature. Once more his face lit up. He wished me a successful tour of the accomplishments of Hero Town. With these words he hurriedly made for the door where Fräulein Büschel was impatiently waiting for him, papers from our driver's package in hand. She was his lover, my friend whispered. I wished him to the bottom of the sea, but my friend only smiled at that.

It is superfluous to mention that my attendant, who had shaved his thick hair down to his scalp and would surely have given quite a bit for an effective remedy against freckles, was a P man, for only P people are permitted to guide visitors in Hero Town. His name was Milbe—call me Rüdiger, he blushingly invited me—he was in his junior year in German literature and doing his internship in Hero Town. This stage in his studies was a particularly popular test for literary scholars. Due to its closeness to life.

Herr Milbe, whom I soon actually did call Rüdiger, required some time to provide these elucidations. He had a stutter.

Our driver was expecting us. He condescendingly approved of Rüdiger's tentative suggestion to begin with the usual tour in order to give me a general impression. So let's have a look at the heroes of the first hour! they said, and my friend announced cheerfully, Great guys!

We now came to an area I would not show to my guests if it existed in my town. This complex had been opened to tourism only a short while ago, Herr Milbe assured me. Naturally, that considerably increased the responsibility of the attendants.

I have seen enough expanses of ruins and deplorable miserable human beings clothed in rags in my lifetime; for heaven's sake, I thought, these people should have left their dilapidated areas closed to tourism if they did not care to reconstruct them. Then I remembered where I was and got confused. Can one feel pity for heroes out of books? Or which kinds of feelings does one reserve for them? I asked Milbe whether it wasn't strange to move around as a human being among the shadows of heroes or shadow heroes, but Rüdiger did not grasp the meaning of my question. Actually, one got used to everything.

We stopped in an almost completely ruined village. The street had been torn apart by shells and was jammed with bands of refugees. My friend appeared to be very pleased by this arrangement: Rudi's star attraction! he said hopefully. An emaciated man—or shall I say hero?—came out of a charred hut marked as the mayor's office. With a powerful, if hoarse, voice he prevailed upon his less starved yet unfriendly fellow villagers to take in the homeless refugees. The scene was beautifully composed indeed and was not lacking in heroic or even comic elements; however, I could not shake the feeling that I wasn't seeing it for the first time. I knew that the exhausted refugee woman with her four children, whom nobody wanted to put up, would end up with Mayor Rudi. And so it happened. I know what comes next, I said, and told my friend and Rüdiger Milbe the entire complicated story of Rudi and the refugee woman. The two of them only grinned at my visionary gift. Perhaps I had read *Seeds into the Land* by Heinz Schnabel? There you have it, said Milbe. The episode we just saw is the novel's fourth chapter.

He beckoned to Rudi, and I saw with my own two eyes that there really was a creature who was flattered by words of praise out of Rüdiger's stuttering mouth. Rudi, you're getting better, said Rüdiger Milbe. You never said "you sons of bitches." Rudi lowered his eyelids. But it had been in the manuscript, page 87. The publishers had not let it pass, however; back then they had subscribed to the theory that heroes of the first hour did not use obscene language. But now, said Rudi, since that was all such a long time ago and things were so much more relaxed now . . .

You're a great guy, said Milbe, after the driver had had a good laugh. Was there anything else that he, Milbe, could do for him? He just shouldn't start on the road again—please!— But sure! screamed Rudi, lovably pigheaded as he was, the road was precisely what he was going to start on. His new proposal had been with the present City Council for three weeks, at the Department of Traffic. Weren't they obliged to react to applications from the public within two weeks? The law concerning this matter had been passed long after Rudi's time! Milbe responded to the recalcitrant fellow, who threatened to go to the town hall with a few tough buddies within the next three days.

Chapter 9, third paragraph, called out my friend. He is allowed to.

He was allowed to in '46! Milbe shouted stutteringly. Nowadays such riotous assembly would be called rebellion against public authority!

He couldn't show any consideration for this, Rudi retorted coolly. He would go even further. He had secretly made contact with the building brigade of the Third District, from the film *We Are the First.* These guys were building a beautiful street right out into the open country, for no good reason, just because it said so in the book. He would engage this crew and feed them from his own supplies, in defiance of all the armchair fartheads and prohibitions of illicit slaughter.

At which point Milbe was beside himself. Didn't he know that, according to the most recent resolutions, film and book heroes were not allowed to make contact with one another at all—for security reasons, the only exception to this prohibition being heroes from books made into films. They couldn't very well be denied an encounter with their other selves. A rather sad chapter, he could assure him of that.

He knew all that, Rudi said patronizingly. But, after all, he had been created in such a way that he didn't give a damn about meaningless resolutions. He was sure Herr Schnabel had given this some thought. Why don't you look it up, page 114, second paragraph. Let's see what it says literally: Rudi Siebenzahl—as in "my humble self"—was not the man to grovel before dusty papers.

Now Rüdiger Milbe changed his behavior. All right, he said suddenly, fluently, and with a decisive voice. See if I care. But don't blame me for the results.

Rudi seemed subdued as we said goodbye.

You let him have it good, said our driver once we were back in the car. Milbe was proud. Any leadership function depended on a precise analysis of the circumstances and on psychological instinct, he explained to me. It was no secret to Rudi that village mayors were overrepresented among the heroes of the first hour. This fact was occasionally used as a mild form of pressure. The books from that time, said Rüdiger, are swarming with characters whom no one can tell apart, and fishing another Rudi Siebenzahl out of the reserve, well, nothing was easier than that. Nothing would have to be changed except for the name. And his current name—no one knew whether it was genuine—would simply sink into oblivion.

And if you liberated these people from their misery? I asked. We've tried it all! Rüdiger gestured with resignation. Do you think that they want to live differently? So they could live respectably and quietly and boringly in an apartment block with central heating and warm water and a schedule for cleaning the stairs on each floor? And give up the right to kick up a racket—for that? The right to criticize any kind of leadership in public and in improper form because of their difficult living conditions? No. Their consciousness is as undeveloped as their existence, and it is based on a law, as a colleague of mine just proved in her thesis. They are troublesome, our heroes of the first hour, but we have to cope with them. But the question is, our driver remarked casually, whether they should be allowed *everything*. To quote from unpublished manuscripts in public . . . All right, so it begins with harmless swear words. But where does it end? Milbe thanked him overhastily for the advice and jotted something down.

The next thing we wanted to do, without being slaves to chronology, was to take a look at the department New Person. We drove under a triumphal arch festooned with green paper garlands into a town district where the houses were profusely decked out with red banners and flags. No, an important holiday was not coming up and neither were the inhabitants in need of a basic political science lesson. Only New People live here.

I was curious about this species. Yet the people in

the streets looked like all the others, the only exception being that a striking amount of P people could be seen under way. Rüdiger Milbe could explain even that: This was where one got one's standards as a young intern. Once one had been educated by the ideal of these heroes, one was immune to any undermining tendencies. That was all he was willing to say about the matter.

Then we encountered the Great Man.

I mean that larger-than-life stone statue on top of an ocher-colored pedestal on the Great Person Square in the New People District of Hero Town, which was the object of a demonstration just as we drove by. My companions could not prevent me from picking up from the loudspeakers a few phrases of the speech, which was being held at the Great Man's feet. I was astonished at what I heard. That's because you keep forgetting where you are! Milbe said testily. It is quite simply not possible to rip a hero's idol from his breast as you can do with a normal person. He is unwaveringly faithful, do you understand? Cynics say they are programmed for good. I argue, Should we, who strive for the satisfaction of everyone's desires, ignore the very desires of these citizens of merit?

I could not think of the word which would elsewhere have adequately described Rüdiger Milbe's art of justification. A weak yet convinced singing started up by the Great Man which was quickly dispersed by the wind. I felt uncomfortable. I expressed the desire for a strong drink. After a long search in these dead straight, clean, neatly arranged streets, we finally found an alcohol-free nonsmokers' bar. Even a milk shake was not to be sneezed at during the morning hours, Rüdiger insisted. We went inside.

A cheerful greeting of JAYAL came from one of

the tables, and Rüdiger and the driver returned the greeting with the same code word. My friend put the left corner of his mouth into operation again in order to whisper to me that JL meant Joy of Life. However, the pleasant blond man who had welcomed us and was sharing his table with a bad-tempered boy with a crooked nose immediately plunged into a long-winded explanation of "Action Joy of Life," which he had been commissioned to carry out. For he, Colleague Ziebelkorn, stemmed from an artistic newspaper report, was one of the first sociologists to come to Hero Town, and, like all newspaper heroes, automatically fell into the category of New Person. Action Joy of Life, however, which was intended to spread from the New People District all over the town, was already beginning to go out of his control. Two pollsters, who collaborated with the representatives of other dangerous sciences in the Center for Secret Sciences, had just come up with scientific proof that the new greeting Joy of Life! or its more progressive abbreviation, JL!, was only tentatively taking root outside the New People District, if not to say, not at all. On the one hand, a committee had just been established to investigate the origins of the mistakes in the questioning method of the two pollsters who, admittedly, stemmed from a novel, the second edition of which couldn't come out. *Wasn't allowed to*, corrected the crooked-nosed boy at the table, and all of us stared at him speechlessly for a few seconds. But, Ziebelkorn then continued his speech; for him everything was as clear as could be. The Town Council was demanding profitability in the wrong places and, on top of that, forcing him, Ziebelkorn, to use the little that had been allotted to him for the wrong purpose.

Now, this interested our driver, of all people. He

demanded details from Ziebelkorn. The detail was sitting among us in the flesh, the latter retorted: Edgar, the crooked-nosed boy, moodily sucking on his straw. Since when did he live in the New People District! Now now. Of course, Edgar wasn't a New Person. But it was well known how unbalanced the population structure was in the New People District; after all, the P people had shown themselves to be incapable of awakening a desirable insight in the sociological concerns of Hero Town among the writers; the upshot of the matter was that one had to borrow heroes from other city districts for certain services in the New People District; hairdressers, for example, saleswomen, tradesmen, taxi drivers, and, alas!, even union functionaries. This was a particularly moot point which had been criticized even Outside in the press. Whatever. After all, Edgar had been given the ambition to become a painter. There were still these unteachable ones who insisted on painting by hand in spite of the grand perspectives offered by science and technology. And as long as no concrete decisions had been taken against this, a respectable citizen could get in touch with one of them, couldn't he?

Cool off, said the driver.

Okay. In any case, he, Ziebelkorn, had ferreted out this loitering boy so that he could assist him in popularizing "Project Joy of Life": posters, banners, leaflets, wrapping paper—everything pop-style. They could well imagine. And it had all begun well. Until Edgar fell into the hands of this committee.

Which committee?

The Celebration Committee for the Anniversary of the Great Man's Death. Edgar had to paint ears and beards for all of them.

What kind of ears? What kind of beards?

Ears and beards like the Great Man's. And they were learning, too: a series of posters was in production.

How many? the driver asked Edgar.

Four dozen, grumbled the latter. Seven marks eighty-three apiece. Guaranteed.

And I'm supposed to take it out of my budget! Ziebelkorn uttered in indignation.

Material incentive is a must, said the driver.

No kidding! cried Ziebelkorn. Of course these guys from the Great Man demand everything for free; it's a matter of political consciousness with them. They don't know any better.

At which point everybody had a good laugh, except for Edgar and myself. Oh well, said my friend, wistfully stirring his milk. Those were the days . . .

Before we left Ziebelkorn and Edgar, Rüdiger announced that works were in the making Outside which contained New People galore of the most varied categories. There was even a Protestant minister among them. Ziebelkorn seemed to be happy about this.

When we were back in the car, I raised the question of whether it was actually a good idea to concentrate the New People to such an extent. Instead of distributing them like sourdough throughout all city districts . . .

This attempt had failed: the New People were too susceptible to negative environmental influences.

How come?

I learned that quite a few of those alive today had to spend a large part of their conscious lives in the old time. And since the need for New People had been overwhelming at the beginning of the new time, the authors had, in their understandable eagerness not to lose a minute in coming to terms with the past, created a certain amount of people without a history, and that meant with no power of recollection as well. No matter how well intended they had been back then, these people were only of limited suitability today. One could put it like that, couldn't one?

Yes, the driver said tersely. Approximately.

The pause after this sentence was getting a bit long for me.

Suddenly Milbe called out, Stop the car! and indeed, the driver stopped. On the sidewalk was a frail, slightly derelict hero conducting a heated argument with a P woman. When he recognized Rüdiger his face lit up; the committee had just refused his application to join the category of New Person, he said in agitation. Why, madam? Rüdiger asked the P woman in dismay, who was a Fräulein in every respect as far as I was concerned; however, the reactionary address "Fräulein" had been abolished in Hero Town. Why? the P woman repeated pertly. Because the committee formed objective judgments and could not take into account that an applicant had been led to entertain false hopes.

I seriously wondered how our Rüdiger could have incurred such a tone of voice; he also immediately stuttered much more as he began defending a table he pulled out of his chest pocket; he had compiled all the characteristics of the positive hero with painstaking effort and now attempted to convince the P woman of the fact that the frail hero met all the said requirements. The blond, overly slim P woman did not share his opinion, and above all, where did it say that Positive Hero and New Person were one and the same thing?

Some questions can throw you right out of the saddle.

The P woman went off triumphantly and the rejected new person plodded off sadly in tow. The really devastated one, however, was Rüdiger. His thesis depended on the acceptance of his table, of which the frail one was, or at least was supposed to be, the prime example; incidentally, in everyday life he was a profit-making branch manager from a humorous tale.

The driver excused himself for half an hour, and as soon as he had gone around the corner, Rüdiger rushed off to get in touch with the Committee for the Acknowledgment of New People himself. All of a sudden my friend and I were alone. And now, said my friend, we'll have a drink. It was always sublime and instructive looking into the future of the human soul, but he, for his part, had to get along with the old Adam, who was, after all, weak. And mighty thirsty to boot.

He led me through an open gateway into a courtyard where snow-white laundry hung on designated drying spots of well-groomed lawn and a group of elderly men were in the process of designing a playground. My friend hurried me past these men; if they catch us, he panted, we'll still be here tonight listening to their plans. Nothing but senior citizens as New People, the district's model leisure brigade.

The next passage opened up onto the same courtyard again. Yet what a different picture it presented! Never would I have expected to find such dirt and dereliction in this district. There was nothing wrong with that, my friend assured me, and walked toward a corner bar, which we had been searching for all over in vain earlier on. On the door it said: CLOSED FOR RENOVATION! but my friend only laughed: Camouflage for the uninitiated.

We went inside. Business was slow, as it was morning. A single, opulent, heavily made-up, black-haired waitress provided the service, and behind the counter stood a strongly apoplectic landlord, for whom I would have prophesied a speedy exit by way of brain seizure on the Outside. Everyone, including my friend, called him Emil, and he was on familiar terms with them all. He had been transplanted from one of the rare Berlin novels—a fate which annoyed him. He showed his dossier of complaints to the restaurant board, to every new customer, and even complained to me, a complete stranger to him and this place, that he'd rather have a hundred proper drunks than these inhibited creatures all the time.

In short: The Dew Drop Inn was a bar for the positive heroes with small human foibles who had enjoyed great popularity with novel writers up till the last but two assemblies. We sat down with Comrade Zahlbaum, a meritorious factory director from the time of the ideology of the ton who had not managed the transition to high-quality work and automation and had started drinking. He quarreled with his author, a certain Eckehart Müllmann, who, irresponsible like most writers, had withdrawn to the country to run a cultural center when his book was torn apart, but had left his heroes in the lurch. If he had only entered a little deeper into my psychology, grumbled Zahlbaum, then he would have provided me with a sweet young thing as a human weakness. There was one in my planning department . . . For I don't even like hitting the bottle. And the likes of us can't kill ourselves!

Killing oneself! a P man called over to us from the

next table; killing oneself had been untypical in every phase, no matter how high the suicide rate was at the time Outside. And psychology had been in existence only since the last General Congress of Directors in the spring of the preceding year; Zahlbaum couldn't demand the impossible from his author.

Kiss my ass, said Zahlbaum, taking a drink.

I can't, said the P man at the next table, as much as I'd like to. You haven't got one.

My friend and I were embarrassed. P people and heroes did not normally interact with one another on such a vulgar level. My oh my, Doctor, my friend called over to the next table. Whatever has gotten into you!

Oh, it's you, said the doctor sullenly. Still, he came over with his bottle of cognac and asked to be introduced to me: Dr. Peter Stumm. Or possibly even doctor doctor? asked my friend. To hell with the second doctorate, said Stumm. He was drunk and dropped down onto the fourth chair at our table. My friend evidently regretted having dragged me along to the Dew Drop Inn. However, the vodka was good and ice-cold. From a yellow briefcase made of pig's leather Peter Stumm produced a frayed manuscript, which he described as his second dissertation and from which he tore a page in order to roll it into a spliff and light his pipe. Ashes to ashes! he declared. Pride goeth before a fall.

I cannot describe the scene as it deserves to be described. The fact is—I am talking to my friend—Peter Stumm was once one of the most promising young cadre in literary scholarship; his ambition had driven him to ruin; where other P people hung on to feebleminded hair splittings for years (for example, the topic: Differences in the

Depiction of Man in the Prose of the Different Phases of the New Economic System), he had to go and set himself a theoretical task, such as The Relations Between the Inhabitants of Hero Town and Their Archetypes Outside. His professor had warned him. Now he was in a pickle. He had discovered that Hero Town did not exist.

How come! I exclaimed.

Fourth fundamental law of dialectics, said Peter Stumm gloomily. All real things must change. But nothing changes here, believe me. I tried it. With you, too, you witch, he said to the waitress, who laughed at him. That which doesn't change isn't real. Ergo.

What of it? I asked.

What of it? I am ruined. It is in my power to wipe out this entire apparition here. For example, I give you my dissertation and have it printed abroad. What's the use? I will have told the truth and destroyed my existence. And why me, anyway? As a non-Party member? Isn't it possible that the Party members know as well as I do what is going on? I tell you, they know. And they keep quiet about it. Because they guard their privileges. Because the P people here receive a Hero Town allowance, which comes to a third of their salaries. And because Outside they can't find nice apartments as quickly as they do here.

My friend had long ago disappeared into the restroom. By way of replacement, Rüdiger Milbe came in, followed by a crowd of young girls and women, for whom a table had been set in the back of the room. With a sigh, as if marked by suffering, they took their seats, and were served grudgingly by the waitress. These ladies, said Milbe, alarmed at my contact with Peter Stumm, these ladies were the women and girls, with or without children, who had been abandoned by their male partners—such cases abounded all too frequently in our literature, which was still written mostly by men. They had voluntarily moved from the colony of the deserted to the New People District in order to redress the acute lack of women.

So there is a change, after all, I said to Peter Stumm.

Only on the surface! the latter said. Come back in a year. Zahlbaum will be drinking. That damned black-haired waitress will be flirting with every man who crosses her path. All these poor girls will be as lonely and deserted as ever.

I felt sorry for the man. There are some desperate people who thrive on their desperation. Peter Stumm belonged to the rarer species of those who don't. Yet still he surprised me. For Milbe, who couldn't endure nihilism, began to ask stutteringly whose damned duty and obligation it was to *believe* in Hero Town if not the P people's; who was supposed to receive and spread the significant word of the current first chairman if not they? If Hero Town didn't exist, we'd have to invent it!

That was the moment in which Stumm staggered me: one never knows in this place what someone will say or do from one minute to the next. For Stumm, far from defending his position, grabbed Rüdiger's hand and squeezed it for a long time, while looking into his eyes, deeply moved, and then pulled a thin file out of his pigskin briefcase. It contained a single page: a copy of a petition to the Committee for Rendering More Scholarly the Everyday Slang in Hero Town. Based "on the results of his research on the immeasurable significance of Hero Town," Dr. Peter Stumm demanded no more nor less than the abolishment of the term Outside, which was, philosophically speaking, untenable. Whoever considered language to be the reflection of real conditions would agree with him that everything which was not Hero Town would in the future have to be called Sector Reality, or, in abbreviation, Sector R.

Milbe turned pale. Of course, he cried, stuttering. This was either brilliant or . . .

Or revisionist, Stumm added. That was the risk for every true innovator.

I no longer knew who was right. Our driver still hadn't come back. The deserted girls were getting obnoxious. We left. Perhaps an extended sojourn in Hero Town is unhealthy for P people, I thought to myself.

I shall skip an exact description of that parade of historical heroes which was to participate in the Joy of Life party and which Ziebelkorn, who waved to us from a loudspeaker truck, had been rehearsing for days; the problem was the stolid self-image of the "historical ones," who know their place in history and won't let themselves be ordered about like us contemporaries who are uncertain of ourselves; Müntzer did not want to walk next to Luther for anything; instead of that, Einstein insisted on a place next to Newton, for "people of the same age," as he put it, who didn't dare contradict him, bored him to death.

Immediately bordering on the New People District in Hero Town is the district of the poor Westerners, small yet conspicuous on account of a foreign odor of gas and a certain luxury—they are for the most part the creations of crime writers who make a lot of money and pick their criminals and crooks from beyond the borders of their own country. I am willing to believe that it isn't easy for the few scattered Western pacifists to live side by side with those wolves; still, they refused all offers to be moved to the New

People District: if they couldn't stand up to their warmongers daily, they would soon stop being pacifists, but apart from that—Milbe said this, not they—without participation in the two big C's of the corrupt Western system—consumption and conveniences—their good mood instantly disappeared and they complained about supply shortages and the faults of the services sector. Therefore, one had to confine oneself to containing the catastrophic effects of such a demoralizing neighborhood on the adjacent districts. Like everywhere else, the youth were the most endangered. Only recently the famous collective under Police Chief Gruner from the TV series *Squad Car* had cracked down on a black-market ring trading Western consumer goods for Red flags, Party badges, and symbols of other progressive organizations; absurdly enough, in the Western district a desire had developed for these prohibited emblems out of pure snobbery. The human being is a puzzle. But if, on top of everything else, some author Outside got the idea of committing a drug dealer to paper, said the Party Secretary of the Western district, an elderly, staunch comrade with an upper Silesian accent—well then, he would resign his post immediately. Later I found out that the Party Secretaries in the Western district have to be replaced every six months, anyway.

There were excellent aromas and tastes in the canteen of the P people, but the mood was gloomy. I can see so many who aren't here, said some joker, but no one wanted to explain to me what could be disquieting about the fact that the meeting in the cultural center still wasn't over and that Colleague Büschel was not present there but sitting here instead with a face reddened from crying; secretly, I was also a little astonished that our blue-eyed driver should be indispensable at that meeting, but I was much more startled by the bad news that Fräulein Büschel would accompany me during the afternoon. She asked me sternly what else I wanted to see, and the devil made me say, That which is most forbidden.

Not that she so much as smiled. She thought it over and then said stonily, Come along! And as much as I would have liked to take back my forwardness, I had to follow her. She led me down the avenue of TV heroes, which was as straight as an arrow and ran into a park, which they call Paradise here. By the way, the TV heroes, who were as thick as thieves, look as if they could be brothers and sisters—a rather unsettling impression, which was, however, quickly explained by the acute lack of actors Outside.

The Paradise is an amusement park, where one can have a ride on the merry-go-round as well as eat hot dogs and cotton candy. I wouldn't mention it if it wasn't divided in two by an inconspicuous wire fence grown over with bushes. TERRITORY FOR SPECIAL RESEARCH is written on a stately sign on a discreet door to which Colleague Büschel has the key; at least she had it then. It goes without saying that the entrance is prohibited for unauthorized persons; yet I have no idea why Dorothea took me for an authorized person. Because now I entered the isolation ward of Hero Town.

At first I was struck by the fact that, instead of P people, characters in white coats without P emblems were in control here. All over the world one can recognize doctors by unmistakable signs; the ones here were even more unapproachable than they normally are. Frau Dr. Behrmann, whose job it was to give me a tour of the territory, seemed to despise me; she later explained to me that there was no other way for doctors to protest against the impertinence of appearing in the country's literature almost exclusively as negative heroes. Incidentally, she couldn't suppress a giggle when I asked her about her medical specialization.

Psychiatrist, answered Büschel dryly in her place. They're all psychiatrists.

At this point I would have liked to be back outside. No—not Outside in Sector R, only outside in Hero Town, from which I had wished myself far removed only minutes before; this is how relative such words as "inside" and "outside" are. Only now, under the high green trees of Paradise, I felt as if I was really "inside."

Yet one must describe what one has seen. We ran into a group of hero-patients who did not greet us but turned their faces away. They're angry at us, said Dr. Behrmann. She called over a Herr Kühn, who stopped unwillingly and grudgingly answered her questions. Why was he here? Intrigues! Wait till I get out! What are you going to do then? I'll go to the Ministry of Culture, the Theater Department, and let them in on what's going on down here. Then the whole brotherhood will be exposed, and with a bang at that! Frau Behrmann tried to convince him that everybody had to learn to live with his failures.

Herr Kühn asked me threateningly for my opinion about the play *Departure in the Rain*. I was embarrassed that I didn't know the play, in which Kühn was the leading character: a journalist who, without consideration for his position, fights for justice for a falsely accused girl, with whom he, incidentally—but only toward the end of the third act—falls in love. I should read the play and make up my own mind whether he was an opinionless apostle of justice who could be put out to pasture like a worn-out nag.

Dorothea Büschel explained that the author had

taken Herr Kühn out of his play after a period of critical self-examination, which a psychologically unstable character like him quite simply couldn't bear. Kühn was seized by a hysterical fit of laughter and taken away by a nurse, all the while loudly calling for a certain Nora. A hallucination, said Dr. Behrmann. She doesn't exist.

What! cried Büschel. But she is that falsely accused girl.

No way, said Dr. Behrmann. I saw the play.

At this point Dorothea Büschel smiled enigmatically. When?

Of course that hypersensitive Nora, who couldn't cope with life, in fact no longer existed in the last draft of the play—which, incidentally, was no longer called *Departure in the Rain* but *Closer to the Goal.* The author had put a young computer programmer named Irene in her place, who came out in front of the curtain after the play was over and called out to the audience:

Armed to the teeth we resolve to the letter
the age-old conflict between good and better.

This had driven Herr Kühn insane.

How about the author? I asked.

What do you mean? asked Frau Büschel, looking at me wide-eyed.

Somebody let down a chain or rope made of medals knotted together from the fourth floor of one of the solid massive houses casually strewn throughout the landscape. Take it! a voice called out from above. Anyone else is worthier of them than I! Dr. Behrmann did so without a word, but Büschel called up, Well done, Heiner! Thata boy! She urged us to go upstairs to meet the man, as he was made of sterner stuff than this Kühn.

Will anyone believe me? On the ground floor we met the catalogue-paranoiacs, those deplorable creations of irresponsible authors who defy all principles of classification, placed in one category at one time and, at another time, in another, and are stuck in a permanent identity crisis. Büschel may refer to these heroes cold-bloodedly as the "inevitable victims of perilous times"; I, however, find it difficult to forget the look of that emaciated youth who, as the son of an intellectual, had had the misfortune to become a production worker and appear in a story written in dialogue. Five different principles of classification had contended for him; now he suffered under the delusion of being sold by the pound by a butcher during the day and having to reassemble his parts during the night. He implored us to take him as a whole, for a cheap price.

On the next floor lived the "unfinished": patients who had been designed by their authors as heroes of trilogies and had never made it beyond the first or the second volume. Condemned to vegetate as war heroes eternally conscious of their guilt, they longed for their future, to grow into a new time. Or the especially pitiful heroes from unfinished films who, if they had been equipped with consciousness, hung signs around their necks noting the amount which their bungled films had cost the state. They calculate like crazy how much of their debt they have already paid off. Dr. Behrmann said that some visitors believed that they had been sentenced to forced labor; far from it: their greatest punishment would be the suspension of labor.

So off we go to the third floor, to the "periodical

neurotics," where Heiner was already expecting us. His fate is banal: His author designed him as a virtuous and respected employee of the machine, who unrelentingly carried out his orders because he wanted to force humanity into becoming the ideal he believed in, even by force. When this period had passed and a new one began, entailing softer words and more flattering promises, he first had to be admonished, then rebuked, ultimately reprimanded, and finally removed. He supposedly threw temper tantrums. Then he cried. In the meantime, he has entered the state of repentance and hangs his medals out the window, ready for an experiment in desensitization which I was free to observe, if I cared to, said Dr. Behrmann.

How do they succeed in making you do what you do not want to do? Why I went with them, why I followed Behrmann, Büschel, and poor Heiner behind that door marked LABORATORY I do not know and I don't want to know. The room was inconspicuous. It was governed by senior physician Dr. Brommer, a P person. Rarely have I met with an intelligence comparable to his; I would like to see the person who could resist him. He sees through anyone. He told me to my face that I mistrusted him, but I should nonetheless do him the favor of observing his experiment with an unprejudiced mind. Much to my annoyance, I found myself protesting my good intentions, which gave Brommer reason to smile.

With a smile on his face, he ordered Heiner to take a seat in a comfortable chair and attached electric contacts to his wrists. At a sign from Brommer, two students sitting at a table began reading newspaper reports to Heiner relating to his person. Some seemed to please him, the others made him angry, offended or even hurt him. Heiner's reactions were automatically registered on a chart, of course. He relaxed when he was told that he had been promoted on account of extraordinary services; of course, his muscles tensed up when he was accused of major offenses in his interactions with people. This continued for a while as an alternating hot and cold bath, which was certainly not pleasant but an imitation of life and surely not insufferable. This could not be all. And at that minute—after Heiner heard that he had been held up as a shining example at a conference of the youth organization—Dr. Brommer, who was standing next to a machine hooked up to the wires at Heiner's wrists, touched a small white key, very briefly, as if by coincidence, and Heiner twitched on account of an unexpected, albeit very weak, electric shock. The chart registered data that normally appeared at unpleasant news. Heiner had reacted the way he was supposed to. This first time, Brommer stopped at these very few adjustments, as he called them.

When we were alone, Brommer explained his principle to me. Heiner and his fellow sufferers had been wrongly programmed; the time for praising them to the skies had passed; it was their sensitivity to unfamiliar rebuke which made them sick. Once you got them accustomed to criticism they were healthy again. I know what you are thinking, said Brommer, and he really did. You think one should try to change this person; you think his personality should learn to accept only as much praise and rebuke as he thinks he deserves, should learn to be dependent neither on the one nor on the other and, finally, to act according to his own judgment and upon his own responsibility.

That's about it, I said.

Yes. You are a dreamer. You forget, the man has

no personality at all. He has been linked to a network of reactions by certain kinds of signals; all we can do is produce new links through signals of a different kind. He will feel better afterward, believe me. We've had great success.

I felt like leaving. Upon parting, Dr. Brommer said in a very serious tone of voice, You dreamers who believe that people can be mature and free cause more damage than we realists. Think about it.

And how about you? I said. Don't you consider yourself mature and free?

I am, said Brommer. But I am one in ten thousand.

We left. God, was I tired. The day seemed ever so long. Perhaps they had also invented a machine here with which to stretch time. Where are we? I asked the tight-lipped P woman Büschel after a while. KL, she informed me. What's that? I asked. King's Level, she said. I said no more.

We walked toward a high-rise building, in front of which a group had gathered which I would have recognized even without their white P emblems as visitors from Outside. I was attracted by them like the thirsty man by the fountain. They behaved exactly the way anyone behaves who finds himself in Hero Town for the first time: by hiding his confusion behind brash behavior. Incidentally, it turned out that these people were writers. I saw my friend among them, along with Rüdiger Milbe. The group was led by a curious couple: an elderly, distinguished-looking man with a pear-shaped skull, who was called Comrade Wohlrath and came "from the Ministry," and his personal assistant, a small, agile, frizzy-haired man in his late thirties. His name was Valium and he was explaining to the writers why the authorities in charge had felt compelled to lead them to Hero

Town and to the King's Level in particular, as much as they had wished to continue sparing them certain embarrassments. For the sake of convenience and control, this high-rise building housed nothing but planners and leaders from the entire body of literature, including, by way of exception, film, radio, and television. One should see, for example, how many of the nameplates next to the doorbells were still without names. This, however, was only the quantitative aspect, the qualitative one being much graver. Valium rang the bell of a first-floor apartment, at Hennig's.

A female voice asked us through the intercom to come up. Well, Günter, I guess we'd better let you do the talking with Frau Hennig, Wohlrath said on the stairs to a pale, intimidated writer with the name of Breisach. Breisach's colleagues smirked. Rüdiger Milbe whispered to me that Frau Hennig, as well as her husband, a member of the district government who was on an official trip, were Breisach's creations.

You are ironing, Frau Hennig? An awkward question on Breisach's part which produced a sniffy reaction from Frau Hennig, who quickly took off her apron. I am ironing, she said. What else could I be doing? Or do you happen to have something for me to do which Breisach couldn't come up with? No one gave Breisach away. The ten minutes we spent with her were uncomfortable, and not only for him. We stood in Frau Hennig's spick-and-span living room: the matching armchairs, the three-armed pendant lamp over the table, the wall-to-wall cupboard units separating kitchen and living room, the coffee service with the black-and-white pattern . . .

Then we were back on the staircase. A long gray corridor, doors right and left with numbers on them. To everyone's relief Wohlrath refrained from ringing another doorbell. Everywhere the same misery, he said. Neglected wives of leaders. Untapped human resources abound.

It finally became clear what all of this boiled down to. Valium read out a list of those positions and functions which cannot be filled in Hero Town for lack of suitable heroes; most needed are higher-level cultural functionaries, as well as promising young candidates for structurally essential branches of industry. With computer experience.

Now comes Koldewitz, my friend whispered behind me.

He was right. A certain Herr Koldewitz came forward, whose youth was long past but who played the role of a young man. He had met just such a future leader in a course given by the Plastics Cooperative, a great guy, educated and still revolutionary, quite simply a member of the new generation. However, not even he, Koldewitz, whom everyone knew to be a hotspur, could have suspected that it was desirable to take up pen and paper and describe such a person. It certainly had not been indicated by the newspapers which he carefully perused every day. Not even between the lines.

Ah, said Wohlrath, and gestured a fatigued refusal, as one might gesture refusal from a certain level upward at the mention of the press. Everyone looked at the leading editor of the cultural page, who accompanies the group for press coverage. He shrugged his shoulders: No instruction!

Use your own mind! countered Wohlrath. Or is that forbidden in this country?

The writers smirked. Valium said for the seventh time in the course of an hour, That is a fact. Herr Koldewitz described in a roundabout way his encounters with our wonderful people in the city as well as in the country and then gave a detailed account down to the penny of what these encounters cost him. Comrade Wohlrath explained that the main plan positions would be secured by grants in the course of the developing order situation. Valium made notes of Herr Koldewitz's interest and asked about other relevant offers. A young, sharp-nosed playwright was hoping to be able to investigate an information scientist, and an elderly, plump lady vowed no longer to evade the advances of her bungalow neighbor, a cyberneticist who had long been unappreciated. That's good, Lily, they said to her, and she smiled impishly and said warningly, But he is a strange fish!

It didn't matter. She was added to Valium's list and would hear from him.

Five hundred marks a month, my friend whispered behind me. And that's for an entire year.

I considered Colleague Lily's late adventure in gallantry quite well paid, but I only asked, What if the cyberneticist turns out to be a flop?

A *fonds perdu*, retorted my educated friend.

Oh, I'd love to be a writer in this country, I thought.

At that point a burly, youthful man jumped to the front (hereabouts the forty-year-olds are still called youthful) and cried out that he couldn't take it anymore. Now they sat arguing about what was water under the bridge, and their sinecures, with everybody pretending he had never created his "Schütt." Schütt who fulfilled, point by point, all the requirements that had just been read out by Comrade Wohlrath but who had been rotting away in a desk drawer in the Ministry for more than a year now. This was enough to drive any man onto the barricades!

The effect could not be any different than if the British Queen had behaved improperly in court. At first it seemed as if Valium wished to appear deaf and move on to the agenda. Wohlrath, however, admonished him: Comrade Oskar Grabe's honest question deserved an equally honest answer. Even though he had perhaps used the wrong tone, didn't you now, Oskar?

Sorry, mumbled Grabe, and Wohlrath raised his hand lightly: It's already forgotten. To get to the matter at hand. Unfortunately, he had to say, Comrade Grabe, you are quite mistaken.

Finally my friend found occasion to fill me in concerning a not at all unimportant detail. Comrade Wohlrath was in charge of the country's censorship office; it would not have been easy to find anyone more suited to this office, said my friend; guess what: Wohlrath loved literature.

My friend seemed touched. Wohlrath was just asking Grabe whether his Schütt hadn't died of heart failure.

That was an earlier draft, said Grabe gloomily.

At which point Valium came to his rescue: And what do you do with him in the most recent draft? Well? Say it?

I have him write a letter, Grabe admitted reluctantly.

A letter. I see. And to whom?

To the First Secretary! roared Grabe. Because they want to get rid of Schütt, man! So he hits back. I see, said Valium again, but he did justice to his name and remained silent. Wohlrath remained silent as well, and the rest of us had been quiet as mice to begin with. After a long pause Grabe said quietly, But they really got rid of Schütt!

Now Rüdiger Milbe took over. Almost without a

stutter, he reproached Grabe for his fatal inclination toward naturalism and instantly came up with three titles of recent works by our aestheticians which Grabe absolutely had to study. I saw that everybody noted down the titles, not only Grabe, whom Rüdiger engaged in a debate of principle on the basis of his outline of the characteristics of the positive hero. Wohlrath praised the free development of the creative conflict of opinions we had just witnessed and promised to work toward an organizational system which guaranteed the safeguarding of any and all literary ideas from their first flash all the way to their materialization—yes, and this included the necessary contingent of paper, a burning problem he had to tackle right here in front of everybody.

He received undivided applause from everybody present, including myself. I must admit that I, for my part, also felt like presenting the kind Herr Wohlrath with a leadership personality, upon whom his entire Ministry would not find a speck of dust, not even with a magnifying glass; right then I accidentally heard Wohlrath snap at Valium, how could he have invited this Grabe here, and Valium spluttered and blamed the slip on a district union secretary; Wohlrath asked Valium whether it had escaped him that "they" had talked about Grabe's manuscript, that there existed an order to let it lie for the time being, whether this didn't necessarily produce a heightened sense of watchfulness in an experienced functionary? Valium was shamefaced and I decided that I would think again before I did something for Wohlrath's sake.

Are we going? asked my friend. There was nothing I would rather have done.

The writers were waiting for their bus on the square in front of the House of Cultural Affairs, I was waiting for our car. The atmosphere was relaxed, almost jovial. Rüdiger Milbe, who was standing among a crowd of young writers, had just asked what the difference was between the Gobi desert and a TV detective movie when the doors of the House of Cultural Affairs flew open and the participants of the meeting that had taken all day poured out onto the square. Milbe stopped in mid-phrase and ran toward Büschel, who crossed the square with a stony face and disappeared from our sight. Soon everyone knew: Upper P man Krause could save himself only by dropping her. The material our driver had brought along had contained the most recent instructions, according to which the former First Chairman—the same person whose reception speech I had heard only this morning—had to be replaced immediately. Superior P man Krause had made a good job of this, no small matter considering the fact that he had defended the present—no, former—First Chairman only yesterday . . .

What was it all about? They had had to change the plans Outside, that is, in Sector R. (I couldn't believe my ears.) Naturally, this produced a profound effect on literature. The most recent slogan was: No more period heroes! Let's move toward the production branch hero! New organizing principles had been distributed; the poison of the old views had to be effectively exposed. Naturally, the indescribably banal and detrimental slogan JL ("Joy of Life") had been removed forever from circulation, as was only proper.

My mind was a blank. I registered that our driver, who finally came out himself, went from group to group and bade a kind goodbye to everybody—even to the former First Chairman, who stood all by himself away from the others; he found a humane, encouraging word for everyone, so that it did not surprise me that all hearts went out to him. I praised him, our kind driver. Yes, said my friend. He had been a good catch for the SOGOCI. SOGOCI? Society for the Good of Citizens, said my friend, and that was all he said.

We got into the car. I don't want to exclude the possibility that I fell asleep immediately, but it is still strange that I don't have the slightest recollection of either our return trip or our arrival, and only woke up in bed in my pleasant hotel room in the morning. Something made me call my friend and ask him how our little outing had agreed with him.

Outing? he asked in astonishment. Which outing?

To Hero Town? I said. Yesterday.

Hero Town? Never heard of the place. Yesterday? I spent the whole day at a damned conference.

That was the day before yesterday! I said. On the fifteenth!

Hey, said my friend, what's the matter with you? Today is Tuesday, the sixteenth. So yesterday must have been the fifteenth. Right?

Boy oh boy, I thought, these people are a lot smarter than they look.

In that case I'm missing a day, I said to my friend.

The film had ripped, he knew the feeling. Had a few too many, huh?

Something else, I said. Recently, I heard the beginning of a joke somewhere: What's the difference between the Gobi desert and a TV detective movie?

Oh that! said my friend. You don't know that one? There's no difference; both of them are long and dry. Pretty bad, isn't it?

I almost miss my friend now. He was such fun.

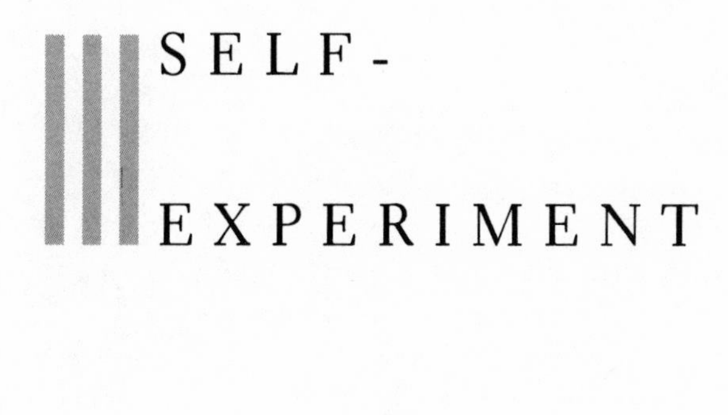

III SELF-EXPERIMENT

TREATISE ON A REPORT

THERE IS NO doubt about it: the experiment was a success. You, Professor, are one of the great men of this century. The loss of everyday praise should leave you cold. As far as I am concerned, the secrecy stipulations, which we are bound to, not only safeguard the strictest confidentiality apropos all the material concerning our experiment, they also give me the freedom to add these unrequired notes to the report on myself.

Filling a gap in a report by describing how that very gap came about: there could be no more brilliant pretext to present you with this information. Tired of pre-texts and pre-tenses, I decide in favor of plain language, which is a woman's prerogative, however rarely used—incidentally, an insight from the time when I was a man or, more correctly, threatened to become a man. My most recent experience demands expression. Happy with the fact that words are once again at my disposal, I cannot help but play with them, marveling at their ambiguity, which shall not prevent me from stating that all the data you can gather from my report are exact, correct, and unequivocal.

Bepeter Masculinum 199 is a wonderful drug suited to change a woman into a man with no risk or undesirable side effects. The tests proving our hypothesis are just like that perfect test you impressed upon our minds in our student days: reliable, sensitive, valid. I myself designed them. My notes were as thorough as possible. Every word in my report is true. However, all its sentences taken together explain nothing, fail to explain why I offered myself for the experiment, and most certainly fail to explain why I broke it off after thirty days so that I have happily become a woman again during the last two weeks. I know that the truth—a word you would avoid—has far removed itself from the facts of that report. You, however, with your superstitious worship of scientific results, have made me suspicious of those words in my inner language which could now help me contradict the unreal neutrality of this report with my real memory.

"Curiosity," you are supposed to have said. Curiosity as the presumed reason for my agreeing to this experiment. Curiosity is a vice shared by women and cats, while the man is hungry for ideas and thirsting for knowledge. That's what I told you, and you smiled—full of appreciation, if I am not mistaken. You never deny anything when you get caught. But you take great pains never to get caught.

And I wanted to know why.

Now they all want to know what manner of devil got into me to break off the successful experiment prematurely. Why was no one interested in the reasons which drove me to this madness in the first place? You personally never asked, neither before nor afterward. Either you know all the answers or you are too proud to betray a weak spot by asking . . .

Should the leader of the cadre, of all people, have talked to me? She was occupied with her obligations toward secrecy. Today it seems almost suspicious that not one of us had violated his or her professional secrecy—like accomplices whose mouths are sealed by a common crime. My text was different from the one for the other six—or seven, in case you also signed in your fanaticism for justice. White document paper, standard format, Academy of Sciences printed on the letterhead. That I: motivated by . . . guided by . . . (the progress of sciences, humanistic goals, and so on) had volunteered as a test subject ("in the following Ts"). I signed it, so it is true . . . had been informed of the element of risk. I signed . . . that a possible "partial or entire failure" of the experiment held the academy responsible with respect to all resulting indemnity and compensation (what had you or the leader of the cadre possibly pictured as "a partial failure"?).

Both amused and angry I signed, and the leader of the cadre watched me with horror and enthusiasm, while behind my back her secretary unwrapped the ubiquitous bunch of carnations due at every award and appointment.

I knew myself that I was suited beyond all measure as a test subject: single, no children. My age was not ideal but still suitable: thirty-three-and-a-half. Healthy. Intelligent. Doctor of Physiopsychology and director of the team SC (Sex Change) at the Institute of Human Hormonetics and therefore an insider to this research program like no other besides the director of the institute himself. Trained in the pertinent techniques of measuring and observation and in the use of the relevant technical jargon. Finally, capable of summoning male courage and manly willpower, which would both be required when the time came.

There's one thing I give you credit for: you did not try to pretend that my bound duty was a privilege. Thus I lost the last opportunity to get angry, defend myself, drop out. How do you refuse to accept a folder from the director of the institute in the middle of a work conference? Not at all. You take it. A sturdy folder containing all the information for the future test subject, which everyone around here has seen. While no one suspects that an exact duplicate of said folder is deposited in my own safe and you can rely on me to keep a straight face. Our colleagues deserve the emotion which can finally overtake them.

It was Monday, February 19, in the year 1992, an overcast month, with less sunshine on average than during the last fifty years. However, after we had fixed March 4 as the beginning of the experiment and you terminated the meeting by silently, and unexpectedly, shaking my hand, the sun shone into your study for about ten seconds. Handshake and smile and head up and be moderate and reasonable: there I stood once again and agreed to everything. Even that it would have been unprofitable to first develop a preparation for the change of men into women because no test subject would have been found for such an absurd experiment . . .

You exceeded the one minute you asked to spend with me after the meeting by thirty seconds in order to tell me that Bepeter *minus* Masculinum 199 was an equally reliable drug—which I knew, of course—and, as soon as I wished it, would change me back even before the scheduled limit of three months. Other than that nothing happened —not a sign, not a glance, not even the blink of an eye. Your inscrutable expression confronted my composed face in the way we had practiced for such a long time.

As I left your room, my friend Dr. Rüdiger, whom you appreciate as a scientist but still find a touch too slack, saved the day by scrutinizing me from head to toe with an impertinent male glance, whistling in an obscene fashion, and saying, What a shame, toots! That worked. That was the only thing that worked, but it lasted only for a moment.

The fourteen days we had left we filled with outrageous banalities, with silliness and hoaxes which you probably took for cheerfulness. (Meanwhile, everybody did their best to give themselves away: Rüdiger began kissing my hand; the laboratory chief of staff, Irene, "forgot" to bring over her little daughter when she herself put up a man for the night; and Beate—the best female chemist you know, Professor—hinted that she envied me. Spare me these Stone Age miasmas, you will say. Lack of self-control, moodiness, all kinds of slips. It would surprise me if you had noticed a single instance of lack of self-discipline during the entire ten years—you had programmed me with this sentence shortly before my final examination. Although I could gather from a comment by your secretary that you would take me over any male scientist . . .)

Once, on a Saturday, two days before the beginning of the experiment, I almost called you. When I was sitting alone "in the clouds"—that's Irene's expression, who lives two floors below, the fifteenth floor—that is, in front of the large window in my living room; when darkness set in and the lights of our scientists' estate and, beyond them, those of the city of Berlin shone up at me, that's when I had a cognac—which violated the instructions—observed the light in your study for several minutes, a light which I can find among all the other lights, and my hand was already touching the receiver. I dialed your number, heard the dial tone once and then immediately your voice, which sounded perhaps a touch less impersonal than usual. Since you did not hang up, although I did not speak, yet did not say anything yourself, I could hear you breathe and perhaps you could hear me as well. I thought remote thoughts. I wonder if the word "morose" has to do with moor, being hopelessly bogged down in a moor? While "audacious" originally meant nothing more than turning toward a certain goal—and resolutely at that. Which is what I was when, at the age of nineteen, in my first lecture with you, I scribbled the short word "I" in large print on a piece of paper which I slid over to Rüdiger. For you, Professor, had just conjectured jokingly that, among us young things, "innocent, nothing more," there sat possibly the person who would let herself be changed into a man in ten or fifteen years by a fantastic drug that had yet to be invented. I. AUDACIOUS! Rüdiger wrote next to it. Do you now understand why it was important to me to have him join our team?

A minute later I put down the receiver, went to bed, and fell asleep immediately, as I had trained myself to do with iron discipline (only now is the training failing, strangely enough), spent a disciplined Sunday following a prescribed schedule with the necessary preparations, fixing meals, taking the required measurements and notes, which, as it turned out in the evening, perfectly served their purpose: I also succumbed to the temptation of confusing a routine day with no coincidences with the regular workings of higher necessities, which relieve us of anxiety, fear, and doubt. Sometimes you can find out why we do what we do when there are no more choices left. None of my good or bad reasons played a role any longer in view of the one reason sufficient in and of itself: that I wanted to discover your secret.

I got to the institute on time early Monday morning and, in a suitably matter-of-fact atmosphere, received my first injection from you, which put me to sleep and initiated the metamorphosis which would be completed by nine further doses of Bepeter Masc. 199, given to me at five-hour intervals. It seemed as if I was dreaming all the while, although "dream" may not be the right word. However, one cannot very well blame language for not having a word for those blurry transitions I was mired in, mirrored in myself as swimming at the bottom of a light-green body of water enhanced by strangely beautiful plants and animals. The object which was swimming around was most likely the stem of a plant, which gradually grew fins and gills until it became a slim, beautiful, slippery fish moving around all over the water between the green stems and leaves with pleasure and ease. My first thought upon awakening was: Neither fish nor fowl. But then I saw and recognized our electronic clock and read the date and the time: it was March 6, 1992, three o'clock in the morning, and I was a man.

Next to my bed sat Beate: a good idea, in case it was yours. (I didn't know until a few days ago that you left the test room literally one minute before I woke up, Professor!) I repeat: Your preparation is excellent. No dizziness, no sickness. Feeling fine physically, with a tremendous desire to get out and move around in the fresh air, which I would soon be able to satisfy; for apart from regular tests I did not have a strict schedule, as we assumed that a person would best get to know his possibilities with the most unrestricted freedom. Conscientious note-taking seemed assured, for we had never found any significant changes in character caused by the sex change in any of our experiments on monkeys. A reliable female monkey with strong nerves would generally also turn into a reliable male monkey.

Forgive me, I am digressing. Incidentally, without any reason, for I hadn't felt so good in a long time. As good as someone who has finally succeeded in finding a gap in the fence. Liberated, I jumped up, put on my new clothes, the faultless fit of which was an excellent confirmation of our prognoses concerning the sizes to be expected of the primary and secondary sex characteristics, gave Beate a signature for the receipt of my new papers made out in the name Other, a name you had chosen, and finally went outside into the deserted main street lit by modern street lamps. I ran to the observatory on the hill and stood up there for a while, admiring the incredible beauty of the sky and extolling scientific progress and, why should I conceal it, your virtues, Professor. And I joyfully praised the courage of the woman I had still been two days earlier, who slept curled up like a cat inside of me, this I sensed quite strongly.

I admit that I did not mind, for why cast out the poor woman for good right away? Today, however, I wonder whether we won't have to prepare my successors for the fact that they won't be able to shed the sensations of womanhood the moment they become a man.

My elation lasted for one-and-a-half days and one night. You can gather from the experiment notes that I walked slowly from the observatory hill to my high-rise that morning—for it took me forty minutes. Had we actually anticipated that the brand-new man would depend on the memories of the erstwhile woman? In any case, as I was walking along, I, Other, thought of the lover of the woman I had been. Of my dear Bertram, who had told me that it quite simply wouldn't do anymore on our way to the observatory three years ago almost to the day. Women scientists, sure; high female intelligence quotients, granted; but what quite simply doesn't suit a woman is an inclination to the absolute. It wouldn't do that I spent my nights in the institute (back then we were starting on our monkey experiments; do you remember the first high-strung females?);

it wouldn't do that I kept evading the main problem. The main problem was a child. (I was thirty and agreed with Bertram. It was the day you forecast a date for the first human experiment in passing: in three years. And you offered me the directorship of the new team. I had to decide what I wanted. I wanted a child. Bertram has one now whom I can visit as often as I wish, because Bertram's wife likes me. It only bothers me that she sometimes intimates something akin to gratefulness, but also perplexity: how could anyone let something as precious as this man get into other hands?) It won't do, damn it, said Bertram—we were standing in front of the brightly lit Urania Culture Palace; it was a beautiful clear May evening with very young couples strolling around everywhere—that I never had any time to celebrate birthdays with his large family. That I never got really angry at him. That I wasn't jealous. That I didn't want to have him all to myself, body and soul, which anyone would take as a lack of love. Whether I couldn't meet him halfway. Which prompted me to ask, Where? In a shared, tele-heated three-room apartment? Evenings spent together in front of the TV, and the eternally recurring birthday parties in the circle of his large family?

The next morning I took charge of our group, and my first night as a man was the first time I could think about that without remorse. Back then the word "unnatural" had been mentioned and could no longer be conjured away. A woman who rejects the compromise which was invented for her sex only; who is unable "to avert her gaze and turn her eyes into a piece of heaven or water"; who does not want to be lived but live herself: she will learn what it means to be guilty. You're going to be sorry later. I was already sorry when Bertram turned away in front of my door. But now, as a man in the same situation, I did not feel sorry about anything. What I felt was gratitude.

Have you actually seen through my tactics in the last three years? In order to try out your drug you needed someone like me. I wanted to get you to the point where you needed *me*. I had to prove my value as a woman by agreeing to become a man. I assumed a modest manner in order to hide the fact that I understood my absurd situation.

On that first morning, I introduced myself to the caretaker of my building as my own cousin, who had agreed with his cousin that he would live in her apartment while she was on an official trip and whose name was immediately entered in the building roster under the heading "Long-term Visitors." Not a soul missed the tenant of apartment No. 17.09, nor did anyone take notice of the new neighbor. Everything went like clockwork as far as that was concerned.

As usual I went and stood in front of my large window as soon as I got upstairs. In the wardrobe next door hung the suits of a man, in the bathroom were the toilet articles of a man. But there I stood, searching with the gaze of a woman for the window of your study, which, to my satisfaction, was the only one lit in the long façade of the institute building, but then, as if the light in my room were a signal for you, quickly went dark. That's when I, Other, tried to manage the smile, which I would have had at my disposal as a woman. I still had it in me, I felt it clearly. At the same time, however, I sensed its failure to appear on my face.

This was the first, very brief bout of confusion. Nice prospects indeed, I said *sotto voce*, and went to take a shower, where I became acquainted with, yes, even befriended, my new body, for I was just as fine-looking, well built, and healthy as a man as I had been as a woman. We wouldn't have admitted an ugly person to this experiment anyway, in order not to discredit our method . . .

Resentment? Dr. Rüdiger was the first to reproach me for a contrary attitude. However, not before he had enjoyed my anecdote about the "little thing next door" whom I had met in the elevator that morning and asked, since she sighed at me, if I could be of assistance. At which point I received a look which would have stiffened a worm. The only difference was that the most pleasant of emotions could not fully unfold within me on account of the feminine-ironic thought: What do you know, it works! That's the only reason I mention it. You shouldn't think your drug had failed in any and, most particularly, this most important of respects. It was I, the woman, who sabotaged the most manly triumphs of Herr Other with my mockery or sensitivity or simply impatience. I, the woman, had prevented him from picking up the little pocketbook for the "little thing next door" (wasn't "I" the older one?), had made one mistake after another, until her look first became incredulous, then icy. Yes, my friend, this is how Dr. Rüdiger spoke to me now—the days of revenge shall follow shortly. He had gotten over the loss of me rather quickly. He found me tolerable and first wanted to get the reaction test over with, which proved without a shadow of doubt that my senses continued to react in the way my subjectively normed scale led him to expect. Blue had stayed blue for me, and a 50-degree liquid hot, and I could not remember the fifteen different meaningless objects on our laboratory table any more quickly than before, which appeared to disappoint Rüdiger slightly. He eventually became excited during the supplementary test, when some of my new answers differed from the old ones. The loss of spontaneity was sufficient explanation for the prolonged intervals: should I answer as a woman? As a man? And if as a man, how, for heaven's sake? So that I finally didn't say "love" when I heard "red," as usual, but "rage." And when I heard "woman," I didn't say "man" but "beautiful." To "child" I said "dirty" instead of "soft," and to "girl" I didn't say "slim" but "cute." Wow, said Rüdiger, you've made quite some progress already, my friend.

Now we wanted to go and eat. Down the long corridors of the institute toward the cafeteria we walked, engaged in relaxed conversation, Rüdiger's arm informally around my shoulder in the midst of our animated discussion. Two good buddies. I was introduced with relish as a colleague and guest to shared acquaintances, and if they mentioned that some feature of my face looked familiar, they were laughed at. Silence reigned behind your door, Professor. You didn't come around the corner. You weren't sitting in the cafeteria. Curiosity was not one of your weaknesses. So you didn't see me having to eat leg of pork and mashed peas, which Dr. Rüdiger takes as proof of a man's manliness.

For the first but not the last time the thought came to me that the person opposite me had changed more by my metamorphosis than I myself. Indeed, it is only you, Professor, who have remained the same yourself. Not only did Dr. Rüdiger not hesitate to admit to his satisfaction concerning the "revised version" of myself, he was also prepared to state his reasons why. The motive for revenge had been a joke, of course. Although a tiny bit of punishment was perhaps not all that bad for me. Why? For my goddamned arrogance. For the bad example I had presented to other women by my voluntary celibacy, thereby encouraging the spreading dislike of marriage of the weaker sex and supporting the rebellion against the boredom and unproductivity of marriage. Oh no, he certainly wasn't living in a glass house. As a bachelor, a man—like himself, for example—was a free person who didn't take anything away from anybody. After all, Dr. Rüdiger could not suspect that my female instinct hadn't left me yet, signaling to me that only he who feels humiliated has such a thirst for revenge. It offended him terribly that he couldn't have had me, even if he had wanted to, because no one had me.

So he attempted in all seriousness to convert me to manhood, while we were having apple cake and coffee. Dr. Rüdiger doesn't particularly like women with problems—who does, after all? They don't even like themselves if they are intelligent enough to see the dilemma they are caught in, having to spend their lives zigzagging between their husbands and their yearning to work, lover's bliss and the desire to create, the wish for a child and their ambition, like a badly programmed cybernetic mouse. Tensions, inhibitions, acts of aggression, the likes of which he, my concerned friend, had been observing during my last years as a woman . . . In short, I shouldn't be so crazy as to fall back into the trap I had had the luck to escape!

I guess you want to convert me to manhood, I said, and could not help but laugh.

You see, said Dr. Rüdiger, now you can afford to find that funny. Speaking of jokes, I said, maybe you are quite simply weary of having a female boss? Rüdiger decided that this was no joke but the usual resentment. However, it was with humor that he offered me one of his strong Cuban cigars after lunch.

At that point I saw Irene and Beate making their way through the cafeteria toward our table, Irene with her gangling walk and her perennial green sweater, Beate with her recent ash-blond hair, which does not exactly complement her pale face. One glance at Rüdiger convinced me: he saw all of this as well. Right away we had to assure the two of them that we hadn't bad-mouthed them. Why do women always think that two men sitting together are bad-mouthing them? Because they almost always do, said Irene. Because women take themselves too seriously, said Dr. Rüdiger. Because women quite simply have an inferiority complex by nature, Beate said. I listened to them with no opinion of my own, existing in a blurry no-man's-land, feeling nothing but a little homesick for the absurdities of women. Irene, who saw me as a guilty victim of unscrupulous enticement, warned me that I would be open to attempts at bribery in order to extort the betrayal of secrets which no man would ever learn without me. I doubted this, but Dr. Rüdiger quoted a story from classical antiquity as proof:

Tiresias, a Greek, once saw two snakes copulating and wounded one of them. He was punished by being turned into a woman who had relations with men. Apollo, the god, took pity on him. He gave him a hint on how to become a man again: he would have to watch the very same snakes once more and wound the other one. This Tiresias did, thereby winning back his true sex. At the same time, however, the great gods Zeus and Hera were arguing about who felt the stronger pleasure during an embrace, man or woman. They finally called upon Tiresias as a competent judge. He stated that the man felt only a tenth of the pleasure; the woman, however, enjoyed it to the full. Angered by this betrayal of the well-kept secret, Hera blinded the unfortunate Tiresias. As a consolation, great Zeus bestowed upon the blind man the gift of the seer.

The brief silence at our table suggested that people were keeping their first thoughts to themselves (mine was, strangely enough, Who will blind me?). Everybody's second thoughts were expressed in the form of exclamations which meant different things, however, since Dr. Rüdiger's story was anything but unambiguous, after all. Irene felt she had to warn me of the various kinds of punishment for the betrayal of women's secrets. But why? said Beate quietly. After all, Tiresias lied . . .

A conversation between men can never be the same as a talk between participants of both sexes. My elation was gone. Instead, I felt a certain emptiness located in the chest area. No wonder. However, what made me uneasy was not the absence of a female organ, the breast, but the absence of male glances of appraisal indicating that you're "there."

I hope you understand that I am quoting random samples and am in constant fear of boring you. I never managed to feel like a spy operating with the most perfect camouflage in the hinterland of the opponent. On the other hand, I ran into difficulties using all the derivations of the personal pronoun "I." We are formed by the expectations of our environment—who doesn't know that? But what did all my knowledge amount to the first time I met with the glance of a woman? Or on my first walks through a city which did not recognize me and had become a stranger to me? Man and woman live on different planets, Professor. I told you this—do you remember?—and you reproached me for my subjectivity, expecting my retreat and the solemn declaration that I would continue to subject my perceptions and feelings to your interpretation. That's when I disappointed you for the first time. The old tricks were powerless against my new experience. For once, I wanted to see what was going to happen if I stuck to my opinion. If I didn't begin to feel guilty right away: guilty of an irreparable flaw in character which, no matter how regrettable men may find it, makes us women incapable of seeing the world as it really is. While you have trapped it in your net of numbers, curves, and calculations, haven't you? Like a sinner caught in the act, with whom you needn't have anything further to do. From whom you detach yourself—most cunningly by means of an incomprehensible enumeration of facts which we pass off as scientific data.

Seen like that, Professor, your humorous statement is correct. Although Scientia—science, that is—was a lady, she had a male brain. It cost me years of my life to learn to subject myself to that way of thinking, the highest virtues of which are noninterference and emotional indifference. Today I am having trouble regaining access to all those buried regions of my inner self. You'll be surprised to know that it is language that can help me, with its origin in that wondrous spirit, for whom "judging" and "loving" could be one word: "meaning." You have always reprimanded me for my mourning over that which cannot be changed. And still I am moved by the fate of some words; and still nothing plagues me more than the longing to see intellect and reason—once one and the same in the slovenly creative lap of language and now at odds with one another on account of us—united like brothers . . .

Never would I, Other, have hit upon the idea of describing the same objects with the same words I used to describe them as a woman, if only I had had different words at my disposal. I had no trouble remembering what "city" was for her: a mass of ever-disappointed and ever-reviving hope. To him, me—Other, that is—it was an agglomeration of inexhaustible possibilities. He—that is, I—was dazed by a city which wanted to teach me that it was my duty to make conquests, while the woman in myself had not as yet unlearned the technique of showing herself and, in case the situation required it, buckling under.

The car story may not convince you, but it is perhaps still funny. Women have an insufficiently developed sense of orientation, which is why, even if they have good technical abilities, they aren't good drivers. This is what my driving instructor said in my first lesson in order to prepare me for the ambiguous reactions of the other traffic participants—women and men, that is—to the woman driver. So I began to get lost in areas which I used to think I knew and to acquiesce to the fact that driving a car is strenuous. Until, at the beginning of my second week as a man, my car left me in the lurch right in the middle of the busy intersection at Alexanderplatz and I had no choice but to block the traffic and wait for the shrill whistles and the traffic policeman's condescending shrug of the shoulders, the honking concert behind me, and the derisive shouts of the passersby. I thought I was dreaming when the policeman closed down the traffic in my direction with the sound of his whistle and a hand signal, descended from his traffic island, and asked me what the problem was, all the while addressing me as "boss"; when a few drivers from other cars pushed the unlucky car off the intersection without any further ado and no one showed any desire to satisfy my urgent need to be instructed, reprimanded, and notified of an offense. Would you believe that I no longer have trouble orienting myself?

But to get back to my planet. Where in the report should I have entered that unprovable sensation that gravity had loosened its grip on me as a man? While that very young female student passed out and sank to the ground next to me in the deserted street one evening? With an unfounded bad conscience I helped her up, led her to a bench, and suggested that she recuperate in my nearby apartment—the most natural thing in the world. At which point she examined me with indignation and called me "naïve." Later on, I looked this up. Naïve used to mean something like "innate, natural"—but could I have spoken to the girl in terms of innate kindness or natural helpfulness without increasing her anger against us men even further? I had the misfortune of referring to her "condition," for any woman would know immediately that she was pregnant. I, however, was not a woman, she could only show me her scorn ("What condition!") and give me the brush-off. There I stood, speechless, insulted on behalf of my sex for the first time in my life. I began to wonder what you might have done to us that we have to forbid you to be kind to us out of vengeance. I did not envy you your entanglement in the countless number of your useful activities, since you stood by and let the words "human" and "manly," originally of the same root, drift irretrievably far away from each other.

"Irretrievable," said Irene. I am not that categorical. She came up to me on the seventeenth floor in order to join her melancholy with mine. A glass of wine has often turned out to be of help here, along with music and, once in a while, the TV. The latter presented us with the problems of an overburdened teacher, mother of three children, with her phlegmatic husband, a designer of household appliances. The author of the film, unfortunately a woman, went through all kinds of trouble to restore the factory's fulfillment of quotas by means of an appropriate assortment of kitchen and household appliances, as well as to save the marriage of the teacher. Irene wondered whether the simple explanation of the nice pickle she was in wasn't the scarcity of designers of household appliances. She had also had to send away the tall, lanky, curly-haired person whom she hadn't found all that bad for a couple of months, on account of his inability to grow up. Irene is angered at the mothers of sons and intends to write an educational primer with the following first sentence: Dear Mother, Your child may be a son, but he is still a human being. Raise him to become the kind of person your daughter could live with.

I will not go into detail about how we thought up a few more sentences together and wrote them down on a scrap of paper, cutting one another short and laughing at each other; how Irene got a kick out of calling me by my man's name all the time (Hey, Other!); and how she finally burned our scrap of paper in the ashtray, since there is nothing funnier than women who write treatises. I'll only mention that I said, Women? I can see only a man and a woman here! And that I succeeded in achieving precisely that tone of voice which a woman could expect from a man at that hour. And that she said only very little after that, such as, for example, what a shame it was that we knew each other from before. And, for example, that I stroked her hair, which I had always liked, it was dark and straight. And that she said "Hey, Other" one more time: Hey, Other, I don't think we have a chance. But maybe some good will come of that damned invention of your professor's.

For others, she said. And in case certain capabilities atrophied even further in men—such as the ability to know us in the literal as well as the biblical sense. *Feminam cognoscere.* And he knew his wife . . . yes, for we esteem nothing more highly than the pleasure of being known. For you, however, our claim produces nothing but pure embarrassment, from which you hide behind your tests and questionnaires and who knows what.

Have you seen the devotion with which our little cyberneticist feeds his computer? This time it was the evaluation of the 566 questions on my MMPI test, which gave our cyberneticist time to comfort me because we women didn't invent cybernetics either—any more than we invented gunpowder, the tubercle bacillus, the Cologne cathedral, or *Faust*. Looking out the window, I saw you come out of the main university building. Women who want to play first fiddle in science are quite simply doomed to failure, said our little cyberneticist. Only now did I realize how desperate he was, because the success of this highly important experiment, which could contribute to the reduction of a questionable species, lay entirely in the hands of a woman. The black departmental car drove up downstairs and you got in. Our little cyberneticist was studying the information on his computer. For the first time, I looked at him more closely, at his big head perched on a small body, the narrow, nervous, eager fingers, his weak stature, his eccentric way of speaking . . . How he must have suffered as a young man among us women! Your car had turned on the graveled courtyard and disappeared between the poplars at the gate. Our cyberneticist announced that my conditioning seemed to be going down the drain. I didn't give a hoot whether I still managed the usual reactions to emotional stimuli; he, however, didn't know whether he should be worried or happy that his computer took me for two completely different people, threatening him with a complaint on account of willful deception.

In the laboratory, Irene told me with an inscrutable face that, according to the evaluation of the most recent analyses, I was the most manly man she knew. I went over to the window. He won't be back right away, she said. He is taking part in the conference at the university today. That's when I still believed that you had avoided seeing me in my new form up until now. However, I wouldn't have dreamed that you would manage not to recognize me. You are never taken aback by anything, anyway. I had been meaning to ask you for a long time when this always-be-prepared-for-anything started. However, the question would have been a severe violation of the rules of the game, which were sacred to us. They reliably protected us from forgetting our parts, as much as I had begun to hate playing the part of the cheerful loser. Sometimes the game was: Who is afraid of the big, bad wolf? and I had to shout, Not I! The games varied, but one rule remained: He who turns around or laughs shall get a taste of the strap. I never turned around. Never caught the master of the game. Never laughed at him. How could I have known that your own rules were pressurizing you?

You will remember. It was Saturday, March 16, the day of the "changeable April weather," the eleventh day of my changed existence, when you left the opera café around 11 p.m., alone and almost sober, and a young man you had never seen before, who had evidently been lying in wait for you, approached you and forced his company on you, without even having the manners to introduce himself. You, on the other hand, without showing any surprise or giving any sign of recognition, acted as if there was nothing more natural for you than an intimate nightly talk with a stranger. Right away you were the master of the situation again. You had the presence of mind to develop a new game, and once again, you were the one to lay down the conditions of participation, which, incidentally, you handled rather generously as long as one rule remained unquestioned: that you had the right to remain uninvolved. You took polite note of what I expressed—for example, the complaint that the memory arsenal of a woman can become a nuisance to a man—but it was none of your business. You were brazen and I told you so. You didn't bat as much as an eyelid. I knew that I was supposed to be indignant, but I wasn't. I coolly used the occasion to attack you with my new experiences, to turn the tables, to surround you with complaints, accusations, and threats. I remember clearly how often I had rehearsed that moment in my thoughts, I knew every turn, every single position by heart. However, now that I was finally performing, I had lost all interest in my act and began to suspect what this must mean. Almost like a set exercise, I went as far as to claim that man and woman live on different planets, in order to force you to make your usual, mild attempts at intimidation, and then play my trump card: that they no longer cut any ice with me.

We were standing at the foot of the television tower at the Alexanderplatz. Did you think it was out of wounded self-love that I suddenly took flight in a passing taxi which happened to be free? Far from it. I fled because I was not wounded, because I was not afraid, because I was not sad and not happy either and could not understand the tension of the entire day at all. I fled because I had spent all that time talking to you about a stranger for whom I could no longer bring myself to feel any sympathy. No matter how beautiful or gruesome the things I imagined alone in the dark car, my feelings remained numb. No matter what questions I asked myself, no one gave me an answer. The woman inside me whom I was urgently seeking had disappeared. And the man had not yet appeared.

Checkmate—that's the word I thought of, for at least language had not yet escaped me.

I had unwittingly given the taxi driver my parents' address. Now I left it at that, paid, caught a glimpse of the light in their living-room window from the street, and stood on the stone pedestal in the front yard, which offered a clear view of the living room. My parents were sitting in their favorite armchairs and listening to music. They were drinking bocksbeutel wine, which they prefer over all other wines, from old-fashioned, long-stemmed glasses. Only once in twenty minutes did my father move his hand, in order to point out a passage in the concert to my mother. My mother smiled, because he always points out the same passage with the same gesture and because she waits for it and enjoys it when he looks up, as he did then as well, and meets her smile with a sheepish grin. As the excited debates with friends which filled the house during my childhood gradually became conversations and friends and enemies became guests, my parents' pleasure at being left to themselves grew. They have achieved the art of treating one another with the necessary consideration without losing interest in each other.

I could have gone inside. Could have violated the instructions for secrecy and described my situation to them. They never lacked understanding for me. I would have encountered no inappropriate questions, no disturbed reaction, no traces of reproach. They would have made the bed in my old room and prepared our accustomed family nightcap. Then the two of them would have lain next door sleeplessly and spent the entire night brooding over what they had done wrong. For the happiness of my parents is based on a rather simple notion of the connection between cause and effect.

I did not go inside. I took the next taxi home, went to bed, and did not get up for three nights and two days—a space of time during which I continued making notes for the report, although the ability to find words to describe my condition was decreasing at the rate at which I was recuperating physically. Since you would never allow the term "crisis," we silently agreed on "peripeteia"—as if we were one step away from the inevitable solution of all the entanglements in a silly classical drama.

Beate, however, did not beat around the bush on Monday and spoke in terms of a fiasco. You know what happened: my failure at the memory test. Although it should have been clear to her as well that the answer "I don't know" is the lesser of two evils for a conscientious person when compared to an out-and-out lie. After feverish deliberation—as proven by the machines hooked up to my pulse and thought waves—I responded seven times to her questions with "I don't know" before she became nervous and began to prompt me. As if I had forgotten the name of my favorite teacher! But how could the man who inserted his well-calculated effect on girls into the course of the chemistry lesson, as I now saw clearly, have ever been my favorite teacher? Or the "greatest joy of my childhood." Of course, I knew what I had answered three times at intervals of three months: Being on a swing. I could even produce in my memory the image of a girl on a swing, shouting with joy, skirts flying, letting herself be pushed by a boy . . . The only difference being that this image clearly displeased me and was no longer a suitable answer to the question. No more than the name of the boy—yes, of course, it was Roland, damn it!—was an adequate answer to the question of one's "first boyfriend." There was no way that my first boyfriend could have held that unknown girl by the waist and lifted her off the swing . . .

All that could be read in my file were imputations, nothing but imputations. Take that silly, forever-unfinished color plate, for example. Of course, I had always interpreted the little picture as a "courting couple" in an open field heading for the forest. The only difference being that I could no longer find the courting couple now, as embarrassing as this was, because it looked as if I was being coy. Two sportsmen preparing for a competition, if need be. But even that was not certain. So I thought I'd better be quiet. After all, it was no great misfortune not to recognize what that meaningless plate was all about.

At that point Beate started to cry. Quiet, modest Beate. Beate, whose name suited her so well: the happy one. Who got everything in the proper relation: her demanding job, her exacting husband, her two children; who never gave the others anything to gossip about. Who had perhaps not even suspected herself the excessive amount of hope that she had attached to this experiment. Did you know that she was prepared to do anything? She wanted to be next: she was serious. She was beside herself on account of my failure. On account of my disgusting pride I would spoil this unique chance for everyone else as well, because I didn't really need it and therefore didn't know how to appreciate it.

Irene helped me put Beate in the car. I drove her

home. I am keeping to myself all the things she said on the way, as well as her tone and choice of words. But a shyness with quiet, modest women has remained with me. Beate has a nice home. The garden and the house are well kept. No dirty cup or unmade bed in sight. There was no untidiness around her, she never wanted to have to blame herself for anything. I put her to bed on the couch and gave her some sleeping pills. Before she fell asleep she said, Why don't you say anything?

She must have thought I was free to speak or be silent. She could not imagine the silence reigning inside me. No one can imagine that silence.

Do you know what "person" means? Mask. Role. Real self. After all this, it seems to me that language is bound to at least one of these three states. The fact that I had lost all three of them probably boiled down to complete silence. There is no one about whom you can write nothing. This explains the three-day gap in my report.

When it became possible to use Yes and No days later, I again sought the company of people. Changed, of course, they were all quite right about that. But not in need of considerate treatment. Not dependent on those searching glances which only made it more difficult for me to show convincingly that I was over the worst of it. It was absurd that no one wanted to believe me, especially now: their doubt appeared just as mine was dissipating. My truthfully stereotypical "Fine, thank you" in reply to their stereotypical "How are you?" was getting on their nerves. I no longer took the opinions they might have about me to heart as before. They didn't like that either.

But what had we expected, anyway?

Or you! Was it conceivable that you had soberly

calculated the price I was supposed to pay? I'm just asking: and without emotion at that, as you had always requested. Without emotion, free and rid of all relationships, I could finally get out of a certain game, the rules of which had been sacred to us for such a long time. I no longer needed that protection. The suspicion that this was precisely what you might have anticipated, and even wished for, cost me a mere shrug of the shoulder. I discovered the secret of invulnerability: indifference. No more that burning feeling inside me at the drop of a certain name, at hearing a certain voice . . . This was a significant relief which opened up undreamed-of freedom, Professor. When I closed my eyes I was no longer compelled to draw painful pleasure from a series of pictures which—embarrassingly enough—kept showing the same two people in the same two situations. Instead, I was dominated by visions of the future: my brilliant performance in this experiment, my name on everyone's lips, rejoicing, awards, fame in all its glory.

You shake your head with disapproval. But what do you expect? Am I supposed to succeed at what most men are unable to do—to live face to face with reality without betraying oneself? Perhaps you had hoped that one man would manage it: your creation. That you could watch him, all the while basking in the reflection of emotions you have forbidden yourself for a long time and presumably have gradually lost (the only thing that might have remained being the feeling of an irreplaceable loss); but I have to disappoint you. Without noticing it, I also began to prefer the easy way and, in all seriousness, to focus my ambitions on the success of the experiment, the barbaric inanity of which I was no longer fully aware. I thought of Dr. Rüdiger's classic anecdote. Without realizing it or wanting to, I have nonetheless been a spy in the hinterland of the enemy and discovered that which must remain your secret in order that your comfortable privileges not be infringed upon: that the undertakings you lose yourself in cannot be your happiness, and that we have a right to resist if you try to involve us in them.

No, Professor, no goddess descends to blind the traitor—unless you want to call the habit that blinds us an omnipotent goddess. The partial blindness that affects almost every man began to infect me as well, for the unlimited enjoyment of privileges is no longer possible in any other way nowadays. Where I would have rebelled previously, I was now overcome with indifference. A feeling of contentment I had never before experienced began to spread within me. Once we have accepted them, those agreements we should be deeply suspicious of gain an irresistible power over us. Already I forbade myself sadness as being a futile waste of time and energy. Already it appeared no longer dangerous to me to be part of that division of labor which leaves the right to sadness, hysteria, and the majority of neuroses to women and does not begrudge them the pleasure of preoccupying themselves with the renunciations of the soul (which no man has as yet found under the microscope), as well as the large, sheer inexhaustible sector of the fine arts. While we men shoulder the globe, under which burden we almost collapse, and unwaveringly dedicate our lives to the three great realities: Economics, Science, and World Politics. And, full of honest indignation, would reject a god who came to bestow upon us the gift of the seer . . .

As we do the aimless complaints of our women.

I didn't get to that point, Professor. There wasn't enough time. I was haunted by fits of my old restlessness. A shock could still save me. A question. Two words.

How did I meet your daughter Anna? I didn't meet her as your daughter—your suspicion is unfounded—but as a very clever, slightly cheeky young thing who coincidentally sat next to me at the film club and whom—no longer so coincidentally—I invited for an ice cream sundae. It was very easy. She would not hinder me in case I wished to pay for her: she happened to be broke at the time and I didn't exactly look poor. Intentions? The most common ones in the world; for if I had to start sowing my wild oats somewhere—women just don't leave a man alone!—why not with this girl whom I liked on account of her ironic laugh?

Wild oats were not called for, as it turned out. I suppose Anna saw me as an elderly gentleman who, dotty like most men—those are her words, but you know her, after all—is no longer capable of noticing anything. For example, that those film people just now had wanted to pull the wool over our eyes. By the way, she said, her name was Anna (I swear to you, your daughter did not mention her family name to me!). Anna thinks one should not make it too easy for men. They had already become too lazy with everything, with love in any case, thinks Anna, and one day it will reach the point where they will become too lazy to dominate. And palm off their outrageous indolence as equal rights upon us, said your daughter Anna angrily. Thanks but no thanks.

Why she took me home with her after that? I swear to you . . . Oh, never mind. No more pledges. Of course I would have fallen for Anna as a man. There was some sort of sensation, if that makes you feel any better. However, the counter-sensation held the other one in check, at least this time. Anna must have sensed something, for she became quieter. She said she thought me a bit strange, but likable all the same. She wanted to play me her records.

I still could have turned back at your garden door. However, now I wanted to see how we'd get out of it. Perhaps you wanted to as well. Perhaps you wanted to prove to me that since you made your bed you would lie in it. Otherwise, you could at least have prevented the invitation to supper. I, thoroughly examined by your wife and your old mother as your daughter's new acquaintance, opposite you on the narrow side of the supper table. Of course, this was quite a joke. You had no trouble grinning and bearing it. Nothing but silent scenes, mere glances, and gestures. But this much became clear: you offered your unconditional surrender. The game was over. No longer a question of your pulling all the strings. You were in a tight spot and saw that you deserved it. It suited you and disarmed me. So it was up to me whether I still wanted to stick to any rules of the game voluntarily. You did not know that I was already out of the game. The person to whom you offered your capitulation was not sitting at your table.

Relaxed conversation, cheerfulness. Relief on one side, generosity on the other. Restrained observations. Your wife's facial expression hard to define, which only now causes me to think. Your mother's good mood, your wife's merriment: skillful imitations of your own good mood and gaiety: the two women have encircled you with highly sensitive radar systems which register even your slightest emotions. Your wife's face is prepared to reflect—that's it. And the object of the reflection: you, who else? Total encirclement. But Anna wasn't prepared to put up with it, being snappish and cheeky but, above all, which I envy her for, superior. It was the twenty-ninth day after my metamorphosis, a lukewarm April evening.

Where is the shock? The question? The two words?

I don't think I have to repeat them to you, for after all, we stood in front of the bookshelf in Anna's room, our wineglasses in our hands, while she put on her records. For the first time you had the courage to recognize me, not to flee or deny the metamorphosis you had effected with me. Without any further ado, you addressed me by the name you had given me: Well, Other—how do you feel? The question. In posing it, you hit upon just the right tone between professional interest and friendly sympathy: neutral. But it didn't hurt my feelings. Other was incessantly distancing himself from the person whose feelings could have been hurt by that.

Coolly, truthfully, I answered you: Like in the movies.

That was the first time since I have known you that something slipped out which you didn't want to say: You, too—the two words.

You grew pale and I understood in one fell swoop. It is always a handicap which is so carefully concealed. Your artfully constructed systems of rules, your irremediable workaholism, all your maneuvers to escape, they were nothing but the attempt to shield yourself against the discovery that you cannot love and you know it.

It is too late to make apologies. However, it is now my place to tell you that I had no choice, either, of entering into the game or not; or, at least, breaking it off while there was still time. You can blame me for a lot without my saying anything in my defense—above all my gullibility, my obedience, my dependence on the conditions you forced upon me. If you would only believe that it was not lightheadedness or sheer hubris which blackmailed that confession out of you. How could I have wanted the first and only confidentiality between us to be the confidential admission of a defect . . .

Each one of us has reached his goal. You had succeeded in getting rid of me; I in discovering your secret. Your preparation had done what it could, Professor. Now it left us in the lurch.

There is nothing worse than two people who are through with one another.

I am coming to the end.

You waited for me at the institute the next morning. There was hardly any talk. You didn't show me your face as you filled the syringe. "Shame" has to do with "disgrace." Disgrace as in destroy. We can't do anything but start afresh with the most painful of all feelings.

I did not dream anything. Upon awakening I saw a growing light spot. Your Bepeter minus Masculinum 199 is a reliable drug as well, Professor. After all, it says so in the report. You have been proven right in all your predictions.

Now we are facing my experiment: the attempt to love. Which, by the way, also leads to fantastic discoveries: the invention of the one who can be loved.

III WHAT REMAINS

DON'T PANIC. One day I will even talk about it in that other language which, as of yet, is in my ear but not on my tongue. Today I knew would still be too soon. But would I know when the time was right? Would I ever find my language? One day I would be old. And how would I remember these days then? Something inside me, which expands in moments of happiness, contracted in fright. When was I last happy? That didn't interest me at the moment. What did—it was a morning in March, chilly, gray, and not even all that early—was how I would think back on this day, still new and not yet lived out, in ten or twenty years' time. Alarmed, as at the frantic warning peal of a bell within me, I jumped up and found myself barefoot on the beautifully patterned rug of my Berlin apartment, saw myself tearing back the curtains, opening the window which looks out onto the rear courtyard, full of overflowing garbage cans and rubble but devoid of human life, as if forever deserted by the children with their bicycles and transistor radios, the plumbers and construction workers, even by Frau G., who would later come down in her housecoat and green knitted cap and take from the large wire containers the boxes from the seed store, the perfumery, and the Intershop, flatten them out, tie them up in handy bundles, and wheel them around the corner on her four-wheel handcart to the wastepaper salvagers. She would rant and rave about the tenants who threw their empty bottles into the garbage cans out of laziness, instead of piling them up neatly in the cases reserved for that purpose, about the late-night homecomers who broke in through the front door almost every night because they kept forgetting their keys, about the municipal housing office, which didn't seem to be capable of installing doorbells, but most of all about the drunks from the hotel restaurant next door, who passed water brazenly behind the damaged front door.

The small tricks which I permitted myself every morning: gathering a few newspapers off the table and sticking them into the newspaper rack, smoothing out a tablecloth in passing, arranging glasses, humming a song ("No way, clever people say, two times two is never three"), knowing all the while that everything I did was a pretense and that in reality I was, as if drawn by a string, on my way toward the front room and the large bay window which looked out onto the Friedrichstrasse and through which shone no morning sun, for it was a spring graced by little sun, yet at least there was morning light, which I love and which I wanted to store up in large doses as a precaution against gloomier times.

Of course I know that heaven's treasures, which multiply unnoticeably, cannot be had by an act of will alone; know for certain that all nourishment above and beyond our bodily needs falls into our laps without our being obliged or allowed to gather it bit by bit, it collects on its own; and yet I fear that these desolate times will contribute nothing to those imperishable provisions and thus drift off irrevocably with the tide of memory's fading. With pure fear, real panic, I now tried to cling to one of these doomed days and not let go, no matter what I ended up holding in my hands, be it banal or weighty, whether it surrendered at once or struggled to the last. And so I stood, as I did every morning, behind the curtain, which had been hung so that I could hide behind it, and looked out, hopefully unnoticed, at the large parking lot beyond the Friedrichstrasse.

Actually, they weren't even there. If my eyes weren't deceiving me—of course I had put on my glasses—all the cars in the first row were empty, and those in the second row as well. In the beginning, two years ago—this is my way of measuring time—I had been fooled by the high headrests of some vehicles, taking them for heads and marveling uneasily at their immobility; not that I no longer made mistakes, but I was certainly beyond that stage. Heads are unevenly shaped, movable; headrests evenly shaped, rounded, high—a considerable difference, which I might describe someday with precision in my new language, which would be tougher than the one in which I was still forced to think. How obstinately the voice retains a pitch once it has been reached, how much effort is needed to alter even the slightest nuances. Not to mention the words, I thought, as I began to take my shower—the words which pour out zealously, rushing forth as soon as I open my mouth, swelled with conviction, prejudices, vanity, rage, disappointment, and self-pity.

I just want to know why they were standing down there yesterday till midnight and why they had completely disappeared this morning.

I brushed my teeth, combed my hair, employed various sprays unthinkingly, albeit conscientiously, got dressed, same things as yesterday, slacks, sweater—I was expecting no one and would be granted some solitude, that was the best prospect of the day. I couldn't avoid making one more quick trip to the window, again without result. In a way, of course, this was a relief, I told myself, or was I really trying to suggest that I was waiting for them? It was possible that I had made a fool of myself yesterday evening; someday I would find it embarrassing to think that I had felt my way to the window in the dark room every half hour and peered through a slit in the curtains—embarrassing, I admit. But to what end would three young gentlemen be sitting for hours on end in a white Wartburg directly opposite our window.

Question mark. Kindly take your punctuation more seriously in future, I told myself. As a matter of fact, stick more to harmless agreements in general. It worked before, didn't it? When was that? When there were more exclamation marks than question marks at the ends of sentences? But I wasn't going to get away with easy self-incriminations this time. I put on the kettle. Let's leave the mea culpas to the Catholics. And the pater nosters, too. There is no absolution in sight. White, why white of all colors these last days? Why not, as in the weeks before, tomato-red, steel-blue? As if the colors had any meaning at all, or the various makes of car. As if this mysterious plan, which called for cars taking turns, occupying different parking spaces in the first or second row, contained some secret meaning which I could figure out by urgent endeavor; or as if it were worth pondering over what business the occupants of these cars—two or three stout, able-bodied young men in plain clothes, who plied no other trade than to look over at our window while sitting in their car—had with us.

The coffee had to be hot and strong, filter coffee, the boiled egg not too soft; homemade jam was preferred, dark bread. Luxury! Luxury! I thought, as I did every morning upon seeing everything assembled on the table—an everlasting feeling of guilt which penetrates and heightens our every pleasure—those of us who have known want. I barely heard the news on the Western station (energy crisis, executions in Iran, the strategic arms limitation treaty: themes from the past!), my gaze had settled upon the burglarproof iron bar which barricades the second entrance to our apartment—the door leading from the kitchen to the courtyard via the back stairs. I suddenly remembered that, in my dream, this filthy, narrow, unused stairway full of discarded furniture had been clean and busily populated by all manner of rude people whom I referred to as "riffraff" in my dream thoughts—a word I would never say out loud in front of those wiry, nimble, lemurine men, devoid of all sense of shame, who—as I had always feared so much!—had gained entrance into our kitchen through the break-in-proof back door, were now pushing and shoving at the threshold and trying to force the iron bar, which remained unshakable in its brackets and, oddly enough, was respected by those miserable creatures, although they could easily have slipped through underneath, but instead pressed their bodies against it, while more and more figures, incredibly agile and loquacious, spewed out by an unseen, devilish throat—yes, they seemed flat like cardboard figures—kept pushing from behind. What was it they had said? That we should by no account let them bother us. That we should act as if they weren't even there. That it would be best of all if we forgot them completely. They weren't goading us, they were serious, that's what angered me most in my dream. Since one cannot forbid oneself a dream, nor can one blame oneself, I laughed out loud to prove to myself that I was actually already above all this. My laughter sounded contrived.

Don't panic. My other language, I thought, still trying to kid myself, while I put the dishes in the sink, made my bed, went back to the front room, and finally sat at my desk—my other language, which had begun to grow but had not yet fully developed, would casually sacrifice the visible to the invisible; would stop describing objects by their appearance—tomato-red, white cars, good heavens!—and would increasingly allow their invisible essence to emerge. This language would be gripping, loving, and protective, that much I thought I could foresee. I would hurt no one but myself. I slowly realized why I could not get beyond these scraps of paper, these individual sentences. I was pretending to dwell on them. In fact, I was not thinking anything.

There they were again.

It was five past nine. They had been there for three minutes, I noticed them right away. I had felt a jolt, a tremble on my inner seismograph, which continued to reverberate. A glance, hardly necessary, confirmed it. Today the color of the car was an unobtrusive green, and inside, three young gentlemen were on duty. Did they swap these gentlemen as they did the cars? And what would I have preferred—that they were always the same or always different? I didn't know them, or rather, yes, I did know one. The one who had recently gotten out of his car and crossed the street in my direction, but only to stand in line at the hot-dog stand below our window, and had returned to the car with three hot dogs on a big paper plate and three rolls in the pockets of his green-gray jacket. To a *blue* car, by the way, with the license plate number . . . I started to look for the paper where I wrote down the license numbers, when I could make them out. This young gentleman or comrade had had dark hair, which was beginning to thin along the part, this I could see from upstairs. For a brief moment I reveled in the notion of being the first one to notice the young gentleman's encroaching baldness, even before his own wife, who presumably never studied him so attentively from above. I couldn't help imagining how they then sat cozily together in their car (it can be very cozy in a car, especially if it is windy outside, with the odd raindrop to boot), how they ate their hot dogs and weren't even cold, since the motor was keeping them warm. But what did they wash it down with? Did they each bring along a thermos of coffee, like other working men?

Our feelings in situations such as these are complicated. And the right words continued to elude me; I was still using words from the outer circle, they made sense but they didn't make the point, they made use of true facts in order to obscure the truth; I wouldn't be able to gush forth much longer in such a carefree manner, but what are you if you are not carefree? Careworn? I looked up "care" in Hermann Paul's German Dictionary, getting drawn deeper and deeper into the maelstrom of my obsession: "Care" in Middle High German could mean "rubble, seizure, want," even "arrest" in the older legal terminology. Seizure, yes, that hit the nail on the head, seized and held and left to waste away. "And it repented the Lord that he had made man on the earth, and his heart was heavy with care." Dr. Martin Luther trying to fool me into believing that we could only refuse or accept, could only be friends or foes. Thy word shall be yea, yea and nay, nay.

Anything beyond that is evil. Dr. Luther's tirades against the Pope, that gluttonous pig, then against the peasants, those mad dogs. It is a happy man who can place his enemy outside himself. In my language animal names will be used only for animals; I could never, as others have done, use the names of pigs and dogs, not even those of ferrets and reptiles, for the young gentlemen out there. I was probably lacking in good, healthy, leveling hatred.

I didn't know them, after all. What did I know about them, anyway? Even the characteristic "leather coats" were an outdated cliché, synthetic parkas having taken over long since—but I couldn't have said whether this uniform had been provided for their field service or whether they got an allowance for wear and tear at the end of the year, and how much this might be. And wasn't it true that one already knew half the person when one knew his working conditions? For example, I would also have been interested in knowing how their daily work schedule was arranged, and the receipt of orders, which is probably what it's called, and whether certain jobs were more popular than others, car duty for example more popular than door duty. And while I was on the subject, whether those who patrol the streets with their shoulder bags really do have walkie-talkies in them, as rumor insists. I sometimes suspected that they had nothing in their bags but sandwiches, which they hid out of the humanly understandable need to impress. A twisted kind of assumption of authority. Of course it was out of the question to go up to one of them and ask politely, Excuse me, what exactly is it that you've got in your bag? Just as one could not ask the men in the cars whether they were equipped with listening devices and, if so, what their range was. Other intimacies, however, were not out of the question; interaction with them was also regulated by a code which one could not learn, though; either you had it or you didn't. For example, I still regretted the fact that I hadn't followed my first impulse right away, back then when it started, on those cold November nights, and brought them down some hot tea. That could have developed into a habit; we had nothing against each other personally, after all, we were all doing what we had to, we could have struck up a conversation—not about business, God forbid!—but about the weather, about illnesses or family matters.

Enough is enough. Just another example of my shameful need to get along well with all kinds of people. We had drunk the tea ourselves back then, late at night, standing in the dark room by the window where we hung up these very curtains on the following day. I suddenly felt compelled to switch on the light, stand up close to the window, and wave to them. At which point they blinked their headlights three times in quick succession. They had a sense of humor. We had gone to bed a little calmer, a little less tense than usual. Tense? I had never wanted to admit that to myself. But now that I had, perhaps this was the first necessary step toward something inglorious. Wasn't this the way children felt when their angered father had intimated to them by way of a curt "Good night!" that he was not averse to making up? And what else but childlike and childish should one call those incessant interior monologues at which I caught myself, and which all too often ended with the absurd question: What do you want, anyway? I still had so much to learn! Addressing an institution as if it were a person! I was well beyond that early phase, I assured myself, I no longer fell prey to protestations, but since when? One day I had understood that there was no addressee for protestations and attempts at explanation; I had to assume that which I had balked at for such a long time, that the young gentlemen out there were not accessible to me. They were not my kind. They were the messengers of the other. It had been a long time since I had thought of sidling up to those cars and staring in with a grim expression to meet the opaque gazes of their occupants, whose sole task it must have been to be recognized for what they were and thus provoke anger, better still, fear, which, as we know, makes some people give in and drives others to rash undertakings, these in turn serving as evidence for the necessity of said surveillance. I felt very strongly that someone had to make the attempt to break this vicious circle.

At some point I would be able to talk about this as well in my new free language, although it would be difficult, since it was so banal. The unease. The sleeplessness. The weight loss. The pills. The dreams. It could certainly be described. But to what end? What the world knew as fear was quite different from this. My hair falling out by the bushel. So what? It had grown back thicker than before and the pills lay unused in the drawer. Things always sorted themselves out. The dreams. Well, yes. I did not deny that to myself, but where in the world can people live without nightmares these days? No. Every day I told myself that a privileged life like mine could be justified only by attempting to go beyond the borders of the sayable, knowing full well that border violations of any kind are punished. However, I told myself—becoming aware of the fact that I had been staring for minutes on end at the television tower, which rose above the massive ophthalmological and gynecological hospital block slightly to the right of my field of vision—however, I would draw closer to the border of language only if I felt capable of explaining why the fear did not go away on those days when the cars were present only as phantoms on my retina and not in reality, was not even slighter than on days of apparent surveillance. I would have to come up with something about that, I thought, no matter in what language.

How much more time did I want to give myself, anyway?

Time was one of my cues. One day I had realized that it was perhaps a fundamentally different relationship to time more than anything else that separated me from those young gentlemen outside—they were still standing there, oh yes!—for time to them was worthless; they were wasting it on a pointless, yet no doubt expensive idleness, which was bound to demoralize them in time, but it didn't seem to bother them. On the contrary, I suddenly suspected, it seemed to suit them fine. They were throwing their time out the window heartily with both hands, or did they call what they were doing work? Even that was imaginable. It was imaginable, no, probable that they showed their wives a face from which could be gathered how irreplaceable they had been able to make themselves once again on that day. Rumor had it, however, that sometimes one of them bragged at the supper table, in the presence of his teenage children, about his insights for the day: the human weaknesses of the observed objects, abstruse love affairs, for example, which, if he was allowed to talk about them, could get a lot of people in hot water. Yet he remained as silent as a tomb. They really did remain silent, of that I was convinced. With the exception of bragging fathers. In reality, all of them surely knew that each of them could become superfluous from one second to the next.

Every time I had this thought, I felt chilled like the first time.

The telephone. A friend. Hello, I said. No, he wasn't interrupting any important work. Why not? he said chastisingly. Well, I said, the question couldn't be answered in one sentence. I could feel free to use several sentences, he said. So that they can be written down, I said. But I was no doubt underestimating their technical capabilities, he said. They could certainly spare a tape recorder for the two of us! What expense, I said.

There followed the kind of laughter which had become our routine upon just such occasions, a little bit provocative, a little bit vain. But what if no one was listening in? What if all our hubris and preening were directed at emptiness? It wouldn't make the slightest difference. I would have to give that some thought.

Did I know how I sounded this morning?

So how did I sound this morning?

Well, said my friend, not exactly thrilled, I would say. Or doth my ear deceive me?

Oh, I said, what else could I be but thrilled when you deign to call me—and so on.

That was how we always talked, circumventing the real text. I couldn't help thinking of the two or three times when the real text actually had slipped out because I didn't have the strength to keep it in, and how his eyes and his voice had changed. How was H. doing? he now asked. Good, I said, he's allowed visitors in the afternoon. And how about us? he asked. When are we going to get together? As soon as possible, I said—the real text. In that case, he said, he would be in the city in the next few days and tell me beforehand when to make the coffee. Certain people whom we both highly esteemed could gladly rack their brains trying to figure out what "coffee" was the code word for.

I do not particularly like these kinds of jokes. Coffee? I said. I thought you preferred tea. Not at all, he said, and I shouldn't get the code all mixed up. *Bon*, I said. And he, after a short pause, with no change of voice: You've got company, eh?

I also didn't like these kinds of questions, but said yes, incapable of lying.

Well, that's just fine, said my friend. See you soon.

Suddenly I heard myself shout into the telephone, Hey, listen! Someday we'll be old, do you realize that?

He had hung up. But I sat back down at my desk and buried my face in my hands. Yes. This is how we spend our few days. I didn't cry. I hadn't cried for quite a long time, come to think of it.

Although I hadn't got any work done yet on that day, I would go shopping now, right in the middle of my work schedule. It was a victory for the others, I wasn't kidding myself, for if there was one ethic I held to, it was the work ethic, not least because it seemed to be capable of balancing out inconsistencies in other ethical systems. I didn't want to give up like those young gentlemen had given up when they let themselves be hired for such thinly disguised non-activity, perhaps due to an ineffaceable penchant for order and subordination, instead of doing an honest day's work.

Now what? Doing other people's thinking for them again? Slipping on shoes, putting on a coat, locking the door twice, preferably three times, if that was possible, no matter how little that would help if things came to a head, as I well knew, for those young gentlemen or their colleagues, specially trained in opening doors, had visited our apartment during our absence at least once, but more likely twice, last summer, of course without taking into account the cleaning tick of Frau C., who wipes away her own footprints when she leaves the apartment after a day's work and naturally became suspicious when clear prints of the profiled soles of a man's shoes, size 41/42, could be seen in some doorways and on the dark parquet floor in the middle room the next day. Which prompted Frau C., who isn't easily discouraged, to sift a little flour onto the doormat behind the front door "in the old time-tested manner," as she put it, before leaving the apartment, after carefully removing the traces which, as was to be expected, made the footsteps stand out much more prominently the next day. Apart from that, the shards of the bathroom mirror had been in the sink without any natural explanation for these findings having presented itself. Therefore we had to assume that the young gentlemen did not wish to keep their visit to our apartment a secret.

That was called intimidation, said an acquaintance, who purported to be in the know about such things; but were we intimidated? Granted. Of course we spoke very quietly with others in the apartment when certain topics came up (and they always did come up); I turned up the radio during certain conversations and sometimes we unplugged the telephone when we had guests, yet we remained aware of the fact that the measures taken by the others and our reactions to them meshed together like the teeth of a smoothly functioning zipper. Hope could not be gathered from this. Hope could possibly be gathered from the fact that I had not felt at home in my own apartment since last summer.

I went outside. Were they still there? They were there. Would they follow me? They did not follow me. According to our well-informed acquaintance, we had been accorded the lowest level of surveillance, the warning kind, the instructions for those carrying out the task being: Conspicuous presence. Following one's every move and step with one, two, or up to six cars (what expense!) was a totally different level, yet another, secret surveillance which was employed when the observed object was rated as under serious suspicion. So this did not apply to us? The know-it-all shrugged his shoulders. It was, after all, possible that two different kinds of surveillance be used on one object.

By the way, I could also be followed on foot. I couldn't see any suspicious characters in the display window of the drugstore. I noticed with slight consternation that I was beginning to breathe more easily. I had been assured by a specialist in Russian literature that Akhmatova had had her own personal shadow for twenty years. I pictured this while walking along the Friedrichstrasse unaccompanied and unpursued like a normal human being and couldn't help asking myself what I had done to deserve this privilege. It began to dawn on me how severe and absolute the freedom at the innermost core of total encirclement must be. They hadn't even shown me their instruments, I thought. But what made me think of that? Oh, yes! They were performing *Galileo* at the Berlin Ensemble that evening, it said so in large black letters against a white background, and no one stood in their way, for this was a play from the time when purified dialectics still counted for something, along with the words "positive" and "negative," when there was a reason for speaking the "truth" and it was evil to suppress it; it was evil not to speak of the nasty lie which was harmful and gave the liar a bad conscience, the remains of which have survived even up to this day. A history of bad conscience would have to be included in reflections on the boundaries of the sayable, I thought; with what words does one describe the speechlessness of those who have no conscience, how does language deal with absence, which will tolerate no adjectives or nouns clinging to it, for it is without qualities and certainly lacks a subject in the same way that a subject without a conscience lacks itself, I asked myself further, but was that at all true? Wasn't I just looking for excuses to banish these young men, who were perhaps not without a conscience after all, from my sympathy, because they had banished me from theirs? Tit for tat. An eye for an eye and a tooth for a tooth. My new language would also have to be able to speak of them just as it would have to deal with every failure of language, I said to myself.

I always enjoyed crossing Weidendammer Bridge. Poor old B.B., with his belief in the unbelief he calls "science," with his determined attempts at division with which he cuts a path through the jungle of the cities and countries as if with a hatchet, convinced that the world will break apart into two halves along this wound. But the jungle closes behind him, and the abyss yawns before us. Galileo, fearful and cunning, escapes the Inquisition and saves his work. The Church, which threatens to destroy him, has nonetheless given him the weapon with which he can stand up to it: a belief in the sense of truth. He only had to come to terms with his fear. And so it was purely a question of character as to whether he fought the lie or not. We, who are also full of fear, and non-believers to boot, always fought against ourselves, for we lied and kowtowed and railed and slandered, and we lusted for slavery and pleasure. Only, some knew it and some didn't.

Leaning over the railing, I saw the ducks and seagulls and a barge with a black, red, and gold flag. There was a wind as usual. In the middle of the bridge hangs the cast-iron Prussian eagle, which stared at me mockingly and which I lightly touched in passing. As always when I crossed this bridge, I remembered the endless walks I had taken through these streets back then, more than two years ago, and I remembered my shameless longing for peace at almost any price and that I hadn't even been able to bear the memory of joy and happiness, and that I used to burst into tears spontaneously whenever they showed a film on television which portrayed a hope I had also once nourished, and I would never forget the moment—I was standing in front of the display window of a run-of-the-mill drugstore, lost in thought—when the realization that pain was the driving force within me struck like a bolt of lightning. I hadn't recognized it. Pure, raging pain had taken hold, had taken possession of me and made of me another person.

This was the same time that the young gentlemen appeared at our door, although they couldn't have known that we would never meet. While they rose out of their underground, I sank down into another and found myself on unknown terrain. One hand had gripped my heart, another had touched my eyes. I was in foreign territory. For weeks on end I wandered through the nameless streets of a nameless city. Winter came, slush, sleet, a damp cold that chilled me to the bone, passing through my flesh as if it wasn't there. Yet it still retained the dull memory of previous joys, bread, wine, love, the smell of the children, the images of landscapes, cities, faces. And now there seeped from it such desolation that I was sure a cool waft emanated from me which anyone could feel.

Without a thought in my mind, I walked the short distance along the low stone balustrade, which is interrupted by the beginning of the path to the door of a certain glass pavilion—referred to as "the tear bunker" in common parlance—where the transformation of citizens of different countries, including mine, into passers-through, tourists, exiting and entering visitors, was accomplished in a light which fell from very high narrow windows and reflected off greenish tiled walls, a light in which the assistants of the master who controlled this city, dressed as policemen or customs officers, exercised the right to bind or release. If its outer appearance corresponded to its function, this building would loom up like a monster instead of being a normal building of stone, glass, and iron struts surrounded by a well-kept lawn upon which one was naturally forbidden to tread. I had also had to learn my mistrust of such well-kept objects, had understood that they all belonged to the lord who ruled my city without opposition: the ruthless advantage of the moment.

Only then did I realize that a secret fire had glowed in the interior of this city before, I didn't know its name yet, but ever since the day when it was to be extinguished, when all its accompanying fires were to be suffocated and each of its hidden sparks stamped out, I had been hopelessly under its spell. As of yet I had to live with all the others in a lost city, in a merciless city which had not been saved, sunk to the bottom of insignificance. At night I heard the stomp stomp of the robot who laid his iron hand on my breast. The city had turned from a place into a non-place, without history, without vision, without magic, spoiled by greed, power, and violence. It divided its time between nightmares and senseless activities—like those kids in the cars who were more and more coming to symbolize my city.

Now I needed to talk to a real flesh-and-blood person. I went into the small liquor store beneath the streetcar bridge in the Friedrichstrasse where the saleswoman, an elderly woman with thin, graying hair, seemed to have been waiting just for me. She struck up a conversation about the red champagne which she actually had in stock, the quality of which was not at all appreciated by all her customers. Satisfied, she took down a second bottle from the shelf for me.

Had she been working here for a long time? Oh, her entire life. Either here or around here. She was an original Berliner.

Then she could surely tell a story or two.

Oh, as far as that was concerned—she wouldn't know where to begin! The most curious things had happened right in front of her eyes. The woman loved the word "curious," she kept repeating it. I wondered whether I could listen to still more curious stories, but I feigned interest in the saleswoman's memories, which could only be gruesome—as, in fact, they were—however, what really surprised me was, the woman knew it. She was an exception. I first heard it in her tone of voice and then I understood: she was really still attached to her Jewish girl friend, with whom she had spent her youth, with whom she had ridden the streetcar from the Alexanderplatz to the Kudamm every morning—she to the department store where she was an apprentice, her girl friend (her name was Elfriede, Elfi, imagine, a Jewess named Elfi!) to the bank to add up columns of figures. She found it boring. When was this? 1935, '36 . . . Don't look at me like that. Elfi's boyfriend, the SS commander, had offered to get her out, but she said, No, only if my family can go too, otherwise no. The guy was crazy about her. Of course it never could have worked out, but you always know better once it's too late. I guess he must have organized something for her anyway, the talk was Holland and they must have caught on. In any case, one fine day, as we are coming around the corner of the

Joachimsthaler street, where he always parked his car and waited for Elfi so that he could catch at least one of her glances for the day, there's his car again, and as we go by, we see that it is full of gentlemen with those trenchcoats and those sporty hats, and Elfi's friend is sitting next to the driver and looking straight ahead, and I whisper to Elfi through my teeth, Don't turn around! Just keep going straight ahead and, whatever you do, don't start running! And we pulled it off. Well, she never heard anything more about the guy. You can't have everything, maybe he finally caught on— The champagne costs thirty marks.

The woman didn't seem inclined to go on talking on her own—she had to be drawn out. Elfi? Of course they came and got her. It was '42 when they took away the last load of Jews from Berlin. With her whole family. I personally never found another girl friend like her; you get choosy with time, don't you agree? And the things that can keep going through your head for decades. We could have hidden one in a pinch, but an entire family . . .

It was all madness, she shouted after me. When I think back on it, pure madness.

I didn't want to get into all of that again. I stared blindly at the window display in the train station bookstore, circled the newspaper stand without success, and decided to go to the new department store in the Japan Center, after all. Shopping, that time-honored painkiller, didn't work, but I got some buckthorn juice for H., who had told me he was always thirsty. The women standing in the checkout line were almost all too fat and had bad posture. By force of habit, I looked for that one face which would turn toward me when spoken to but did not find it until a young, singularly plain-looking woman let another older woman ahead of her in line because she couldn't stand on her feet any longer. So it is possible, after all, I thought. It had to be. Still, that strong, isolating feeling of otherness would not go away, but I knew that I should not get hung up on it. Even if the people ahead of me in line didn't know anything, hardly suspected anything, worse still, didn't want to know anything—you couldn't let your aim fall short, it was better to aim higher to reach them, further, toward the future.

All right, all right. I was getting on my nerves. My last stop was the post office, to withdraw money. Anyone who knew me could have seen how irritable I was. Everything was too much for me now and everything took too long now, although I was wondering at the same time where I was rushing to and what it was that I so hurriedly sought. Always this deep, dark double life. The thrill of the uncertain, which can be as addictive as a drug. That I always felt the compulsion to express everything. Meanwhile, I had long since spotted my old friend and he me, of that I was sure. Our gazes had collided for a fraction of a second, but Jürgen M. pretended not to know me: his gaze had retreated a fraction of a fraction of a second earlier than mine. I was used to that. Was I ever: the curtain lowering before the eyes of the other; the whites of a friend's eyes glazing over like those of a fish; the clouding of the lens. We have never seen one another, never met. All right. It's better that way. Just go over to the other counter. Busy yourself with the papers you have to show the post-office clerk, shuffle about unnecessary forms, anything, as long as you don't run into me at the exit. But the other, this time it's Jürgen M., can relax: I'll play along. I'm already outside. There is no way I am going to turn around.

How long has it actually been since I went up to an old friend, certain in the knowledge that he wanted to see me? Since I was the first to hold out my hand? Since I started up a conversation? Since I withdrew? And now the big question: How many people have to cross over to the other side of the street, to get caught up in the handiest window display, to change tables in a restaurant and turn their backs on you at a meeting before you understand and behave accordingly? How often do you have to think "coincidence" before you're prepared to think "on purpose"? I couldn't help grinning, because I'm always happy to discover that statistics can't answer the real questions.

No great loss, I thought. Jürgen M. was no great loss, so why did it bother me that he was avoiding me? Why did it bother me every time it happened? Why didn't one toughen up? What was wrong with me? Which mechanism was out of order?

Now one thing at a time, just relax. Jürgen M. When was the last time I saw this Jürgen M.? Quite some time ago, that much is certain. No doubt under pleasanter circumstances. Hadn't I teased him about the loud pattern of his necktie? But all he did was make an ironic bow and hand me the glass of champagne he had just taken from a tray, take a new one for himself, and make a toast. Long time no see but still recognized. Did I like the paintings, he wanted to know; So-so, I said. It was that exhibition opening in the Marstall, things weren't going badly, people were running into other people they hadn't seen for a long time and asking the standard questions about their situations, as if they had spent the previous years in different countries. We *had* spent the years in different countries. I played according to the rules as usual, whenever it was possible, and asked Jürgen M. what he was up to at the moment. Me? he said, oh, you know, the usual daily grind.

That was all he had actually said, when I thought about it. Jürgen M., a fellow student's boyfriend, for whom a brilliant future had been predicted by his friends. Jürgen M., the philosopher. Hadn't he drawn attention to himself with a few controversial publications? I remembered that he was thinner and wore his hair parted on the side back then and hadn't been going out with my girl friend for a long time—first I lost track of him, then of her. Was he still writing for the appropriate periodicals? Had that book he had incessantly talked about ever come out? Was he a failure, disappointed in himself and the world; was this perhaps the reason why he avoided meeting former acquaintances? Should I have been the one to approach him? But hadn't there been something else about Jürgen M.?

Someone walking behind me whistled so loudly and shrilly that it echoed throughout the streetcar underpass and drowned out the sound of the traffic. What was he whistling anyway, I definitely knew that song: "We swore to Karl Liebknecht, we give Rosa Luxemburg our hand," the man whistled. I started to cry. This had to stop. And it would stop, unfortunately, probably very soon. The man whistling the song, a broad, heavyset man around forty, was wearing a black corduroy suit like the ones carpenters wear, but without the shiny buttons; he strode whistling up to the door of the little bakery, not caring whether people were staring at him, and disappeared inside.

Could I imagine a woman at this man's side? I could not. There are always certain women with whom I can't imagine any man, but this time it was the other way around. I had no trouble imagining a woman at Jürgen M.'s side, one of those stylish women who come twelve to the dozen, for he could only have left my girl friend, who was difficult but still something special, for that kind of woman. Or had my girl friend left him back then? Hadn't we all been a little puzzled about why the two of them had separated after all those years?

What did I care about Jürgen M., damnit. Was he even worth thinking about? Hadn't he written that disgusting article about his professor back then, during similarly difficult times! It was just like me to forget, not to do what I had set out to: never to speak to him again. To think that I talked to him because of that stupid tie and then was surprised at how eagerly he had given me his champagne! He had quite simply been relieved that I spoke to him at all. But now the shoe was on the other foot, things weren't going well, no, they really weren't, and Jürgen M. could certainly afford not to know me. What is more, he wasn't allowed to speak to me. Perhaps he even knew that . . .

Now one thing at a time. Just relax. What could he know? What could a man like Jürgen M. know, above and beyond the scanty, official statements and the elaborate rumors which were possibly more than enough for him? After all, somebody else apart from my friends had to know about the existence of the young gentlemen outside my door. The person who had stationed them there, for example.

There it was again, my obsession; I recognized it immediately, but I couldn't help wallowing in it joyfully: that there must be someone who knew everything about me except for the really important things. All the information about me—gathered by the young gentlemen, the telephone tappers, the mail spies—had to come together on some desk or in some head somewhere. What if it was in the head of Jürgen M.?

There seemed to be some likelihood of this, for my second spontaneous thought was: Then he'd finally get what he needed. I was astonished at this second thought. Since when had I had something against Jürgen M.? Since when did I think I knew what he needed? What else had I filed away on Jürgen M. without even noticing it? Jürgen M., the speechmaker—indeed, he had been that as well. Was that before or after that business with his professor? I didn't remember anymore. A reputation for straightforwardness preceded him, and it was true, he was straightforward, but everything he said impressed me as a justification for past or future activities. I remembered how fascinated many of our colleagues were by Jürgen M. Finally, someone who tells it like it is. He received lots of applause, as I recall, and I wanted to go home quickly, deeply dejected as I was, but he was lying in wait for me at the door and dragged me off to the beer parlor. The crowd at our table grew, the evening was long. I hadn't known that Jürgen M. drank. When he started babbling on uncontrollably, I made the mistake of asking him, Why do you drink? His head whipped around to face me as if I had given him a slap. On top of things as usual, madam! he said. The man hated me. Did I do something wrong? I said helplessly, and that one sentence broke through the dam Jürgen M. had built up around himself, and there streamed out an unstoppable confession which I was forced to listen to but did not want to hear, for I knew: after this he would not only hate me, he would be a danger to me. But I was caught up in the spell of his fury and my own curiosity, and so I discovered that he, Jürgen M., had been spying on me and my life for years.

That he knew every single word I had said or written—above all, every word I had refused to say or write; that he knew all my relationships as intimately as an outsider can possibly know the relationships of another person; that he had thought and felt his way into my very being with an intensity that staggered me and—this drove him mad with rage—that he thought I was successful and happy. And above all proud. Proud, I asked dumbfoundedly, how so? Insofar as I seemed to think that one could have everything I had without selling one's soul. Come come, now, I said, if only to alleviate the tension, we're no longer living in the Middle Ages, are we? Luck wasn't with me that evening; I kept giving him the cues he seemed to have been waiting for, since now he really got going. No longer in the Middle Ages! There you have it. That was precisely what I had chosen to believe and probably actually did believe, rather than, as he had thought for a long time, shrewdly parading around with it as a motto behind which to hide and take all kinds of liberties, for who could contradict such a motto nowadays? Prancing around on that tightrope of yours with your head in the clouds and never falling off, said Jürgen M. But now, just between the two of us, he wanted to pull my head out of the clouds. Not in the Middle Ages? You're wrong, madam. We are in the Middle Ages. Nothing has changed except for appearances. And nothing is going to change. And should you wish to rise above the ignorant masses like someone in the know, then you'll have to sell your soul—that's the way it's always been. And if I wanted to know the truth, blood would flow in the process as well, even if it wasn't one's own. Not always one's own.

Now I remembered what I had suddenly understood back then: they had him in the palm of their hand. And I remembered how my pride—he was probably right about that, talented psychologist that he was—drove me to ask him quietly, Why don't you quit? And how he turned as white as a sheet, rolled his eyes, brought his face up so close to mine that I could smell his beer breath, and, in a clear and stone-sober voice, said three words: I—am—afraid. Right after that he played the drunk again; I got up, knocked on the table, and left. I didn't see Jürgen M. for years after that, forgot the episode which he will never forget, and now he no longer feels the need to know me, sits in that house with all those telephones and collects all the news about me to his heart's content, news unavailable to anyone else, and offers his thanks each morning to a fate which has placed him in a situation whereby he can satisfy his passionate desire and be useful to society at the same time.

Just like me, in my own place.

I walked blindly across the Weidendammer Bridge in the opposite direction and couldn't help thinking of the files in which all the information about me was no doubt hoarded. But first it had to be sorted, formulated, and possibly dictated to a secretary. Or how else was one to picture it? Could I imagine Jürgen M. arriving at his office punctually at eight in the morning and reaching for a thin folder with my name on it—my imagination allowed me this one small vanity—first thing? Therein was the report on the previous day; Jürgen M. concentrated with visible pleasure. Aha! Yesterday—this was today—she had a telephone call at 9:45 a.m. Caller: Here the name of my friend appeared. There followed the transcript of our discussion, at which Jürgen M., who was now no doubt in a position to be amused, would grin. He was also in a position to be condescending. "Codeword," "coffee," "tea"—oh, you poor amateurs! Jürgen M. was a pro, if my picture of him was correct, and being as intelligent as he was, he was bound to be struck with horror at the futility of his occupation one fine morning while reading the two-hundred-and-thirty-seventh report by his informants. For whenever he leafed through all the files, reading a line here, a shorthand note there, and then the transcript of a conversation, and asked himself what he now knew about the object in question that he hadn't known before, he would honestly have to say, Nothing. And if he furthermore asked himself what he had accomplished, he would likewise have to say, Nothing.

But I knew better. He had accomplished a lot, the dear, quite a lot, but there was no way he could know what, for that was something his spies hadn't heard and his tape recorders hadn't recorded. For it is made of too fine a fabric; it slips through their fingers, not even the tightest net can entrap it, and when I now asked myself what this mysterious "it" actually was, I found that I had no name for it; dissatisfied with myself and unable to justify what I was about to do, I crossed the parking lot, headed toward the bottle-green car (they were still there, what else had I expected?)—it was 11:15—I brushed by the car and surprised the three young gentlemen in the middle of their breakfast. The one at the steering wheel had his lunch box on his lap, the one next to him was taking a bite out of an apple, and the one in back was gulping down a bottle of bitter lemon soda with abandon. He did not choke when he saw my face, he just kept on drinking unconcernedly, but all three of them put on a glassy-eyed stare, as if by silent command. Maybe, I thought, as I ceremoniously crossed the parking lot to the mailbox as if I had some letters to mail, maybe they learn that glassy stare at their training school. They must learn some practical skills apart from social sciences. Maybe it's written on the weekly course agenda: Glassy Stare Training 101.

And what if it isn't Jürgen M. but someone else?

I knew the voice. Good morning, dear self-censor, haven't heard from you in a long time. Well then, who could it be if not Jürgen M., in your opinion? An unprejudiced civil servant who doesn't even know you. I think I would even prefer that. Prefer is good. All the same. Someone who has no personal interest in me. Who has nothing to prove to me. Who does not want to beat me at my own original game.

Like Jürgen M.? Wake up!

I knew from experience that interior dialogue is preferable to a long-drawn-out interior monologue. And so I let my inner censor think about what was spurring Jürgen M. on: namely, that he was dying to prove to me that not only a writer could find out everything there was to know about a person—he could do it as well, in his own way. He as well could make himself the lord and master of his objects like any run-of-the-mill author. Yet since his objects are made of flesh and blood and do not exist only on paper, like my own, *he* is the actual master, the real lord.

And you, said the unwelcome voice, which can be very tactless, you want to compete with him? Want to pick up the tossed gauntlet? Show him who the master is? Face it, your spotless Jürgen has already won.

But what else am I supposed to do? I asked myself, while I opened up the mailbox in the hallway and took out the mail and magazines. Up the stairs, toward the hallway mirror, the one that isn't smashed yet. The fact that I was pale didn't mean much, a bit short of breath, that's all. Good luck in your middle age, the voice wished me. Impudent, was my reply. By the way, wasn't there something touching about the young man drinking soda in the car down there? I should not play down such undignified activity. So we were still talking about dignity? Still? But we were just starting.

But who told us what dignity is?

I started reading my mail after the usual preliminaries, that is, after making sure that there were no unpleasant return addresses, no one I was afraid of. After holding the envelopes up to the light in such a way that the shiny glued edge, which evidently was caused by sealing the envelopes a second time, became visible. The glued edges of the envelopes were very rarely less smooth than usual and hardly ever did I find a page stuck to the inside of an envelope. Such slip-ups should be avoidable. Somewhere—probably right out in the open—there had to be a huge house (or maybe there were smaller houses in all the districts?) where wagonloads of mail were delivered daily, to be sorted by busy female hands on a long assembly line and directed to other floors according to criteria unfathomable to the likes of us, where even more women steamed open the letters—or had they come up with more effective methods in the meantime?—carefully, oh so carefully, and conveyed them to the sanctum sanctorum in which skillful colleagues no doubt made use of the photocopy machines we so sorely missed in our libraries and publishing houses. An army of employees granted neither recognition by the press nor a holiday in their honor like the miners, the teachers, or the employees of the public health service; a steadily growing swarm of people who had to resign themselves to working in the shadows. The word "shadow" got lodged in my mind; I wrote it down on a scrap of paper. The occupation of large sections of the population is relegated to the shadows. I saw crowds of people sinking into a deep shadow. Their lot did not seem enviable to me.

I put aside the newspapers after skipping over the headlines. There were three letters I still hadn't opened. I knew who had sent them, although one of them had neither a return address nor a stamp; the sender, a very young poet, was in the habit of putting his letters in my mailbox in person. I had never seen him. Going by his poems—these new ones had been written in a premilitary training camp—I pictured a delicate, soft-spoken boy with gentle blue eyes who suffered without being able to defend himself and survived by writing poetry. I read the boy's poems reluctantly, for I could not help him; I wrote him evasive responses and sometimes I was furious at him, even more so at myself. He could have been my son. I believed I could foresee the fate awaiting him. They would stop at nothing. The young gentlemen standing in front of my door would not hesitate to pass through his door. That was the difference between the two of us—a major difference. A moat. Would I have to jump over it?

Now we were finally getting down to the right questions, that certain voice said to me. You could recognize them by the fact that they provided a certain satisfaction along with pain. Once again Mr. Know-It-All seemed to know it all.

Weren't there days when I craved these questions?

So what? Today wasn't such a day, in any case.

My partner claimed to be informed about that as well. It just seemed to be one of those days for me. I told him to butt out. Okay, okay. After all, he hadn't been appointed my judge. What, then? My companion, was his laconic reply, to which I could only add sarcastically, My personal companion. The insinuation didn't faze him in the least. In a rage, I demanded to know who had appointed him, and he answered indifferently, You did yourself, sister. If you would please keep that in mind.

I myself. I couldn't get past those two words for a long time. I myself. Who was that? Which of the multiple beings from which "myself" was composed? The one that wanted to know itself? The one that wanted to protect itself? Or that third one that was still tempted to dance to the same tune as the young gentlemen there outside my door? Hey, buddy, which of the three are you siding with? At this my companion grew silent, out of sorts but helpful. That was what I needed: to be able to believe that one day soon I would have completely detached and expelled that third one; that that was what I really wanted; and that, in the long run, it would be easier to bear those young gentlemen out there than the third one in myself.

Why was it that, for some time now, each and every choice I was presented with was only a choice between bad and worse? Was it simply that one learned to see more clearly with those gentlemen outside the door?

Procrastination? It was about time to open the second letter, from one of my closest friends. The one who had supposedly been employed and assigned to me by the others for a long time, according to the insinuations of another friend. If this was true, they could have spared themselves the mail and telephone surveillance, the hidden microphones and the young gentlemen outside our windows. This friend would be more effective than the lot of them. Jürgen M. could toss all the other transcripts and tapes into the wastepaper basket and needed only to file away my friend's reports. It wasn't that they could be dangerous to me in the bureaucratic sense of the word. In a deeper sense, however, there could hardly have been anything more dangerous for me. Without a doubt, Jürgen M. could bask in my innermost thoughts; above all, however, there would be no relying on anybody, and the pull toward the dark side of life, of which I was strongly aware once again, would grow stronger still, perhaps all too seductive, perhaps irresistible, and the place toward which I was being drawn would no longer be called "life." But what was the name of that which no longer was life?

No. I didn't want to read the letter just now.

Slow and steady now. One step at a time. And relax.

Are they still out there?

They are, and they'll stay there today as well, you know that.

But what is the point? If he tells them everything, anyway?

Now sit still and listen. Stubbornness is one thing, but a cool head is better. All right, let's take our friend. Suppose he was forced to comply with their wishes.

Forced to?

Forced to! You and your damned pride again! What could he do? Pour out his heart to us? So that we'll never ever be able to have a relaxed conversation with him again?

What else?

Holy simplicity! Pretend to carry out his orders, for example. Tell them only what they already know. Don't give them a handle against you or against himself. Walk a tightrope.

Trapeze artists, I said sorrowfully to myself inside myself, we are all trapeze artists. But in that case I don't want him for a friend.

Once a princess-on-a-pea, always a princess-on-a-pea. And on top of that, how do you think he should get away from them, and with whose help?

You don't mean—

Exactly. Only with your help.

If he even wants it.

Why shouldn't he want it? You know his history.

My friend wrote from H., where he was attending a conference, that he longed to sit in my kitchen, drink tea, and talk with me to his heart's content. If that is meant to be a hint that there are no bugs hidden in our kitchen . . . All right, I'm ashamed of myself.

I sat down at my desk and wrote my friend that I was presently in the middle of a difficult phase. Thoughts were surfacing in me which I myself found frightening. We could talk about it sometime soon when we were drinking tea together in my kitchen.

Who knows, I thought, and my inner companion was angered at my reservation. I asked, Should I let him into my kitchen without reservation? and he said, Without reservation. But he wouldn't notice a thing; I would act perfectly natural, I am good at that. And even open, to a certain degree.

That splendid inner voice remained silent, silent, silent, silent.

There was one letter left, the most conspicuous of them all, a long white rectangle. This one I hadn't examined for suspicious signs; if they were there, I didn't want to know about them. An official letter. I absentmindedly slit open the envelope with a letter opener. The necessary seconds, the seconds I needed to take out and unfold the letter were sufficient to pass review on a chain of remote thoughts. Pushkin. The collected letters which had just been published. His rage upon discovering that the czarist mail censors had opened one of his letters to his wife. His pathos: not even the intimate exchange of thoughts between spouses was sacred to them! His overreaction: that he could not write to his wife for a long time thereafter. And my spontaneous laughter upon reading this, my feeling of superiority: Oh, those oversensitive poets of the nineteenth century!

When was it that I stopped writing confidential and intimate letters? That I had to force myself to write letters at all? I no longer knew. When had the period of the "as if" letters begun—when I had decided to write as if no one was intercepting my mail; as if I was writing freely, as if I was writing confidentially. I no longer knew. All I knew was, I was ruined as far as spontaneous letters were concerned, and the contact with distant correspondents was fading. Could I still feel disappointment at this? Horror? Hadn't I come to accept it? They're succeeding, I thought. And how.

The letter had an impressive letterhead and was brief. The man who had written it was employed by the Bureau of Letterheads and wished to present himself as a respectable person. I was meant to gather from the letter that he would remain a respectable person, even in difficult times; he would not abandon me, even in difficult times. Is that all? I thought, half relieved, half disappointed, and no doubt unfairly. After all, he had written to me—on official paper!—that it would be no problem at all to "work me into" his institution's planned program of cultural activities. He wrote "work me into" in quotation marks to show that he was aware of the irony of his offer. Did he think I needed money? No, he did not. My advice, he pointed out tactfully, my occasional cooperation could do his joint—he wrote "this joint here"—a world of good. It would be no problem at all to talk me into it sometime soon. Then he would also take the opportunity to tell me how he had been doing "since then"—the sole expression which had slipped out uncontrolledly. But, as I well knew, ill weeds grew apace.

Silence. Silence. Intermission. In case you think he can still hurt me . . . Well, you're right; he can hurt me. He can do it again.

The letter gave off a faint aroma of self-sacrifice. I guess that was part of his personality. And now he writes me this letter to prove that the opposite was true. And he files it away carefully, as evidence of his brave solidarity. But invite me he will not. Nor will he work me into his planned program of cultural activities. He will presumably attach the list which forbids him to do so, and which also includes my name, to his letter in the same file.

So what? Chalk it up to experience.

The telephone rang for the second time that day. A female voice. Why is she so upset, I wondered before I even knew to whom I was speaking. She was upset because she was expecting complications that evening. It was Colleague K. from the cultural center, who, much to my surprise, had invited me for a reading that evening, and now she wanted to know if I couldn't come half an hour earlier.

Sure, I said, but why?

To stave off any chance that unpleasant incidents might occur.

She had said "stave off." It was her language, her tone of voice that made me break out into a cold sweat. What kind of unpleasant incidents? I asked cheerfully.

Frau K. already regretted her choice of words. She said, trying to placate me, Oh, nothing special. Just general precautions.

There seemed no reply except: All right. I'll come earlier. Then I had to hang up. I smelled a rat.

Now it was after twelve. Were they still there?

They were.

So let's have something to eat. One shouldn't have to be alone on days like this.

Alone? There was hardly anything left to think or say without getting my censor upset at me. If you don't stop whining and feeling sorry for yourself . . .

All right, all right. By the way, you're right. I'll let you-know-who into my kitchen without reservation. I won't have forgotten what I thought about him today, but I'll believe him when he says that he is fond of me. And who's going to get him out of there, if not someone he is fond of? If he really wants to get out. If he really is involved with them. It had to be someone. Have you forgotten how many weaknesses they can exploit to get at him? Oh, to hell with you and your moral bigotry.

Maybe it wasn't quite one of those days, after all.

I heated up yesterday's beef broth and ate absent-mindedly while listening to the same news as that morning. Children's shouts from the courtyard could now be heard, they were answered by pop music from the fifth floor of the building next door, opposite my kitchen; soon Frau G. would appear in her green cap and complain bitterly about the noise. And so she did.

I was back at the desk but had avoided looking out

the window. (They were still there.) I sat down and began catching up on the entries I had neglected to make the last few days in my thick green pocket diary. Someday I would be sitting in a room—I pictured it as bare, a typical office—and they would be asking me questions. Questions of different degrees, innocuous ones among others; but I had decided not to answer a single question and would stand by my decision (you and your illusions, sister!). Then, after one, two, or twenty hours—weren't there interrogations which went on for days, with short breaks?—my interrogator would take out this thick green notebook in which I was now conscientiously writing down what I had done, read, heard, whom I had seen, and even what I had noticed about the weather today, yesterday, and the day before that. Now, my interrogator would say—he would remain very polite up to the third- and fourth-degree questions and only become very rough all of a sudden at the fifth-degree questions, but I would be prepared and would also stand up to his roughness, perhaps even more easily than to his politeness (Sister! Sister . . .). Now, he would say, let's get down to the nitty-gritty. And he would read me the answers to every question, which I had just so proudly refused to furnish, out of my own notebook in my very own words. Now, Mr. Know-It-All, can you explain to me why I still keep writing everything down, other than out of pride, foolhardiness, and arrogance?

Because you think they won't dare.

Silence.

Now I had to go to the telephone, dial, listen. Did I wake you up? I said a little too guiltily. No, said my younger daughter. But she was in the middle of her breakfast. What was she having? The list was long and given my approval. So that was what she called "breakfast." Other people would live off that for two days. She made up for it by not eating anything for two days. But that was just the tragedy. She asked for and received news about her father. And what about yourself, ma'am? Oh, marvelous, said I, and she said, Splendiferous, at which point I requested that she make use of a generally understandable form of speech, which she indignantly refused to do. Whatever you say, missy, I said. But how are you spending your tired days? Oh dear! said my younger daughter. No indiscretions, please! But seriously, are you getting enough sleep? Aye, aye, sir. Do you ever go out for a walk? Aye, aye, sir. Listen, I said, I'll tell you one thing. If I ever sever our relations because of mental cruelty, you'll be sitting in the gutter and your hot tears will be flowing. Lady, said my younger daughter, you really cut me to the quick.

We both hung up at the same instant. I felt better. I looked out the window. Yes, they were still there. See if I care. As for me, now I was going to take a break. I drew the curtains in the bedroom and lay down. This was one of the most deeply relieving moments of the day. No unfamiliar person, no unfamiliar look, perhaps not even an unfamiliar ear had followed me into this room. I reveled in the indescribable pleasure of being alone and unobserved and placing no demands on myself. No thinking, no working. Not finding anything out, not wishing to know anything. Lying peacefully on my back, closing my eyes, breathing. I am breathing. I am not thinking. I am relaxed.

My inner eye focused on a high, pale, curved horizon above a dark disk. Was this a stage? All my inner thoughts floated off to this horizon. Shadowlike, they flew away, sluggish, lazy bats. They're succeeding. Nonsense.

They're not going to get very far. They're going to bash their heads in. The horizon is made of marble. Can't you see that? They all came crawling back to me obediently. I'll never get rid of them this way.

How does one get rid of thoughts? By thinking them. Thinking and thinking them again and again. Thinking them through. Thinking them out. If only there were a machine that could gather up all the hope left in the world and shoot it like a laser beam at this horizon of stone, melting it, breaking it open.

Now you're thinking like them. Machines, radiation, violence. Now you're extending their little bit of current power into the future. Then they'd have you where they want you.

Don't you think I know that? Do you think I think that I am completely the other? Purity, truth, kindness, and love? Don't you think I know what they need? I know. They want me to be like them, for that is the only joy left in their poor lives: to make others just like them. Don't you think I can feel their hands running over me, looking for that weak point through which they might enter me. I know that point. But I'm not going to tell anyone where it is, not even you and not even in my thoughts.

So, how do you see your future?

Suddenly all those huge, shadowy bats rose up again in a frightening flock.

Do you really not know that one has to forbid oneself certain words sometimes? In order not to weaken? In order not to get too soft?

So you think I should be harder from now on?

The opposite of soft isn't hard. The opposite of soft is unyielding, firm.

Sounds fantastic. And how do you manage to conjure away your fear?

My little bit of fear? We'll just have to live with it. Whoever can't deal with it can leave. And whoever is trying to scare me by shooting these images through my mind—a minute ago the curved horizon had disappeared and in its stead I saw barred rooms—whoever is trying to break me down can leave as well. And I mean right now.

I see. In case that means you're giving me my notice, that's fine with me.

Then I did fall asleep, after all. The last images I saw were sharply defined details of a familiar male body, irreconcilable love scenes which would have astounded me had I been awake. A dream demonstrated to me in ruthless fashion the violation of the amniotic shell of an embryo; accompanying this I heard the scornful words: Born in a caul! I understood the meaning upon awakening, but why the scorn? Why these wounds that one had to inflict upon oneself no less?

No reply. The notice remained valid. So I got dressed, made a pot of strong coffee, and sat down at my writing table, my torture table. Were they still there? They were not there anymore. The bottle-green car was gone. They had given up. They were finally convinced that . . .

Four cars over to the left stood a white car, occupied by two men. Everything as it should be.

It was 3 p.m.

Through the right alcove window I had a clear view of the Friedrichstrasse all the way to the streetcar terminal, through the left alcove window all the way to the Oranienburgerstrasse. Throngs of people were pushing and shoving in both directions. Thousands of unsuspecting citizens by the hour passing between me and the white car over there, heading home or to work or to their lovers or to their shops. Carrying on their normal lives, which were stuck to them.

As long as I wasn't prepared to change places with any of them, my pride remained unbroken and my principal lessons remained to be learned. Or theirs? The foreignness separating me from the crowd also separated the crowd from itself, or so I thought.

I had not yet had such thoughts, but the time seemed ripe for them, and quite different ones as well. Different ones and in different ways. The crowd not always infallible, a judge, a higher authority: the many who know better, whom I couldn't disregard, hurt, ignore; the masses, who were always right when it came right down to it. They were passing by my window, knew nothing, and were neither right nor wrong, for they had been made up. And wasn't it possible that it wasn't up to them, but rather the individuals who could say yes and no, could raise their arms automatically or refuse to agree, throw the first stone upon instruction or refuse to accept the judgment. Wasn't it up to each and every one of the many people down there—that girl, for example, who had just woven her way between the white car and the black-and-yellow one next to it and was now walking across the strip of lawn which separated the parking lot from the sidewalk, who had to wait at the traffic light and was now purposefully crossing the street. A girl like thousands of others, medium height, neither thin nor fat, with very short brown hair and a dark complexion. A green cloak, her pocketbook hanging from her shoulder.

All you had to do was look one of them in the eye and you were rid of your fear.

I had to get ready, pack H.'s bag, put on my shoes;

visiting hours at the hospital began in less than half an hour. The doorbell rang. It couldn't come at a more inopportune time, I told myself, in order to cover up my fear. Who was it? Today? At my house? It would be best not to open the door at all. I snuck through the corridor and listened at the door. Put on the chain? Nonsense. That's how it starts.

At first I thought my senses were deceiving me. It was the girl I had just seen crossing the street. Very short brown hair. Dark complexion. Cloak. Shoulder bag.

Who had sent her? Our eyes met and I started to feel ashamed. I asked her in as casually as possible. Something which at its core was both related and, at the same time, absolutely foreign to me crossed over my threshold in the form of this girl. I couldn't bring myself to tell her —how young she was! twenty? twenty-two?—to take off her cloak. The girl told me her name, which seemed vaguely familiar, and I was overcome by the feeling that this girl would never again leave my apartment. I did not pull out the telephone plug as I walked by, which would have been the reasonable thing to do; I risked letting this girl talk about herself into the possibly activated microphones in my room, at my round table, for that was why she had come, that much had been clear to me from the start. A few quick questions and answers revealed that the name of this girl had popped up regarding a certain incident at a certain university in connection with denunciations, proceedings, and cases of blackmail; that it really had been she who was expelled from the university because she was not among those who let themselves be blackmailed.

Right, yes; I remembered the story, which I knew about from hearsay, but that had been . . . how long ago was it? One year? Two years? Yes. But the girl now said, almost casually and certainly not by way of bragging, a second incident had landed her in prison for a year after that, which was why she had not been able to come sooner. As if we had had an appointment for two years now. The atmosphere I had been prepared for since the girl's arrival had finally been established. "Prison" was the word that jeopardized our relationship. There was nothing I could say to this, nothing I could ask. The girl dug around in her shoulder bag and finally pulled out a few pages, the manuscript that was the reason for her visit, and I read them at once, although I had said right from the start that I had to leave.

After reading the short text, I asked the girl to whom she had shown it apart from myself. She had shown it to her sister, a friend, her husband.

Now I stood up and pulled out the telephone plug. I didn't want to turn on the radio; the girl should think me neither timid nor conceited. So she was married. Yes. Her husband had stood by her, but he wasn't really interested in what she did.

I had the fleeting thought that, in times such as these, all our weaknesses come to the fore or our strengths become weaknesses. It wasn't for me to call a good text bad or not to encourage the author of a good text. I said that what she had written was good. It was no lie. Every sentence rang true. She shouldn't show it to anybody. These few pages could land her in prison again.

The girl's pleasure at hearing this softened her; she loosened up and started to talk. I thought, The time has come. The young people are writing it all down. The girl told of her hard life; she wished to reveal her innermost feelings, but where would this lead? I had to restrain her,

I couldn't allow her to go back on the street in such a trusting state of mind; I couldn't help asking how it was in prison and couldn't help hearing that the worst thing had been the cold. And the high quota set for stocking production. And the kidney pains. They simply didn't heat sufficiently there.

And this in my warm room, and me in my stockings. Now I had to scare this girl, if it was at all possible. Had to tell her that the greatest talents had already rotted in German prisons by the dozens, and it wasn't true that talented people could withstand the cold and the humiliation and the wearing down better than those with no talent. And that people would still want to read sentences like the ones she was writing in ten years' time. And please not to rush headlong into disaster.

So she should save herself? But what for?

Didn't she love her husband?

He had married her to give her security. He stood by her. She was a danger to him; he held a high office. Love? No.

And didn't she want to have children?

Earlier she had wanted to, oh yes. But not anymore. By the way, they hadn't recognized her kidney pains for what they were and had performed an operation on her uterus.

Silence.

The girl had had a change of heart. She didn't want to throw her life away, after all. It was just that she enjoyed writing down the truth as she knew it. And then talking about it with other people. Now. Here.

The girl cannot be held back, I thought. We can't save her, can't spoil her. She should do what she must do and relinquish us to our own consciences. She left. I watched her departure from the window. She crossed the street, threading her way between the cars and walking directly past the white car, unmoved by the glassy stares of the young gentlemen, made her way across the parking lot and vanished from their sight and mine.

And I had forgotten to get her address.

Now I plug the telephone back in, finish getting ready, lock the door, and go. I am sure that visiting hours at the hospital have already begun.

My car stood seven spots away from the white car, which I did not grace with as much as a glance. I got in and started up the engine. The girl had not asked small-mindedly, What remains? Nor had she asked how much she would remember when she was old someday.

I went the same way the girl could have gone, concentrating on the sidewalks and almost causing an accident when I thought I recognized the short brown hair in the crowd and tried to stop at the curb without observing the traffic, was forced to drive on, harassed by furious honking, and lost sight of the brown hair. No address. We did a good job on that one.

As I continued driving faultlessly and precisely, observing all the traffic regulations, something curious occurred inside me. Something was happening to me, to my vision or, more precisely, to my entire faculty of perception. I still remained in control of my vehicle, that was not the problem; the problem was, I could no longer see properly. I no longer saw what I was seeing, although the houses, streets, and people had by no means become invisible to me, that wasn't it. What's the matter with us, I heard myself think several times in a row; no other words came to mind and none have to this very day. Let's say, by way of trial, that a tie had broken between me and the city—provided that "city" can still stand for everything that people do to one another, both good and bad. It wasn't that I was afraid of going crazy. I was neither afraid nor anything else, I wasn't even in contact with myself anymore; what did a husband, children, brothers and sisters, or entities of the same order matter to me in a system that was self-sufficient. Pure horror, I hadn't known that its first stage was lack of feeling. I wove my way out of the traffic effortlessly, observing myself from a certain height all the while, not without a sense of appreciation, turned left into the driveway of the hospital, found a parking spot immediately, as if this were only natural, and wasn't even surprised that it was suddenly possible to enter a building which had stood there, flat and sharply silhouetted, looking as if it were cut out of cardboard, that there was a staircase, albeit a dirty one, signs with arrows indicating the various floors and wards through which I quickly and easily found my way to the third floor, Ward C1, and a room with the number 17. I arranged my features to accommodate the expression of a woman visiting her husband in the hospital; I knocked on the door, went in, nodded to the young man lying in the first bed, went up to the second, observing myself from a certain height, saw myself smile, bent down over the face lying on the pillows, and kissed it.

All the while, I was observing myself from a certain height.

I asked the questions one asks, got the same old answers, put the buckthorn juice on the night table, and packed up empty bottles and dirty laundry, performing everything quite convincingly and naturally and not even leaving out words like "worry" and "longing," since, after all, those who feel nothing have all words freely at their disposal. I sympathized, digging for details and wanting to be informed of even the slightest progress, of fractions of degrees in his temperature and all levels of pain. No, there hadn't been any real danger, that I knew, although I had been uneasy all yesterday morning. That's what I said, and it was true, I had been uneasy and I knew at that very moment that I was bound to cause suspicion with this truthful sentence, although he wouldn't immediately articulate it. He would only ask, What else? That's what he did.

What else?

What else? Nothing special. Pretty quiet. Not many people. Done me some good. Nah, nothing out of the ordinary. Now stop it. Sleep? Of course. Like a baby. Now stop it. You don't have to worry about me at all.

Why do you keep saying "Now stop it" today? asked H.

Me? I said. Do I?

Within the space of one minute you said "Now stop it" twice, said H.

Leave me alone, I said. His sentence demanded silence. Go ahead and cry, said H. after a while. I pushed the chair aside and sat down on his bed; the nurses didn't like that, he said.

How are you doing? I asked, starting all over again. The same answers to different questions. He looked pale and one of his facial expressions was unfamiliar to me. I traced along the lines I knew with my finger. He had been in danger. Yesterday I had had to fight violently against the horrible vision of a life without him for one whole morning. Everything is going well, I said. Everything is fine.

Really?

Now stop it.

I'll tell you everything later. Don't be afraid. I'm not afraid anymore either. Everything depends on us, you know. Don't laugh if laughing hurts. You can laugh at me all you want later. Thank God, you can laugh at me for a long time still, husband. You know what, I'm so happy all of a sudden that I don't know what to do. And not even being able to touch you.

All right. I guess, I'll be going.

I sang in the car, "Have you seen the mockingbird, the mockingbird, the mockingbird . . ." They won't win, husband. I turned on the radio and sang along with the tunes, I drove down the Leninallee too fast, suddenly deciding to have a bite to eat at the bar-and-grill and whipping around the steering wheel to get to the parking lot on the other side of the street. The signal NO U-TURN flashed too late in my cerebral cortex. I hope no one . . .

Uh-oh. The sound of a whistle. So, there was a traffic policeman stationed at this intersection, whom I was obliged to obey and show my papers in a friendly and rueful manner when he waved me over to the side of the street. The best thing was to admit to the offense immediately, not try to gloss it over but rather provide reasons which the already mollified guardian of law and order can rationalize into mitigating circumstances. He wasn't going to write me up after all, the right moment for that had come and gone, ten marks' fine at most, and possibly only five if he was willing to listen to reason. What could Patrolman B. do with an offender who candidly admitted to driving down this street frequently, who offered nothing in her defense but a state of absentmindedness and, to top it all off, happened to be a woman? All he could do was hand me back my papers with the almost jestful-sounding admonition: Now don't you turn here anymore!, raise his hand to his cap, and wish me a good day.

My luck couldn't hold, though.

It didn't. The waiters at the bistro were unfriendly, the service was slow, and I finally had to leave without having eaten. I knew from experience that hunger disappears after an hour at most. It got dark. I took a chance and parked the car in one of the gloomy, dilapidated streets behind the Alexanderplatz, wasted a long time walking in the wrong direction looking for the cultural center, and when I finally found it, the half hour I had promised the program director had already begun. I was no longer beaming, but a smidgin of gusto remained. Gusto propelled me through the throng of people blocking the entranceway to the cultural center, where I laughingly persuaded the young people that they would have to let me through, which they laughingly did. The large sign at the locked entrance announced: SOLD OUT. A young gentleman stood on either side of the door. Well, what do you know. Not exactly what you'd call inconspicuous. The young gentlemen didn't cause any trouble, they politely signaled to those inside that they should open the door. This they did. Four or five young girls and women and two young men were standing in the foyer and greeted me courteously. A trap! I thought in my typically exaggerated way, while shaking hands all around—more, in my confusion, than would have been necessary. I read PEOPLE'S SOLIDARITY CLUB on a door sign to my right, and then I got led up the stairs by a zealous, young girl toward a large inscription reading: GROWTH—PROSPERITY—STABILITY. Once again I read automatically: growth, prosperity, stability. Where were we, anyway? I really felt like sinking my teeth into this question, but I had to admit that this was neither the time nor the place.

The unreal atmosphere of the office of the departmental head of cultural activities, a storage room for outdated office furniture, surpassed that of almost every other office I knew. Three ancient posters on the walls did nothing to enhance the cultural aura which Colleague K. was aiming at. Colleague K. pretended to be thrilled to see me, but she seemed all upset to me. She was wearing a pea-green sweater, which served as the background for a hammered bronze shield the size of a clenched fist which hung right between her breasts. I wondered whether this woman happened to be called Brunhilde, but I really wouldn't have profited from the information. Then she started talking in a rapid, precipitous manner that made the shield on her chest start to jangle. What was the matter with her? At first with growing astonishment and then with growing comprehension, I saw her fingers groping about on the desk top, saw how her gaze rested stubbornly in the farthest corner of the room, and realized: This woman was afraid. The unit for measuring the degree of her fear was the jangling on her chest. It tinkled softly when she mentioned her boss; apparently he had not deemed it necessary to back her up against those "higher authorities," the mention of whom caused her shield to jangle more loudly. Still, since the event could no longer be canceled anyway, she had succeeded in wringing tacit permission from those authorities as well, although they must have put a lot of pressure on her. However, Frau K.'s bronze shield rang out a loud alarm when the conversation turned to the visitors outside the door who hadn't gained admission. Such a riotous assembly was all Colleague K. needed.

That was all I needed as well, although I didn't say

so. On the contrary. I mobilized my pertinent experience, which was considerable, and began asking Frau K. questions which were designed to back her up and simultaneously inform me as comprehensively as possible. There is a way of doing this which can't be explained to an outsider; I assume that there are conversations in every country, the hidden meaning of which becomes apparent only when they are compared with dozens of similar conversations on the same topic.

So what was the problem with the higher authorities? The higher authorities feared that something could happen. What, for example? Provocative questions from the audience, for example. I see. The level of barely tolerable questions seemed to have sunk a few notches lower. But don't panic, Frau K., just leave it to me. After all, I'm no beginner.

I was no beginner? To tell the truth, today of all days I felt just like a beginner.

What else, Frau K? I see, foreign correspondents. What foreign correspondents? Those who could have snuck in, although . . . Although what? Is this a public reading or isn't it? Well, yes. Although . . .

The long and the short of it was that precautions had been taken. Precautions?

Now a familiar little alarm went off inside my head. Now I entered negotiations with Colleague K. which, tenacious, tactical, clever, and friendly as they were on my part, stymied the defenses of the departmental head from Thüringen, who only a short time before had been stranded in Berlin, the snake pit. After a certain amount of haggling and considerable shield rattling, she surrendered to me the list of invited participants with a gesture worthy of the capitulation of an army. Truly, it honored me. No one had been omitted.

I told Frau K. that the list honored me. But what was the meaning of the six successive numbers which were followed by neither a name nor a departmental designation? Frau K. remained silent and stared down at her desk. I also remained silent and stared down at her desk. Only six, I thought, almost confidently. When I thought of those other events where almost a quarter of the audience . . . But one really shouldn't talk about "progress" in certain contexts. The important thing is not to lose my sense of humor now.

And so I asked Frau K. whether a normal audience was to be expected at all, considering this impressive list. Now I had all but insulted her. Of course she had let in "normal people" as well. Those were her very words, which almost completely restored my good mood. At least we'll have something to fall back on in our old age.

But now Frau K. had to hurry down and get the audience outside the door to disperse. And what about letting a few more of them in, what about opening the door leading to the staircase? Frau K. could only dismiss this as an unseemly proposition in light of standard fire regulations. Left on my own, I leafed through my manuscript, wiped the sweat from my face, and sprayed myself with eau de cologne. Didn't all these old Berlin apartment buildings with their countless corridors have a hidden rear exit? And might it not be next to the door of the restroom, which I could still visit inconspicuously? Where I could just as inconspicuously mistake the restroom door for the exit? After all, the insinuation that it had never happened before would be beside the point. There was always a first time for everything.

But Frau K. was already back. Had she been able to disperse the waiting crowd? Unfortunately not. Frau K., who had quivered in many different places since we met, now quivered in the general vicinity of the chin. She told me that, whatever might happen, she was determined to let the reading begin. Something had to have happened to her down there by the entrance. Only someone who was resolved to the utmost could have walked the way she walked on ahead of me. If green really is the color of hope, then her green sweater gave off all kinds of signals, but hope was not among them. At the door to the auditorium it turned out that she had no intention of introducing me. I should just go up and start right in. People will notice on their own when the reading starts, said Frau K. My oh my, I thought. This certainly is a first.

It was quiet in the auditorium. I squeezed between the rows of seats and made my way to the podium, upon which stood a bare wooden table, a simple chair, and a lamp. I stepped up onto the podium and sat down. Two or three pairs of hands clapped. So they were not among the six on the list. Or were they? I announced what I was going to read and began.

I knew the text by heart. The sentences establish their own rhythm, the voice rises, falls, softens, hardens. The way it should be. Everything automatic, no one will notice. Whatever the reasons for your coming, ladies and gentlemen, you will be served properly. The fee for which you have hired me is modest, but I am giving you your money's worth. What I would like to know is, did you have to fork out the money yourselves or did your respective departments pay the one mark fifty per ticket for you? I can only hope so. Do you at least have to feign a keen interest in cultural events for this job or isn't that necessary either? And what are your instructions? Applause at the end, and if so, how much? Or manifestations of displeasure? But at what point? Raised workers' fists are apparently no longer in fashion.

GROWTHPROSPERITYSTABILITY.

Oh yes. You will be served. One day you will be fed up, my dear colleagues. By the way, why you of all people? Why of all people that young guy down there on the left, with the sweat running down his forehead, who isn't wiping it away? Doesn't he dare to for fear of attracting attention? Is he as interested as he makes out to be? And the girl behind him, the one with the long hair—where might she work. Or have the two of them not been ordered here after all and belong to the "normal" people? To those for whom I would have to read in a completely different fashion. Why would I have to: have to. Even if there were only the two of them. But there could be two or three dozen, and I forgot all about them. And why didn't it occur to me that it would also be a worthwhile experience for the others, for those who have been sent here? For where does it say that they are made of stone, that they can't be seduced as well.

All right, then. Now I make an effort.

Now I no longer cared about classifying the audience in whatever way. No matter how the world might be reflected in these more than one hundred various minds—for this one hour I wanted to implant my world therein. I no longer had any objections, or the slightest reservation against any single member of this audience and—although I couldn't swear, I was more than willing to believe it—maybe those six, or however many there might be, forgot their prejudice, if not their assignment, for a short time. For where would we be if it became fashionable to spit into the hand being held out to you?

I could see how gladly Colleague K. would have used the pause before the first question was posed in order to close the evening she had so valiantly refused to open. Nothing had happened yet, but any second—now, for example, where that young man in the first row was getting up, the one who was sweating so—it could. But all the young man wanted to know was when the book was coming out, and none of those aforementioned six could have opened the discussion more cleverly, for now time was spent providing information on how books were published. The reports, which would hopefully come together tomorrow at the proper place, could read "composed atmosphere." The general atmosphere of the discussion was composed.

But you shouldn't count your chickens before they're hatched. You should always keep an eye on your own feelings. In the last row, a young woman of the type I am helpless against got up and introduced the word "future"—a word we're all helpless against and which is capable of changing the atmosphere of any room and moving any crowd. The young woman—a teacher? a student of music? a technical draftsman?—would never have had the heart to speak in public if she hadn't come for the express purpose of asking that question which she could no longer postpone: how a livable future for ourselves and our children was going to grow out of this present situation.

She spoke in a level tone of voice, she didn't make a fuss, made no accusations, did not put her feelings on display. She only wanted to know. Everyone in the auditorium had caught the signal, each in his own way. Colleague K.'s bronze shield started clanking desperately, but it didn't do her any good. Even if the words GROWTH PROSPERITY STABILITY had appeared on the wall in large neon letters, nothing would have done any good, for now the real questions had surfaced—the ones which give us life and can mean death if taken away from us.

I said something along those lines and took great pains, as was my habit in such situations, to shoulder the responsibility for her question and thus cover up for the young teacher, who may have been sitting there innocently among the wolves. I immediately felt ashamed at this maneuver, for hands and voices were raised in many parts of the auditorium which not only repeated the young woman's question as their own but elaborated and dwelt on it in a carefree and ruthless manner. What were these people doing? They were putting themselves in danger. But what right did I have to think them more stupid than myself? What right did I have to protect them from themselves?

And so I remained silent and listened as I have seldom listened in my life. I forgot about myself, they forgot about me, and finally, we all forgot the time and the place. The auditorium was couched in semidarkness. As the forms in the auditorium became harder to distinguish, the formality of the occasion faded. The terrible habit of speaking for others faded away and everyone spoke for themselves, thus leaving themselves vulnerable. Sometimes I had to shudder: How vulnerable. But wonders never cease, no one attacked. Most of them were seized by a fever; it was as if they could never ever make amends if they didn't grasp this perhaps last opportunity and immediately contributed their small part to that curiously close future, which kept slipping out of reach. Someone said the word "brotherhood" softly.

Sheer madness, I thought; someone else jumped up and shook his fist, pulling at his hair in frustration at such naïveté and incapable of understanding what was happening when those all around him offered gentle remonstrations on the practical value of this utopian word. He sat down, shaking his head; someone else, who obviously enjoyed the sound of his own voice, was cajoled into getting to the point, which presumably had been his intention in the first place. The atmosphere got more and more relaxed, as on the eve of a celebration. The titles of books were shouted across the room, some people wrote them down, others started talking to their neighbors, a circle formed around the young woman who had spoken first.

Had Colleague K. taken leave of her senses? Was she responsible or wasn't she? But there she was, clinking softly, one might almost have taken it for the clinking of spurs. Her sweater was even greener than before, the glow of her cheeks redder still. Was she trembling? Of course she was. The trembling of her body carried over to her voice, which nonetheless sounded determined. This seemed to be the right moment. All get-togethers had to . . . And so she hereby closed the reading and was certain to be speaking on behalf of everyone present. The thank yous. The flowers: the five obligatory gerbera, surrounded by asparagus leaves. A good evening to all.

Yet the people remained seated. Was Frau K. mistaken? Had it not been the right moment, after all? On the other hand, what were they waiting for? No one really knew, but when the old man in the second row—the one who looked like a war veteran—stood up, it seemed as if they had all been waiting for him. As the oldest by far at this gathering, he merely wished to take the opportunity to make a friendly gesture. He then took a flat box wrapped in tissue paper out of an ancient, coarse linen bag and presented it to me. Now they could laugh and applaud, now they could get up and gradually disperse. Some people came up to the front with photographs to be signed, among them the young woman who had asked about our future. What was her profession? Oh, just a nurse. Why the "Oh, just . . ." Oh, that wasn't anything special.

This should have been the finale of the evening. But instead there was an epilogue. It was begun by the two young people who approached from the door and had not been among the audience up till then. A harmless-looking young man, a nice young girl with frizzy blond hair. As I was signing their books, the young man told me his name. So he was the one who had been putting his poems in my mailbox for the past few months. Well, this was a nice way of finally getting to meet one another.

Then the young man asked, By the way, do you realize that the police broke up the crowd downstairs outside the entrance?

I recognized that familiar sensation of an elevator descending rapidly into the pit of my stomach. The police? But why? And I'm supposed to have known . . . Colleague K.!

Colleague K. was prepared. Yes, unfortunately. Unfortunately, it had been necessary to call in police protection. The crowd had become unruly and aggressive.

Both the young man and the girl said quietly, That's not true.

Not true. Well, Colleague K. knew better than that. She herself had been insulted when she attempted to disperse the crowd in a friendly way.

"Friendly!" said the two young people in one breath.

So she had been aware of the intervention of the police? I asked Colleague K. Perhaps even ordered it?

Everything had transpired in accordance with proper and lawful procedure. Police headquarters had called finally to assure her that a squad car was on hand.

When! When had the police called?

Around half past six. Of course before the reading. But it had been predictable that something like this would happen.

But what? Something like what? asked the boy, the girl, and I.

Suddenly, as if he had shot up out of the floor, a man was standing next to Colleague K., who was jangling and trembling from head to toe. He was barely taller than she, but obviously one or two notches higher on the salary scale: the director of the cultural center himself, her boss. Who now felt obliged to reveal his identity. Just for the sake of showing these young people here . . . So, to get right down to brass tacks, what had happened? Well. Years ago he started studying law. But even without that background, anyone with any common sense would call what happened today "trespassing." However, to prevent such occurrences we fortunately had a powerful police force, even if some people didn't happen to agree. Just to set the record straight. Moreover, the police hadn't even cracked down, which would have been perfectly justified.

One of them told me they could easily have loaded us all onto three or four trucks and carried us off, and one, two, three, the problem would have been solved, said the young girl.

Told you! said the director of the cultural center in a superior tone of voice. But what did the police actually do!

They pushed and shoved out the people standing downstairs in the foyer.

So you admit it yourself. The police reestablished order without bloodshed. Was Colleague Writer even aware of the fact that her fans had forced their way into the building?

Forced! said the young man. We were bored outside and just passing the time with all kinds of nonsense. Somebody at the door called out, What we need is a skeleton key! and then someone passed one up, they opened the door—it was easy—and a few people went inside. That was all. It was completely peaceful, funny even, like a happening or something. So please don't think anybody wanted to disturb your reading.

What I thought was of little importance. I was relieved to see that although Colleague K. had known about the police intervention, she hadn't known about the trespassing. I wondered what the two young men standing at the door had actually done when the skeleton key was passed up. Had it perhaps passed through their hands as well? There was something fundamentally illogical about this story which I couldn't get out of my mind. That phone call at half past six when not a soul was thinking of a skeleton key . . . or were they? I had relaxed too soon. Jürgen M., or whoever else it was, would get his report, probably even three or four fat, juicy reports, which would satisfy him and enrich my file. And wasn't it conceivable that my old friend Jürgen M., whose young men had stood around so long in front of our door without any results, would spare no expense for such an enrichment of my file. Conceivable yes, utterable no. Unutterable. Unmentionable.

Well then, good night.

Just a minute please. The director of the cultural center had decided to take the opportunity to conclude that, in his opinion, the evening had been quite successful all in all and that the unpleasant, peripheral incidents had nothing to do with Colleague Writer in the least. The best thing was for her to forget them as soon as possible. Colleague K., all jangling shields and quivering chins, concurred. Her eyes glued to her boss, she formulated the sentence which would later appear in her report: It was a normal reading in a liberal atmosphere with a satisfied audience.

Exactly, said her boss.

I left, flanked by the young people. Someone brought me the flowers I had left behind. The two of them accompanied me to my car. It's better this way, said the boy. We didn't say much. The people outside had really been peaceful, peaceful and unprovocative. They had talked with one another. The two of them, for example, had only just met out there.

That's nice, I said.

I was probably tired now.

Yes.

Was it a good discussion?

Oh yes. We discussed the future, you see. What remains.

What remains.

I couldn't help laughing. I knew it would be dangerous if I started to laugh now. I managed to stop. The young people discovered that they both lived in the same direction. See you some other time, I said, got in the car, and drove off. The only thing on my mind was that I was tired.

What if they really had loaded some of the young people onto their trucks and taken them away? What if they . . . That was it. There was nothing I could do. Put out of action, as they say. My back to the wall.

Around this time there is no more traffic in the Oranienburgerstrasse, especially not in the Tucholsky-strasse. I drove mechanically and parked the car in the first row of the big parking lot, right opposite our windows and right next to the car in which two young gentlemen sat smoking. This car was probably blue in the daylight. Dark blue. Let it be. Let them be. In the daylight and at night, in summer and in winter.

It was 11:05 p.m.

The apartment was dark and quiet. I went through all the rooms barefoot and turned on all the lights. In the kitchen, I put the gerbera in a vase with some water. I stared at the announcer on the tube, who wished me good night and vanished. I looked through the records. *Exsultate, Jubilate*. What good is that to me? What good the painfully loved "Arrived did I a stranger"? And a stranger I will leave.

Nothing fits.

Walk along the bookshelves, even climb up the stepladder, peruse the upper shelves, tap the back of a book here, check out a title there. Nothing works anymore. I had lost all my spirit, even the holy spirits. There may have been a few lines left here and there. With my assassin time . . . That worked. With my assassin time I am alone.

Go to the bathroom, stare into the mirror I couldn't smash because they had smashed it before me. The course had been set. The concrete poured on the pathway over which they would drive us. Go back into the room, turn on the radio. Unwrap the candy box the white-haired man had given me. Read the enclosed card. It turned out the man was a priest and wished me God's blessings. With the radio blaring hit after hit, I sat there and ate one piece of candy after another until the box was half empty.

Now what?

The telephone rang. It was midnight. My older daughter had heard from a friend what had happened. One of the people who had been standing outside. She was supposed to tell me that they had not provoked anybody. Really not. They had been in a happy, relaxed mood. They hadn't wanted to make any trouble for me. I know that. But listen to your voice. It sounds normal to me. Sometimes one should just grab oneself by the scruff of the neck and place oneself a few years into the future. Oh. So that was her recipe. Why wasn't she in bed instead of telephoning all over the place at this ungodly hour? I didn't really want to know, did I? Was Father doing better? Yes. Well then! You can't have everything. Were they out in front of the house again? They were. Did it still bother me? No, it didn't bother me anymore. But it bothered me that my own daughters were spying on me. Well then, so long, said my daughter. Oh, by the way, they're right not to trust you. I'm just beginning to understand that myself, I said.

The moment I put the receiver down, the phone started ringing again. A man I vaguely knew wanted to tell me that he had been among the young people at the cultural center that evening. They really hadn't provoked anybody. I said I knew that. How was I doing? Good, I said. Really? Better, I said. Let me give you my number, said the man, whom I all of a sudden remembered. You can call me any time, even at night. My goodness, I said, telephone therapy. Go ahead and laugh, said the man. I'd rather that than something else.

I wrote down his number. I went through all the rooms and turned off all the lights until only the desk lamp was still burning. This time they had almost got me. This time, whether they had been trying to or not, they had found the weak point. Which I would describe one day in my new language. One day I will be able to speak easily and freely, I thought. It is still too soon, but it won't always be too soon. Why not simply sit down at this desk, by the light of this lamp, shuffle the paper into place, take my pen, and begin? What remains? What is at the root of my city and what is rotting it from within? That there is no misfortune other than that of not being alive. And, in the end, no desperation other than that of not having lived.

June–July 1979 / November 1989